NATURAL SHOCKS

RICHARD STERN

COWARD, McCANN & GEOGHEGAN, INC.
NEW YORK

Copyright © 1978 by Richard Stern

SBN: 698-10865-5

Library of Congress Cataloging in Publication Data

Stern, Richard G.   1928–
    Natural shocks.

    I. Title.
PZ4.S83943Nat   [PS3569.T39]   813'.5'4   77–22952

Excerpt from "The Piccolino" by Irving Berlin on page 118.
© Copyright 1935 Irving Berlin.
© Copyright renewed 1962 Irving Berlin.
Reprinted by permission of Irving Berlin Music Corporation.

PRINTED IN THE UNITED STATES OF AMERICA

This book is dedicated to Arthur Heiserman
JANUARY 10, 1929–DECEMBER 9, 1975

I

1

Three years after Frederick Wursup moved across Lexington Avenue and turned his office into his home as well, he discovered that he could see the old apartment—where his ex-wife, Susannah, still lived with their two sons—from the roof. He'd never paid any attention to the cross-planked square on the ceiling of his back bathroom, but it was through this that Mr. Spunkel, the janitor, admitted the roofers one September afternoon. They climbed through and Wursup followed, hoisting himself up from the lidded toilet seat. While they checked for clogged spouts and worn asphalt, Wursup surveyed the avenue.

Sixteen floors up, only feet higher than his usual perch, but unceilinged and with full compass, the view was terrific: the southern flow of busses, cars, cabs; the miniaturized hominess of brownstones; the cramped silvery punctuation of the Episcopal-church steeple; the fraternity of nearby roofs with their odd brick structures—for elevator motors?—and gardens (potted boxwood, small pepper and locust trees in deep clay urns). Two roofs south, a gray-haired couple in sweat suits threw a deck-tennis tire back and forth over a net. What a sporty world it was up here. In the other direction, the Hotel Carlyle, noble, snowy, remote, alpine. Frightening. How could window washers endure the scare, the dazzle, racket and smell?

And then, surprise—what couldn't be guessed from his windows—there, eighty feet away, were the front windows of Susannah's apartment. He could see the green leather grandfather chair (where he'd spent how many thousand hours), the gold love seat and the mosaic table he'd carried home from Damascus twenty-odd years ago. If his eyes were better, he could see which books were on it.

"Oh me oh my."

"Yessiree, Mr. Double-U, you can really get you a breath of air up here," said old Spunkel.

For weeks, Wursup didn't go up again. (It wasn't all that easy pulling his hundred and eighty pounds through the hole.) But one October evening, feeling especially lonely, even abandoned—his girl, Sookie Gumpert, was giving a paper in San Diego—Wursup went up with field glasses to see if he could get a glimpse of Petey or Susannah. (Billy had gone back to Cornell.)

There she was, sitting in his chair, reading, smoking.

So strange to see the head that he'd known so well in this new way. For so many years, the sight of it had eased him; and then, for years, the same sight had gripped his stomach, infuriated him.

It was a head at peace with itself. Once, his description of Susannah's temperament was "armored stupor." "She has a fanatic's serenity," he'd said to Will Eddy, their oldest friend. "She lives by exclusion." (It was the time of their divorce.) "How lucky to have such psychic armor." Almost the worst part of the breakup was seeing how much ugliness the armor concealed. "There's such fury under that opacity," he told Will.

10

"She doesn't have your verbal spout to clear it off," said Will.

Three years later, Wursup and Susannah were more or less easy with each other; friendly, if not exactly friends. In fact, for a year or so, there was almost nothing he learned about her that did not touch and sometimes rend him. Three years away, the body that wrinkled and unwrinkled her clothes was stranger to him than any body in the world. Its look, feel, temperature and odor were erased; yet, unlike a newly strange body, he had no desire whatsoever for it. "Desire must be like alcohol," he told Will. "It's the first thing that evaporates from the pot." But he wished Susannah well; he cared for her well-being, and he guessed that meant he cared for her too.

These days, at the first whiff of any disagreement, each of them turned tail or tried to give in to the other. Both remembered—neither wanted even a souvenir of—the terrible, laconic battles of their last year together. Their relationship existed in a special part of the universe of feeling, a kind of miniature black space where the gravity of suppression was so powerful that no spark showed. Within its rigid unintimacy, they were friendly, almost affectionate; they reminisced, and could laugh at, as well as with, each other. Will said they looked closer than they'd been since he'd first known them, more than a quarter of a century ago, back in Chicago. "It's as if it took uncoupling to turn you into a couple again."

Wursup undeceived Eddy. "We treat each other the way you treat other people's pets."

Not quite.

Wursup almost never saw Susannah at home. He seldom went over, because all the boys had to do was turn around the corner to be at his place. When Susannah visited her mother in Chicago, though, he stayed there, because it was more comfortable for Petey to stay in his own room. And it was then he felt more deeply about her.

Susannah had never been a sterling member of the Consumer Society. She bought her clothes in department-store basements and resale shops. (Though he made five times the money he'd made when that was necessary.) Since she was slim and tasteful, she looked fine; and more, felt fine. Her taste was not limited by penny-pinching or penury; it was part of an aversion to self-display, a form of egoism as coercive as a stoic's self-assertion. When Susannah's old pal Adele Doyle gained forty pounds and sent her a trunkful of designer-label clothes, she gave them away to cleaning women and to a couple of the girls who worked with her down at *Chouinard's News Letter*. (Maybe it was because Wursup had thought she'd looked so terrific in them that she gave them away. As if to say, "Care for me underneath.") The sad foolishness of Puritanism. To work against sexual tedium even with verbal flourishes froze Susannah. Her sexual imagination was—as far as Wursup knew—as narrow as an animal's.

Of four years of high-school Spanish, Susannah remembered best the proverbs of abstinence and thrift: *Quien mucho abarca, poco aprieta*—"Who grabs too much, squeezes little." (That was her one bed joke with him.) *Poco a poco se va lejos*—"Little by little takes you far"—did for food, clothes, study. For life itself. *No es oro todo lo que reluce*—"all that glitters . . . " and so on. The genius of Spain shrank into a *vade mecum* of caution.

Since the divorce, Susannah's life seemed constructed to arouse pity. She gave their bedroom to Petey and moved into the tiny back bedroom whose vista was the neighboring air shaft. The bed was assertively single, monkish. (Not that a larger bed would have fit.) The room's other works of carpentry were a bed table and a straight chair. There was no dressing table, no mirror; her clothes were in a closet, blouses and sweaters folded on shelves. The single ornament was a red silk panel on which stood an epicene Japanese saint holding a golden jug. Susannah and he had bought it at the ancient wood temple, Horyugi, when he was doing the Japanese articles which became his first book. Long, pleated, indented with the Beyond-You smile of Buddhist saints, the Kannon's head was overwhelmed with spadiciform flame (immodest equivalent of the western halo). There were a hundred reasons Susannah shouldn't have it in her room. She'd trimmed as many reminders of their life together as economy permitted. (No madeleine cakes to undo her emotional diet.) But there it was, this icon of renunciation.

Wursup himself was no great hauler of historic luggage, a rare attender of weddings, christenings, funerals, no singer of anthems or saluter of flags; but Susannah's uninvolvement, her carelessness about the signals and symbols life throws up, seemed to him quasipathological. A no-nonsense woman, fine, she'd had much praise for that (from him as well); but to believe that almost nothing on earth stood for more than its face, stomach, or flesh value removed too much from life. She used to overlook the boys' birthdays with a regularity that became a not always funny family joke. For Christmas, he'd lug home a Scotch pine—instead of, say, the broomstick fir she might allow herself to buy—and her green eyes glittered with an amused tolerance far more telling than voiced disapproval. "The toys of morons," was what he read in them. Susannah's face was noble, modest, oddly sensuous. Sculptors loved the fine bones of her temples and cheeks, the beautiful lips, the elegant chin. Her color was splendid—lime-green eyes, rose-and-peach flesh coloring. Yet it was mostly artists who saw her beauty. She did not consider herself beautiful and made none of the gestures which suggest beauty to the unobservant. Her modesty was a counterpart to what he'd first seen as her realism, her commonsensical practicality. (Later he regarded her abstemiousness as a form of torpor.) In the beginning, he'd been charmed—and relieved—when she said of course she didn't need, in fact wouldn't wear, a wedding ring; that she'd married—in the Seventh Arrondissement *mairie*—in a dress she could have worn any other day. But everydayness became her cult. No, not quite. For instance, her distaste for ceremony was so great she could take part in it without feeling hypocritical: it was beneath notice. So she decorated the Scotch pine, and, reminded, she gave the boys birthday parties. "It suits them; it's not worth an argument. The habit doesn't make the monk. A birthday cake won't ruin anybody." So the Japanese saint they'd bought together in the gift shop of the ancient temple hung over her bed, a mild defiance of nostalgia and—perhaps—of symbolism itself. Susannah would not debate the symbolism or the mode of defiance. You couldn't top Susannah, anymore than you could outargue an analyst.

What upset Wursup most about her life now was her calendar. It was an ordinary handout from Somayo's Cleaners on which Susannah wrote the month's engagements. What in hell was the matter with their old friends? Didn't they realize what a terrific person she was? Underneath all that No-Nonsense frontage, there was a grand, true-blue human being. (At the worst, he'd never ignored that.) One night, maybe two, in a month, she'd be invited somewhere. (Of course, she wasn't all that hospitable herself.) What had happened? Their marriage had been festooned with hundreds of dinners and parties all over the world. She'd loved going to and giving them. The white blanks of Susannah's calendar had the resigned bareness of exile. Were their old friends turning her into a No-Person? People were swine.

Of course, Susannah did have friends at work—the Miyakos, the Bennetts, "Dame" Mae Twiddy—so she wasn't like one of those poor wrecks police find after Christmas, stiff in their armchairs in front of a burned-out television set. Still, night after night, the calendar—and then his field glasses— saw her at home.

She seemed married to the *Times*, to television and the books on Latin-American politics whose titles he now made out with the field glasses. Saturdays, though, she did go— Petey told him—to museums and galleries with Dame Mae or

Libba Bennett. Susannah did love painting; she'd painted as a girl, going down to the Chicago Art Institute school every Saturday morning for lessons. Through their twenty years together, she painted, mostly landscapes copied from postcard reproductions of Corot or Pissaro: the paradise retreats of twentieth-century urban nostalgists.

According to Petey, she wasn't painting much now. "She says the price of paints is crazy since the oil embargo." Wursup had no love for the moguls of the world's second-commonest fluid, but this expression of Susannah's tightness was something he particularly hated. Spanish proverbs couldn't disguise such contortions of meanness. The first years, it hadn't bothered him, he'd hardly noticed it; economizing is one of the games of young middle-class couples, like the little languages of sex or playing cribbage. Yet when he began to make and then spend money, her distaste for it ceased being a game. When he bought an old Mercedes, the distaste was so skillful a torture of silent looks he took a bath on a trade-in for a Chevy. When, marriage coming apart, he bought a Porsche, she understood. (She was a fine interpreter of the symbols of revulsion.) Now she filled Petey's head with the prices of life. Vergil's most famous line was the "tears of things"; Susannah's was mean-spirited and unworthy of her: *the cost of them.*

"Tell her I'll buy her paint enough for *The Last Judgment.* If she can't find canvas, I'll buy her a chapel."

Petey relayed very little of such messages. Earlier ones had met with refusals that were as barren of gratitude as the Arctic of buttercups. Wasn't *doing without* life's essence? Petey didn't seem to mind it. He and Susannah economized in the old cribbage-game spirit. And he did love her so, it made everything else unimportant. The boy suffered when she didn't get a raise she was after (Wursup didn't think she should let him in on this); he bragged about articles she'd researched, about her good looks, her humor. He was a real companion;

he understood Susannah's loneliness, encouraged her to go out, and when Wursup took them out for supper, Petey tried to draw Susannah into making good talk. He was so sweet and good-humored about all this, there was neither excess nor warp in it; he was just one terrific twelve-year-old.

Petey knew his mother would take nothing "extra" from his father. He'd heard her refuse offers to pay for cleaning women—"I don't need one, I don't like strangers around"—vacation trips to Europe—"Very nice of you, but I can go myself if I want. I've seen enough of it anyway." He admired his mother's independence, yet appreciated his father's generosity. Now and then though—Wursup noticed—Petey seemed fatigued by the *insistence* of abstinence and began regarding his mother's life as a special case. "It's the way Mom is. When she feels bad enough like painting, she'll break down and get some canvas. But thanks, Dad."

The first year of separation, Susannah didn't just bother to ignore his offers. If Petey carried over a rug Wursup had picked up in Kashmir for their apartment, she managed—when Wursup himself showed up—a kind of grunt which his knowledge of susannahese interpreted: "This would be a 'thank you' for anyone else, but please do not try to control me with gifts. All you can give me is your absence." In that first year, the proximity of his office-home was an oppression to her. Lexington Avenue was populous enough so that they didn't see each other in the street more than once or twice every month or two, but she had to see his building, she knew they could meet. When they actually did, panic stiffened her, the lime-green eyes shrank into a tunnel vision which excluded as much of him as possible. Thank God, he thought, she didn't know what Sookie looked like—did she?—or that he watched her from the roof as she read, smoked, stared.

With the field glasses, he observed smoke gushing through her nostrils, her fingers playing around in her hair—"a dump of brown gnarls" he'd described it in one of the unwritten novels of his insomniac divorce-time. It was still brown (still a dump). No gray at all to speak of in either of their middle-aged heads. Will Eddy had gone gray at thirty, was a Santa Claus today. What message was relayed to the surface by those molecular dictators? "You are still young; keep the doors unlocked"? "You've had it, get ready for the end"? Across the thirty yards, Susannah was blocked by the window into portraiture: *The Reader; The Puffer; The Ex-Wife.* (Not, though—for he didn't have the requisite psychic distance—*As Seen by the Ex-Husband.*)

"Ah, Susannah," thought Wursup, standing in the night air among the television antennae, "if only someone would see what a little champ you are."

It was a strangely quiet time in Wursup's life. He was not flying around the world, harvesting the annual crop of stars and villains, wasn't coming home to family dinners. "Lying on the bottom, he has stopped sending bubbles to the surface," he read in the *Penguin Anthology of Latin Verse,* his week's toilet reading. ("When you give away at one end, you bring in through another" was his explanation of this habit to Susannah, who found it disgusting.) He passed this bit from Persius the satirist to Will Eddy over a lobster lunch at King of the Sea.

"Success is agoraphobic for you. Except you'll learn its pleasures. You'll huddle with your peers in the rooms reserved for celebrity."

"In the cages, you mean. Attention's a pressure to repeat. Celebrity's the vengeance of the unfamous. They turn the famous into stage settings. It's a way of paralyzing them."

Three years before, a series of articles Wursup had written about American statesmen, industrialists, bankers and educators had been fused—partly by Will's editorial laser—into a book about the disastrous brilliance of recent American leadership. *Down the American Drain* sold three hundred thousand copies in hardback, ten times that in paper. The world sales alone brought in more money than Wursup had made from all his articles and three other books. Conscious of the string of successes John Gunther had had decades before with his "Inside" books, Wursup's publishers saw golden feathers in his flesh. They contracted for Asian, European and African *"Drains."* Will sketched out the sorts of thing he could write about: "Oil policy, currency manipulation, multinational technology, funding, bloc politics, electronic dependence, Third- and Fourth-World Counterforce, the new national-ism—Uzbeks, Bretons, Lapps, Balinese—the Switzerlandiza-tion of the world, OPEC, OAS, GATT, IMF. And the types who run them—Harold Geneen, Howie Page, Davy Rocke-feller, Walt Wriston, Bob McNamara. Then the mercenaries and maniacs—the Amins, Stroessners, Qaddafis, Perons; the sheikhs, shahs and shamans for color, craziness, backspin. A world spun by greedies, goons and loons. And you're the cool correspondent à la Montesquieu or Heine, zooming in on starship *Galaxy Soul-Pure.* It'll be a world epic. No one can do closeups and panoramas like you. You'll mail Talese, Hal-berstam and Mailer to the dead-letter office. *Drain* was just your milk teeth breaking through."

An hour with Will, and an author felt that all he had to do was go home and type. "If you were around in Homer's day," said Wursup, "he'd have been more productive. Moses wouldn't have come down with a lousy ten commandments; there'd have been a thousand. We'd all know where to spit and shit on odd Tuesdays."

"It seems I've got you cooking."

Sookie Gumpert said that Will Eddy was like a bank with all its money lent out two and three times. "Investing, investing, investing, in everybody else. No wonder he looks older than Father Time."

Wursup knew several Wills. The one without confidence who, at parties, introduced himself and spelled out his name:

"E-d-d-y. Simple, but hard to remember." In a celebrity-heavy world, anonymity was sometimes despair (though it could occasionally be potential celebrity, buried treasure). For Will, who had been raised in a family of scientists to be a poet, anonymity was a death's head, but one hidden like a hair shirt beneath the cheer. He and Wursup had known each other since they'd been students at Chicago, in the forties. They'd met in Professor Macfarlane's famous survey of Western philosophy. (Humans had been held together by weaker bonds.) Macfarlane, a head-breaker, carried a chip as big as Mars on his abstract shoulders. He'd read ten thousand books which he dumped on heads left and right. His pedagogy, a fusion of terror, mesmerism and granulation, victimized not only students but the dead philosophers: Aristotle clubbed the Eddys, Wursups, Doyles and Knoblauchs en route to mugging Plato and Plotinus; Aquinas mowed down mystics; everyone moved in to cream Hume and Kant.

Will, a Macfarlane addict, had taken three parts of the survey. "Like Colette after leaving Willy," he said. "'The mouse sometimes misses the claw of the cat in its side.'"

The red-haired philosopher chewed up systems and notions in a soft voice, sweetly burred with a defect that turned *th* into *z*. "It's why he never says 'Thanks,'" explained Will. "Why Thales and Pythagoras aren't on his Murderers' Row."

Will had been called many a name by his mentor—"Cretin," "Hamburger Head," "Faker," "Parlor Snake," "Dummy," "Buggsie Blueeyes"—but Wursup, who never spoke in class and quoted Macfarlane liberally in his papers, crawled through unnoticed, till one day, when called on to summarize Leibniz's "vicious doctrine of internal relations," he cited Bertrand Russell's criticism of it and received a full blast. Macfarlane's hair looked like orange rinds on fire, the little gray eyeballs of malevolence popped violently against schoolmarm specs. Russell was Public Enemy Number One. (Academic rumor had it that he had sliced up the young Mac-

.farlane in these very seats.) Macfarlane's shot pinked Wursup left and right: "Marinating intellectual garbage"; "Rear ends leading rear ends." Wursup, dying in his seat, heard Will Eddy break in to ask what exactly the doctrine of internal relations was: "Did it say that someone whose father dies without his knowledge is intrinsically altered by it? Is that the one, Mr. Macfarlane?" The interruption drew Macfarlane from the Wursup kill and was the beginning of a twenty-five-year friendship.

Wursup wanted to dedicate *Drain* to Will. He had been in on it from the beginning. They'd argued about its conception, organization, tone; about paragraphs, sentences and words. "What Louis Bouilhet was to *Madame Bovary*, you've been to this book."

"I'm doing my professional job. I get paid."

"You practically wrote it."

"Not even theoretically. I couldn't have written one word of it."

Which, oddly, was true. It wasn't a question of marks on paper. Will could not commit himself to the prosaic description of a person, a scene, an action. He enjoyed circling ideas, he had a nose for falsity, for rotten sentences, for authenticity, but he could write nothing but business letters and the most periphrastic, abstract poems.

"All right," said Wursup, "I'll dedicate it to Dante."

"You could do worse." (The Master's Essay Will didn't finish did have a dedication page: "To D. E. across years and seas." "D. E." stood for "Desiderius Erasmus.")

"I never trusted men with two first names. Or who grow beards in mid-life. Erasmus wasn't too devious to shave."

"Dedicate it to the boys."

"They each have a book."

"How about your pop?"

"He only reads poems and obituaries." Poppa Wursup had retired from reading meters for People's Gas in Chicago, swapped his retirement gift—a hi-fi stereo—for an electric typewriter, bought a mountain of scratch paper and begun filling it with doggerel (much of it about the last years of famous old men).

There was no dedication. Which didn't keep *Drain* from floating to the top of the best-seller list, where it stayed for twenty-two weeks. Tania Pullen, Wursup's agent, fielded the requests for interviews, speeches, awards and talk shows. For the first weeks, Wursup relished the attention, put his face in front of cameras and lost successive engagements as sit-down comic to talk-show hosts, actors, politicians, professors and poets.

This was when Nixon's accelerating fall dominated American life. With the rest of America's sages, Wursup turned into a fountain of opinion. "And for nothing," groaned Tania. "Write up this stuff you're giving away gratis. *After the Drain.* We'll have two books fighting each other for the top of the list."

It was a—silent—Wursup boast that he could pluck the real story out of a thousand clumsier reportorial hands, but the Watergate story had no savor for him. Still, he did write a "think piece" on it for the *Atlantic*.

Wursup had grown tired of his old methods. "Making stories out of little surgical cuts of appearance and talk. Prosopography. The glint in the eye explains the guy's ideas. I'm fed up with it," he told Will. "It stinks of surface. Dog piddle. I read a sentence of Brecht's about realism not just showing the way things are, but the reasons they are that way. That's what I want. I'm tired of these squints and glints. Long views. Marx. Machiavelli. Weber."

In the Watergate piece, he'd trotted out a few: "the terror of the new Horatio Algers discovering the perverse sources of their purest impulses"; "the democratic diffusion of individuality in a modern state which required computerized information which itself compromised individuality and—that Victorian luxury—privacy." At first, he was intoxicated with this philosophic ether. He felt he'd explained the fury, hubris, contempt and naive fervor of the Nixonians; their boys'-club secretiveness, heroics, vanity and nervelessness; the emotional poverty in the little marble capital; the hunger for theater- and history-making; and then the stripping of Tartuffian holiness from the shriveled neurotic who was its totem. But the piece didn't work. Farsightedness bored Wursup. When people tell you to watch the stars, keep your hand on your wallet. To get to the heart of things okay, but en route there was a heap of rhetorical flab. Was anything worse than Faulkner's Nobel Prize meowing? (*Corruptio optimi pessima.*) To backtrack on his own meowing, he ended the piece with a chunk of doggerel called "To Salivate at Watergate, or He Picks on the Ticks on Nixon" (which Tania made him remove).

Tania—"the sentimental Iron Maiden," Will called her—sat Wursup in one of her ten-dollar wire-backed chairs and told him he had to screw himself up to the mark. "You're messing up your emotional map. You don't know what you're doing. Let the colors of one country run into another, the map's useless." Tania was losing her hair. Tiny black curls covered less and less of her Augustan head. She hated this—in fact, hated her looks—but her perfect lover's lips and passionate, glittery, Tokay-grape eyes excited no small fraction of her authors (all men). She was confessor, mother and prosecutor as well as advocate, advance man, paymistress and occasional easer of sexual tension.

"One emotion per story" was her Poe-esque principle. She cowed most of her authors into swallowing it. Wursup, more difficult now, was an old favorite; she let him get away with more than most. "Don't pull the tablecloth out and think the dishes aren't going to break."

"I'm sick of it all. I can't even see straight."

"How lucky you don't have to anymore. You're not starving. Anytime you want to close your eyes, you can. Look at me. I didn't have to stay with what I was given." She touched her head. Wursup *had* noticed something new but, full of his own aches, hadn't said anything. (Like hanging, or a psychiatrist's couch, Tania's chairs drove you toward self-absorption.) Tania's alteration was a handsome mess of black curls, not originally Tania's. "Twelve hundred bucks. The best. You didn't say anything."

"You look terrific, but what's new about that?" (Augustus had turned into Caligua.)

"If I wasn't afraid of ruining it, I'd lock the doors here and now."

"You wouldn't find me useful. If Sookie didn't take it on trust these days, she'd have to have it sent in from Bloomingdale's. I'm not worth a goddamn."

Tania's desk gleamed with the tiny apparatus of her industry: pencil points, pens, silvery typewriter, cigar holders, roach clips, lighters, bottles and glasses for the sunken, the risen or rising authors who opened their veins on the hard chairs, or who were trussed up and given marching orders. The new curls also shone in the white noon light. "You're the real thing; you stamp the bullion. Don't sit there moping. I'm going to find you something lovely. This afternoon."

"Maybe Sleeping Beauty needs sleep."

"Then you'll sleep." Perfect little teeth spread in her wonderful cheeks, gleaming amidst the small lights hopping off her desk. "But I'm going to do some calling. Tania knows where the fish are."

The next day, Mike Schilp called him at home. "Tania said you felt like doing a piece. Want to go to Africa?"

"I can't make it to Central Park."

"Okay. I've got a job you can do in your armchair. Reading."

"That I can do."

"I want you to do a piece on dying."

Wursup made a punched-in-the-belly noise. "Don't make jokes about everything, Michael."

"I make nothing. For two years now, these death books have been storming in. An avalanche. It's the new topic."

"Yes, it's a very clever device. I wish I had the patent."

"Just listen." That was superfluous. Schilp had a basso boom, and was, in Sookie's phrase, the "Mussolini of telephones." "When he speaks, my bones melt. If I hadn't seen him, I'd be terrified." Schilp was chubbier than Tania, but almost shapeless, like a beefsteak tomato. Sookie said his voice box was thirty percent of him. "You've done the country, you're doing the world. Where else is there? Mars? Not your meat. You want to change sex like Jimmy Morris? Turn black like Jack Griffin? Shrink like Alice? Pose as a bunny? What? What can you do now?" ("Now" was a key Schilp word.) "Death is still 'undiscovered country.'"

"I don't think you know what's coming out of your mouth, Michael."

"I'm not telling you to shoot yourself. Here's the way I see it. There are twenty books a month coming in for review on death and dying. You know the way subjects"—the punched-belly noise came out of Wursup again—"rise out of nowhere and take over. One year the courts are filled with First Amendment cases, two years later there isn't one."

"That's different. What you're talking about has been a fact—a fact of everything forever."

"And I'm saying it gets rediscovered every fifty years or so. And for good reasons. Whenever there's a cultural saturation point, death's trotted out, front and center: the graveyard poets in the eighteenth century, the death preachers in the seventeenth, Jeremy Taylor, Bossuet. No accident they're still the prose classics of French and English. Ever read the *Oraisons Funèbres?*"

Schilp was the most literate editor in America. He'd done a thousand-page dissertation at Berkeley entitled "Violence in

the Country," which was not about assassination but images
of slaughter in pastoral poems from Theocritus to William
Carlos Williams. It had exhausted his academic ambition. Ed-
iting was his métier. He was born to oversee the conversion of
The Everyday into The Sensational. For him, writers were
like individuals to deathless genes—necessary conveniences.
He speed-read through the publications of Europe and America, thousands of pages a week; his memory was fantastic—so
good, thought Wursup, that sometimes his notions came
through glued to feathers or even whole organs of swallowed
matter. "It's the best French ever written. Turn a good writer
loose on death, and you've got something. It never fails."

"I'm fed up with all the death crap. I thought your job was
diverting people."

"That's the kicker. Do it right, there's nothing more diverting. One way or another. The blues send people through the
ceiling. *Last* quartets, *last* plays, *last* words. Irresistible."

"Not to me."

"All over they got these courses in thanatology. That Ku-
bler-Ross lady started it in Chicago. Every slut kicking off in
the wards is propped up to lecture interns. Feifel, Choron,
Glazer, Strauss, Rosvetchki—there's quite a bibliography. A
literary *campo santo*. Beacon just reissued that book by Wertenbaker's widow about his last months. When she helps him
cut his wrists, I busted out weeping."

It must, thought Wursup, have sounded like Victoria Falls.
Still, it was nice to know Michael's eyes were connected with
his feelings. Except for an ugly man's hatred for ugly people,
and his lust for print, Michael usually seemed unconnected
with feeling, a kind of growth germinated by Alexander Gra-
ham Bell. "Now, Freddy, these books"—Wursup heard the
slaps and grunts of books dropped on one another—"*Choos-
ing a Lot, Explaining Death to Children, Grief and Mourning, Reaching Those Gone, Omega: A Journal for Dying, Suicide and*—get this—*Other Lethal Behavior,* they're all sitting

25

here. Here's my idea. Most human energy is spent, necessarily, on the human middle." (Wursup's head filled with the
neckless tomato on the other end.) "Improving, changing,
making. The feeding-nourishing-propagating world. Then,
every once in a while, there's this stir about beginnings and
endings. Like the sluts' push for rights to their frigging bodies
started all the gas about defining Beginning: cells, embryos,
fetuses, what the fuck, protons. So all this transplant, eu-
thanasia, pulling-the-plug stuff drives people to think about
Ends: What's death? What's dying? How to croak? Croaking
right, croaking wrong. *That"*—the boom was *pianissimo,* a
huge pianist, a Richter or Gieseking, crouched over a tinkle, a
summery rumble—"is your piece."
  "You've just written it."
  "Don't slither. This is going to be a new color on the Wursup palette. The underworld of *Drain.* Orpheus going down
for Eurydice, a poet in search of a great subject. Luscious lips
in the netherworld. The singer in the pubic forest."
  Who'd interrupt Bach improvising in the Gewandthaus?
When Schilp took breath, Wursup said quietly, "It's an interesting proposition, Michael. As you spell it out, anyway. But
I'm not your man. I'm a little nervous about turning into a
shade myself."
  Eleven-thirty in the morning. His work time. Usually he
unplugged the phone. Schilp knew that. Was the word
around he wasn't working? Of course, Tania had told Schilp
he wanted to do a piece; but Schilp had a mean genius in his
nostrils. Had he smelled something? Something deeply
wrong? Maybe he thought he could get a blow-by-blow story
of a writer's last days. "I don't see why you found this piece for
me." He'd forgotten Schilp's first offer was Africa.
  "For one thing, you did that terrific Groppenza piece for
Look. Of course I thought of you."
  "That's right. I nearly forgot."
  Leo Groppenza: A little golden fellow, mild as a corn

muffin, who hurdled flames and leapt gulches. His slogan was "dying others." "We need that verb form. Not everyone can kill himself." Leo did, in an Idaho canyon, two weeks after Wursup's piece came out in *Look*.

"Dear old Leo." Slots of visibility opened in window rime. Through one, Wursup could make out the peak of the building which blocked Susannah's, a red-brick doghouse which sheltered the air-conditioning generator. The sun was making merry through iced New York, gold braid in the white crystals. "Leo was a man, dying's a—a what?—a thing, a subject, an idea, a state. And gloomy. You need someone like Candy Bergen. She could pull corpses out of the ground and make them laugh."

"And talk like Barbie Dolls. Ever meet a lady reporter with an ear? Never. Even Colette. In her fiction, fabulous. In reportage, the ear turned tin. What a little meatball she was." (The burning bush had turned frying pan.)

"I'll think it over, Michael. I'm grateful you thought of me."

Monday morning, Wursup called. "Find a gloomier Gus, Michael."

Two hours later, he saw a picture of Will Eddy's father sitting on two columns of Ollie Fenchal's mortuary gas on the obituary page of the *Times*. Old Professor Eddy, with his snow-blond hair and his pinstriped suits, tie clasp, collar pin and French cuffs, wearing a button of the Légion d'honneur, telling stories out of the nuclear epic—Oak Ridge, Los Alamos. Wursup had gone up to his Maine island to record them for his book *The Big Thought and the Big Bang*—the Minnesota farmer's son coming into his own at the Metallurgical Institute under Fermi and, later, with Szilard and James Franck, assembling the scientific community behind civilian control of atomic energy. In retirement he translated Icelandic sagas. "There was little the old fellow couldn't do, once his will was set," said Will on the phone. "Ha"—for he'd caught his own name in the noun, painfully. His father's accomplishment was a corrosive—though unmentioned—rebuke to him. "He was a terrific man." And, groaning, "The past tense is so quick. All I think of is the way he handled the ashes." The elegant old fellow let his cigarillo turn into an ash parabola, which, unfailingly, he'd catch in an ash tray .

"Do you need anything, Willie?"

"No. I'm sure he left everything in order. The ash tray's on its way to the ash. I just have to put it back on the table."

From his day on Swan's Island, Wursup remembered a sentence Professor Eddy loved. It was Galileo's. "He'd been rebuked," said Prof, "for pushing God too far off into space. So he said, 'The sun which has all the planets revolving around and dependent on it for their orderly functions can ripen a bunch of grapes as if it had nothing else in the world to do.' What a model."

Wursup called Mike Schilp back and said he'd try the article.

The odd thing was that in forty-four years Wursup had had no close touch of death. His parents were in their seventies (separated, but alive); he had been too young to feel much about the death of his grandparents or, later, his mother's brothers. (Her three sisters were still-rollicking octogenarians.) He had seen lots of dead and dying men in Vietnam, and it was true that now and then a death—a six-year-old girl in a village near Danang, a Chicano corporal with whose platoon he'd gone into the mountains in 'sixty-five—had gone through him like a poison; he had felt it in the stomach for days. He'd seen stacks of corpses carted into ghats along rivers in India and Nepal, but they had next to nothing to do with that vacancy which the end of the little girl or the corporal or Leo Groppenza had put into the world.

Only two or three times had his own death touched him. (Waking at night around a terrible hollow.) He couldn't handle that; no point in it. Such sensation destroyed capacity. Didn't eyes have lids for such protection?

He spent a couple of weeks reading: Bushido Death, Stoic Views of Death, Psychoanalysis and Death. Freud claimed death fear fused anxiety about mother loss with anxiety about castration "projected upon the powers of destiny." Freud himself was said to have one of history's worst cases of death terror, *Todangst*. In fact, the most vital people were the greatest death-fearers and death-dodgers: Goethe, Tolstoy and Dr. Johnson were divisional champs. They were examples of what Wursup called his Koufax Theorum. The famous pitcher had said that his terrible arm pain derived from the same calcium deposit which gave him extra throwing power. So death torture gripped the libido of the world's most living livers; they exposed themselves to it again and again. The hope was to inoculate themselves.

Now Wursup swam in death texts. Some cheered and exalted him (Hume's decorous stroll with stomach cancer); some (the death of Paul Dombey, or the Wertenbaker death, which had made Schilp weep) devastated him.

Seeing his long face about to collapse in sobs one night, Sookie said, "You can't take much more, Freddy. Every night a funeral. When are you going to wind up?"

Lanky, awkward, sharp and charming, Sookie was one of those double beauties who looked gorgeous either unmade-up or as the creation of the dust and syrup of five hundred plants and animal bladders. Her long head sprouted a snub, Renoir nose that told the air, "Come to me." She had a fashion model's emphatic cheeks, which she rouged with a hundred shades of blood; huge, dense, almost violet eyes which were outlined, italicized, sparkled, veiled; a Dover cliff of forehead was topped by a mass of red-gold hair, which, two or three times a week, she metal-tortured into Versailles shrubbery.

In the morning, she was even more delectable. Subtle power streamed from her sleep-undone beauty; there were delicacies of color in her cheeks. This beauty was infinitely more appealing to Wursup than the manufactured beauty which could be lifted off and left in a museum. For Sookie, though, that made-up beauty was not just necessary mask but escape from an old conviction of ugliness instilled by a thousand sisterly digs and a girlhood of unfavorable comparison to the models in *Mademoiselle, Glamour* and *Vogue.*

To the current queens of appearance, Dominique Sanda, Catherine Deneuve and Jacqueline Bisset, Sookie's spirit paid terrible tribute. To every inch of them she gave an eye trained to read the subtleties of terrestrial slippage. Jacqueline's broad shoulders and big waist, Dominique's small, floppy breasts, Catherine's stick legs, were lights of hope in her despair over these celebrities of beauty (who themselves, said Wursup, probably despaired over the perfection of a salesgirl's nose, a secretarial bust).

Made or unmade, Sookie's beauty diverted Wursup. Only that industrial middle state which converted ore into currency disturbed him. Once, he said, "Your dressing table is like the Ruhr. Or Gary. You're the General Motors of your own appearance."

Sookie's face leaked tears. A mature, a brilliant, woman, a geophysicist who lectured all over the world on what made it tick and rumble, she was a permanent adolescent about her looks. Not a month went by without an invitation to pass on her notions in Berkeley or Bogotá, Rome or Amsterdam. And underneath all this earthly science were the shifty plates of her physical insecurity.

Professionally, she was a rock. After a hydrographer attacked her description of a river basin, Sookie said, "It's hard enough to know what goes on in a bathtub."

Of her work, Wursup made little. Indeed, of Sookie herself, he made little. Purposely—or so he told himself and her. "The less we spell each other out, the longer we'll last. It's a good reason to keep separate apartments." (Sookie had a place off Central Park on Sixty-eighth Street and spent about half her nights there.)

"Is longevity such a virtue?" asked Will, whose long marriage had become a prison. "You're not planning to have kids."

Sookie wanted no children. And the idea of marriage belonged to the Dark Ages. Still, she and Wursup had spun a thousand marriagelike threads between them. They knew each other's tastes, habits, gestures, love and battle movements, and now and then, they were pleasantly surprised to find themselves not just in one of the states of passionate affection they refused to call "love" but aware that they were indispensable to each other.

"It'll wind up when I write the piece," he told her. "It's not going to be a book."

"I hope you're done when I get back from the Gulf." Sookie was part of a team funded by Texaco to assess an offshore site for a superport. "You go on much longer, the only sheets you'll be fit for will be shrouds."

Sookie too had waked at nights feeling misery in her chest, her eyeballs popping with imaginary tumors. This was some of the static Wursup's project installed in their recent nights.

"It's so big," he said to her. (These days, "it" was death.) "In a way, there's nothing to say about it. Yet life's soaked with it. Until you deal with it, there's no culture. Every *polis* has a *necropolis*. Death sits on life. It dominates economy: social security, debt, conservation, pollution, the Pentagon. Half the world's stories circle it. One way or another, millions are in the death business."

"I'm not," said Sookie. "Death is nothing in my work. Life's just a little carbon zone dangled between ice ages. No technology's going to touch that. Death's a local sample of the Great Ice. I care about what it leaves behind. A chunk of coal, a little gas, calcium. Take a long view. Relax. Life's a haphazard coagulation of inorganic soup."

31

"Beautiful," he said. "Can I have it?" Already appropriating—*writing*—it into the accountant's ledger he used for notes. Three hundred of the long, gridded pages were stuffed with death notes. "And I haven't begun," he told her. "What's the Chinese line about love? 'There are an infinite number of steps to my heart. You've climbed perhaps one or two of them.' I'm nowhere."

"I know," she said. "I know you. You've got to get things right; and you've got something you can't get right. So you knock yourself in the head." She was taking off her work-clothes, the tailored jeans which on her long, lean knob-kneed legs were like ideal, platonic jeans (exhibitions of what they concealed). "You push too hard, too. Take your time. Mama used to say, 'Grass grows when it's ready. You can't pull it up blade by blade.' 'A time to sew, a time for silence, a time to speak.'" Over the rust-gold rings of hair came her green cashmere. Sookie's breasts were heavy—"significant breasts," he'd described them to Will Eddy. "She thinks penis envy is nuts. 'Wouldn't you rather have these?' she asked me."

"'A time to love' and a time to stew."

The mortuary grip relaxed. What a thing is man. "'We're fundamentally what shouldn't be, which is why we stop being.'" This out of his file. Schopenhauer. He watched Sookie's torso grow from the discarded clothes, the butterfly motion of the hips. "What shouldn't be, but is. Oh, my Sook-heart."

It was a corollary of the Koufax Theorem that attention to something tended to promote it. Wursup's absorption did not, he had to believe, cause anyone to die, but in February, he did write four letters of condolence to survivors of friends. The last of these went to Susannah's boss at *Chouinard's News Letter*, Kevin Miyako, whose wife had died after a long, wicked cancer.

In March, from his post on the roof, Wursup spotted Kevin

in Susannah's living room. He didn't notice him immediately; noticed only that the room was brighter than usual, that Susannah was talking, and using her hands, which, talking with Petey, she never did. Listening, her head bobbed expressively: *taking in.* She was a wonderful listener. That had attracted him from the beginning, back in Paris. (Later, he believed that Susannah listened but didn't understand.) Now, watching her rock along in self-effacing, surely comforting attention, he knew someone special was receiving it. (She was the best of mothers, but the boys did not get that kind of attention.)

He'd gone up without field glasses, more or less as a security check, but now he climbed down to fetch them.

It was Kevin. Small shock.

But why not? They were inevitable partners, hardworking, old-fashioned people, scornful of frills and theatrics. Peggy Miyako had suffered genuinely and terribly, but she'd been a flamboyant complainer. (Was that another form of future-inoculation?) Kevin and Susannah were stoics, self-anesthetizing anesthetists.

"Zookeepers" was Will Eddy's term for the Kevins and Susannahs of the earth. "They throw in the meat, pull out the splinters, deliver the cubs." He'd said it of Susannah years ago. "You needed a keeper, Freddy, and you got the best."

Maybe he was jumping the gun. Kevin and Susannah were *talking.* Period. Kevin was handsome. Only an ugly guy like himself noticed that. A Japanese Dubliner. When Susannah, years ago, had first described her boss, Wursup conjured up *Ulysses* with Kevin sitting in for Bloom. Kevin had a big Western jaw and northern, cream-and-berry cheeks on which perched small black eyes ready to take off at a harsh word. *Mister Butterfly.*

Wursup lost himself in the field glasses. He knew the form sheet here. Susannah would like—*did* like, she'd said— Kevin's East-meets-West looks, his to-the-point, don't-fiddle-around manner. Kevin dressed as an expert dresses a manikin, for sales. Now he wore a maroon turtleneck and double-knit slacks colored by Disneyland. The clothes didn't relate to him, either as expression or contradiction. All right, Susannah saw the outfit; the price tag was by the cuff. And in these days of loss, the price was low.

Why not? Kevin, walking steadily away from the long death watch, could find in Susannah the undramatic vividness and good flesh which had surely accumulated a terrific balance in the sexual bank these years of working side by side.

Good old Susannah. No more empty holes in Somayo's Cleaners' calendar.

He stopped looking. An hour later, feeling another breeze of curiosity, he climbed up again and saw that the lights were out.

No, not yet. They couldn't be in bed. (She'd have to have a bigger bed. Not that Susannah's lovers would need much room.)

Two nights later, Kevin was back. Wursup got a report from Petey. (The field glasses were inadequate; and he was not going to bug the living room. He told many a journalism class, "Don't be buggers. Reporting isn't voyeurism.")

Petey usually came for supper Tuesdays or Fridays. Tuesdays, the meal was cooked by Constance, the cleaning woman. Fridays, Wursup had meat, onions, garlic, cloves, tomatoes, basil, parsley and anchovies bubbling in the iron pan for his special spaghetti sauce. If Petey didn't feel like coming, Wursup made no fuss. No pressure on the boy.

Like Billy, and like Wursup himself had been, Petey was a late grower. Which entailed some humiliation and much evasive strategy, including a sweetness and charm for pacifying bigger, meaner boys. Petey was a dear fellow. He had a large, Wursuppian head and Susannah's coloring, that wintry rosiness that made Gregory the Great call the Angles "angels." He wore a Sherpa hat—fox fur sewn to dark-green suede—

Wursup had bought for him in Katmandu. The fur flaps covered most of his cheeks. All one saw of the features was a little square nose and chin.

Over the spaghetti, Wursup slid into reportorial gear. "You know, Petey, I sure wish Mom would find a nice friend."

"She's got friends." Meat-red sauce on the miniature Wursup face.

"I mean men friends. You know. It's hard for a woman as attractive as Mom not to have men friends."

"Hard for any woman, isn't it? Anyway, she's got a friend."

It seemed that Kevin had been over five or six times, and though Petey had known him as part of Kevin-Peggy and as an office name, he knew him now as the kind of friend his father meant. "You know, Daddy, it'd probably be a good idea if I stayed over with you every once in a while. You know?"

"That's grown-up of you, Petey. You may have something. Maybe Mom and Kevin would like to be by themselves occasionally. And you know I like to have you around here."

"It won't cramp *your* style, will it?"

"You're my style, sweetie."

So things were working out. Hiroshima, mon amour. Banzai. (Maybe the Kannon from Horyugi had done the trick.) Mysterious are the ways of Eros. East meets West, Dublin and Osaka, Yankee and Samurai. May they enter the Lotus Land of Bliss. Though Japanese men had wicked erotic reputations. Mothers handed down to daughters the smooth, masturbatory stones—smoother each generation—which consoled the injured caverns of pleasure. There was—Wursup had read—an old tradition of shrinking the vagina with alum so the Japanese macho could know a rapist's terrible joy. Dear God. Poor Susannah.

2

"It's one of these glassed-in ant farms," said Wursup of *Chouinard's News Letter*. Though not to Susannah, who was one of the ants, and for whom the struggles Wursup miniaturized were grim business. Chouinardians referred to Wursup's "sort of journalism" as "gigantism" and, even before Susannah's divorce, thought of his work as a mastodonic grinding down of the truth. "You looking for big research staffs?" Kevin asked new staffers at *Chouinard's*. "Junkets to Paris, your copy rewritten on editorial assembly lines? Then trot on down to *Newsweek*."

Most new Chouinardians had already been there, and to all the other journalistic mastodons of New York. Still, it was not bad at *Chouinard's*. The *Letter* was turned out on the fifth floor of an apartment house overlooking the sculpture garden of the Museum of Modern Art. "The land John D. Rockefeller, Sr., lived on when he moved here from Cleveland," Kevin told new staffers. "And Nelson said he learned his politics there," pointing over the crib of bronze, shrubbery and marble to the dull white building.

New staffers sometimes thought that Kevin was a Rockefeller intimate, that the *News Letter* itself was wired into that great family empire. It was—conspicuously—not; but it was Kevin's feeling that newcomers should feel part of a grandeur five cluttered rooms and twelve thousand subscribers didn't permit. Guides become part of what they show, and Kevin's introductory references to "Senior," "Junior," "The Brothers," "The Cousins," "Suite 5600," and his versions of intimate, as well as corporate, anecdotes at times obscured, even for him, his lack of any but topographic association with The Family.

The apartment was not zoned for business of any sort; only the amiable, almost domestic nature of the *Letter* allowed them this rent-controlled shelter. They had more mail coming and going than the other tenants. There was a teletype in the back room, and the apartment received tidings from Santiago and Stockholm, but it was still an intimate enterprise. Its version of the world's prospects, mailed each month to libraries and a few executive and professional people around the country, had the regulated passion that could come from a well-informed, public-spirited family over a good dinner. Many of the subscribers would as soon desert their parents as cancel their subscriptions.

The *Letter* had been started in the nineteen fifties by Auguste Chouinard, the son of a French-Canadian farmer, who'd begun as a writer of film reviews for a short-lived rival of the *Village Voice*. When it folded, Gus Chouinard took his book of clippings up to the *George Masterman News Letter* and was taken on as a researcher specializing in entertainment industries and markets. These were the years television was altering not only entertainment but business, politics and social life. Chouinard's ambition was little more than to lose himself in celluloid dreams,. but he found himself making sense of amalgamations, spin-offs, stock options and corporate territoriality. Even though it looked as if he might be in line for Masterman's own chair, it was too much. He set up his own *Letter* in his own apartment.

Kevin was his first employee. A shy, handsome; uncertain young man, Kevin had seen his father narrowly escape deportation to a Montana camp for California *nisei*. As it was, the family fruit store was sold for half its worth, and the family moved to St. Louis, where Mrs. Miyako's brother worked for the Myelius Shoe Company. For the next four years, Kevin suffered the taunts, then the—largely imagined—detestation of .his classmates. His name, his eyes and his father marked him as the—always useful—enemy within. A stubborn timidity became his shield. Even before pro-Japanese sympathy replaced the gook-hatred of the war, he'd become a class pet. His looks, formerly his curse, now—to his surprise—became an excitement. At Washington University, he was approached, courted and initiated into amorous and fraternal life. In his junior year, he fell in love with an editor of the school paper, Peggy Spitteler. Interest followed love: hooked on journalism, he switched his major from business, and, at graduation, got a job in the business office of the Chicago *Daily News.* A year later, he saw an advertisement in *Editor and Publisher* for the new *Chouinard's News Letter.*

When Susannah Wursup came to work for the *Letter*, in 1967, Kevin was its editor and owner. Gus Chouinard had called him in the day after Johnson's election, in November, 'sixty-four, and said the life of deadlines was killing him; he'd let Kevin buy him out for thirty thousand dollars. By then, there were five paid and two unpaid staffers, and subscriptions brought in two hundred and fifty thousand dollars a year. Kevin had been registered as cotenant with Chouinard, so the rent raises could continue at the controlled rate. It was a fair, even a charitable, offer. Kevin borrowed money and became *Chouinard's*.

For the *Chouinard's* staff, the best of life went on in the office. Each staffer had his bailiwick and his area of expertise. Susannah, starting as secretary, file clerk and go-fer, turned her high-school Spanish on to Latin-American newspapers and journals and became house expert on the business, politics, society and art of a hundred million South Americans. At first, she didn't risk anything more than rewrites of accepted expertise. In time, though, her confidence grew enough so that she affixed queries, then barbs, and finally criticism of the authorities.

Kevin too was happiest when, in his vanilla blazer and raspberry slacks, he surfaced from the IRT and jogged toward Fifty-fourth Street. He and Peggy had been an exceptionally loving couple. Instead of children, their bond was trouble—economic, social and physical; but between getting established in New York and Peggy's last illness, there'd been an intermission of tranquillity which offered nothing to combat. In the office, there were the world's battles. And also, there were Susannah, the "Bennett Twins," Terence and Libba—unrelated, unalike, but called that: he, a stooped exile from the defunct newspapers of New York; she, heavy lipped, great breasted, hungry voiced, the *Letter's* "Man in Consumerland"—and "Dame" Mae Twiddy, a friendly little old lady who wrote their most impressive forecasts. There were floating personnel as well: Old Bennett brought in discards from dying newspapers; Libba, alumnae of Mount Holyoke and girls she'd met at the Manhattan Theater Club.

Every day at ten, the Chouinardians had a conference on the last twenty-four hours: politics, the markets, hot items in technical journals (they largely relied on *Scientific American, Nature, Petroleum News,* and the *Journal of Modern Business*). Kevin parceled out research areas and inspected stories. There were twenty or thirty small nations which had less-efficient intelligence than *Chouinard's*.

The tutelary divinity was I. F. Stone. "He never needs an interview," Kevin told new staffers. *"The Congressional Record, Le Monde,* the *Zürcher Zeitung,* books. He sinks more shafts into the world than a thousand commissions. Maybe his politics were toasted in the thirties—they don't have to be ours—but he doesn't need junkets to Paris and research assistants. If you do, go down to the *Times.*"

It was like the mayor of Waukegan or San Bernardino telling a subordinate that if he was *that* kind of planner, he'd better try the White House. *Newsweek, Time,* the *Times,* the *Post* were terms of abuse at *Chouinard's.* They stood for labyrinths of intelligence-gathering in which accuracy was more victim than quarry. Terence, ex–police reporter for the old New York *World-Telegram,* and Dame Mae, who'd had two years in a corner of the *Journal of Commerce,* stood at *Chouinard's* for those who'd rejected expensive distortion for the chop-your-own-wood simplicity of the *Letter.*

Kevin debated putting the slogan *Tempus occidit, litera vivificat* ("Time kills, the letter giveth life") on their logo, but it seemed too ambiguous, cynical and limiting. "If our name were *Eternity,* we could use *'Tempus'* to stand for those who live by the minute, but this way we'd only upset some of the readers. After all, our bunch read Latin."

Our bunch. Our crew, our gang, the Readers, unsere Leute, les nôtres, watashi domo no uchiju (Kevin occasionally fetched *our family* from his father's language)—these stood for the persistent twelve thousand who sent in the checks which guaranteed them the *Chouinard's* view of the world eleven times a year (July, August and September were collapsed into two issues). No survey had been taken of *Chouinard's* "readership." Kevin didn't want to know: "Suppose it's the robot list that just takes everything?" Letters of correction, rejoinder, appreciation or denunciation were so rare that when one came in, it was passed around to everyone in the office. Ignorance permitted the handsomest assessment of their readers; and as Kevin assumed general classical knowledge on the part of Our Bunch, it could also be assumed that *Chouinard's* readers, repelled by impurer media, waited breathlessly for their monthly supply of pure intelligence.

Now and then, the *Letter* would be quoted in *The Nation* or *Barron's;* and one of Terence's pieces (on the decline of candy sales) was picked up and rewritten—"condensed"—by *Reader's Digest.* The staff pretended nonchalance before the astonishing evidence that they belonged to a greater system of information. If someone mentioned "that piece of Kevin's *The Nation* mangled" or joked about the *Reader's Digest's* "incinerator journalism" which reduced "Terentian diamonds to uniform ash," the others throbbed with comprehension.

For all the loyalty of the subscribers and the smallness of the staff salaries (Kevin's sixteen thousand a year was two thousand more than Dame Mae and Terence's, five more than Susannah and Libba's, four times that of the recruits), postal and printing rates drove them ever closer to bankruptcy. They gave up the teletype ("It was more for show," said Kevin. "Fast-breaking stuff was never our thing"), gave up the cleaning woman, coffee maker, morning pastry. It wasn't enough. The next triennium their rent would rise seven percent; and the higher costs of printing, taxes, and postal rates were a murderous hand on their throat. "Should we up the subscription rates?" It terrified them. At twenty-five dollars, they might coast through the inflation, but if they stuck their heads up along with the rest, who knows how many of Our Bunch would foreclose the luxury. That was the last thing to risk. They'd never had advertising. Maybe it was time to have a page or two. *The New York Review* had book advertisers; so did *Public Interest.* Only Izzy Stone did without, but his *Weekly* had stopped before the worst rise; it also had a bigger circulation, and Stone and his wife had done nine tenths of the work on it.

Crisis time. Kevin said he would feel out advertisers. Some of "our corporation people" might be willing to support them. To draw attention to their financial weakness was also risky, but the risk must be taken. No alternative. Susannah worked up a letter describing their unique audience and sent it to four hundred firms which advertised in any publication which resembled the *Letter* in quality, policy or general intent.

The result was poor: thirty-eight replies, which led to only three takers, two of which, small publishers, requested special rates.

A dark time. The cheery office limped toward night. The staff saw one another as survivors of a wreck. The wonderful bustle of Twiddy, Terence, Libba and the recruits, the white waterfall of the ten-o'clock mail, the bulletins of the radio news station (substituting for the teletype), were the gallant chatter of sailors as the sea crawled over the decks. "Three more issues," Kevin told Susannah. "Even if we stopped paying the recruits, it'd only be four or five. You better start looking for something else." This was in the six months before Peggy's death. For Kevin, the terrible prospects fused.

For a year, Susannah had relished the economies. She brought in a broom, a vacuum cleaner, a hotplate for coffee. Spanish caution revived on her lips: "The best sauce is hunger," "Who grabs too much, squeezes too little." The Chouinardians would have to hunker down and wait out the storm. That was life's best test. Clothes don't make the man. He who doesn't have a straw tail doesn't fear the fire. Better the mouse's head (*cabeza de ratón*) than the lion's tail (*que cola de león*). What was said of George Wallace's political strength— that like a rock's it didn't grow but didn't squeeze, either— would be true of theirs.

The proverb that turned out to be the one that applied best was not one Susannah had memorized: *Dádivas ablandan peñas*—"Gifts soften rocks."

Libba Bennett's latest recruit was a quiet young woman named Abby Schlosserberg. Kevin had taken to her strongly, in part because Kevin's favorite Rockefeller "cousin" was Abby, the feminist, whose essay "Sex: The Basis of Sexism" he'd used as the prop of a piece entitled "The Cycle of American Fortunes, From the Illicit Adventurism of William Avery Rockefeller (1810–1906?) to the Rebellious Personalism of Abby Aldrich Rockefeller (1943–   )." Abby Schlosserberg was also a feminist, and, more important, also an heiress, though not of oil, steel, railroad and banking fortunes but of a rubber-and-nylon product she said she'd only learned was a condom after her graduation from Mount Holyoke. Distant, courteous, quietly passionate about the *Letter,* Abby looked like a recruit who would stay. She'd majored in modern-European history and soon covered the European press for them—the *Corriere della Serra, Le Monde,* the Portuguese *Expresso.* A piece on the Portuguese military-academy officers· who'd worked together in Africa and started the post-Salazar revolution had been used—without acknowledgment—by *Time* and *Newsweek.* It was one of the *Letter's* proudest coups.

Abby's remoteness had kept her from the financial tremors that filled the office. Only after Kevin called them in and told them that even if they all worked for nothing, it looked as if they couldn't last another year, did she understand the desperation. Even then, it took her a week to connect her own inheritance (her parents had died in an automobile accident the year of her graduation) with the salvation of *Chouinard's.*

"Excuse me, Mr. Miyako," she said—or whispered—to Kevin. "I wonder if I could talk with you." That began the conversation which led to the first office party ever *chez Chouinard's.* Though Peggy Miyako had only six more weeks to live, and Kevin went directly to the hospital from the office and stopped there an hour every morning before work, the wonderful offer of Abby's—"Please take what you need"— turned his heart around. He would not let the extent of his happiness show when he saw Peggy, only telling her that things were working out better than he'd thought they would (he hadn't told her how bad they'd been); but to Susannah he was able to show how much hope lay under the misery of what was happening at the hospital.

Abby, Terence, Dame Mae, Libba, Susannah and the four latest recruits came in a body to Peggy's funeral, and came back to Kevin's apartment with Peggy's mother to see Kevin through. They cooked the roast and sliced the cake. They were a larger, sturdier family than Kevin had known. Then, beyond that, the feelings that he and Susannah had left unexpressed for years began to surface.

3

"Modern urban life"—Wursup, used to carving verbal marble for invisible audiences, was "giving an interview" to Ollie Fenchal, of the *Times*—"is made for the single, the clumsy, the lustful." Ollie, one of the obituary writers, occasionally doubled in features. "Can't cook, you heat up a Stouffer's goodie; cold, turn up the thermostat; in danger, call the cops. Unless the danger's the cop. As for the sexual signal system . . ."

"What was that, Fred? Didn't quite get that."

Ollie himself had carved up enough verbal marble to fill Arlington Cemetery. Tony Spilotto, one of Wursup's pals on the *Times*, said the reason Ollie had a tough time hearing was that he had silicosis of the cerebrum. "Still, once he gets those old fingers round something, the juice pours out."

"Like hell," said Wursup, a Squeezee. "He couldn't even get the color of the eyes right. And he called my place an 'efficiency garret.' It may not be The Breakers,"—this was to Sookie, who'd brought back three copies of the *Times*—but 'garret' is slander. Why didn't he call it a 'prison cell'? You know I love Japanese bareness."

Sookie said Ollie should have seen it before she took over. "It made the moon look like a Victorian whorehouse. You still don't have a blade of living green here."

"I take no prisoners. Who's going to give 'em a bath when I take off and you're in Galveston or Caracas?"

"Susannah will do it, you're so palsy-walsy."

"Don't get on that. Susannah and I are pals because we have no obligations to each other. Beyond the month's check."

"Mighty cozy."

Years ago, while writing a series of pieces on the conversion of physical and emotional war debris into the Japanese economic miracle, Wursup spent four days in a small Kyoto *ryokan* up near the Ko-dai-ji temple. Never had he felt so at ease with habitation. Between the rubbery fronds looking in the window and the bare, subtle room—the blue vase in the alcove, the *tatami* mats, the scroll—was a sort of courtesy of things. There was also a wonderful courtesy between Mrs. Uemura and himself: she bowed when he entered and helped him off with his coat and on with the house kimona and slippers, but there was no obsequiousness, no sense of inequality, only some old hierarchy of host to guest. The towels were odorous and moist with steam; the bathtub was a little porcelain well. The tea service before the inquisitive scarlet fronds became for Wursup an ideal of domesticity: simplicity condensed out of complex choice; much had been tried, much rejected. He'd not been accustomed to associate luxury and precision.

Years after, furnishing the office that became his apartment as well, Wursup tried for the same sort of simplicity. He owned one mug, two spoons, two forks, one spreading and one sharp knife, a few plates, one couch, one large bed, a couple of chairs and tables. "Simplicity!" said Sookie. "You're

just a piker." Only the study contained more than the minimum (desk, swivel chair, bookshelves, file cabinet, tape recorder): on poster-size cardboards, there were pictures of his
sons, parents, friends, people he'd interviewed; on the
shelves, or taped to the wall, were souvenirs—heather from
Dartmoor, maple leaves from the Place St.-Sulpice, stones
from Boroboudur, the Acropolis, Angkor Wat and Lumbini
(Buddha's birthplace), blades of grass from the Birla House
lawn (where Gandhi had been killed), a petrified lime from Picasso's villa in Mougins, a stone broken off Louis Sullivan's
Chicago house, ash trays baked in school kilns by the boys,
and fifteen or twenty postcards—he had a thousand or so
from the world's museums—a Van Eyck from Ghent, a head-
less Aphrodite from Syracuse, a self-portrait of Hokusai (the
old fellow leaning on a beggar's crook).

When Sookie became a sometime part of the household,
Wursup was drinking coffee, orange juice and wine out of one
thick mug. "It'd also make a nice chamber pot," said Sookie.
"Lay off," he said. "It's my pal." He wasn't joking. One day it
dropped and cracked on the radiator. Picking up glazed
chunks which had been so often at his lips, he was close to
tears. "Nutty," he thought. "Nutty," but so it was. His pal,
Mug.

Sookie forced him out of this dream of Oriental bareness.
"Even if you're not going to have any other company, we
might decide to drink at the same time. I don't mind straws,
but you might not be drinking what I want."

In three hours at Bloomingdale's, they bought cups,
glasses, skillets, pots, blankets, chairs, lamps, a gold love seat,
a second bed. "Can't tell, some of your pals might come and
talk with us some day. Maybe even two at once. And don't
you want an extra bed for the boys? Divorce doesn't exile you
from humanity."

Will Eddy had told Wursup that the scholar C. S. Lewis's
dream of heaven was lounging in a garden reading the epic

47

poems of Ariosto, Pulci, and Boiardo. Wursup didn't invest in the next world, but an ideal life in this one was not complex: stuffing an orifice or two with nature's offerings, letting the mind out on an easy leash. Now he had that. Adrift between books, ducking most assignments, occasionally responding to editorial requests to name The Ten Most Beautiful Women, The Five Worst Presidential Decisions, Wursup felt he was coming as close to the sweet *nada* of the West as he'd ever been. After a long professional life of asking people questions, now he was questioned. Why not? He turned out to have as much guff, vanity, curious opinion and nerve as anyone else. He knew how to seem modest, how to beat a fluent retreat (and then another, and another). He was becoming one of the most-interviewed "seldom-interviewed" celebrities in America. A verbal Houdini: "It would take me a month to answer that, Gracie." "You put it better than I, John."

"You're basically hostile," Sookie told him. "All this sweetness is killing something in you."

"You think so." So mild. "I wonder. I'm treading water. Marking time. I don't have anything better to do."

Sookie came out of the shower, a Titian fruit goddess, rosy, golden, a towel wrapped around her thick hair, another around her long middle. What a way to score points. "You're just throwing it away. Giving it all to the gulls."

Her own self-consciousness helped her sense tremors elsewhere. And her hard line concealed a depth of feeling for what counted most. She believed deeply in Wursup; they both knew it, and the knowledge was their ultimate attachment.

Still, she did not alter his strange calm. The only rifts there now were his death texts and his queasiness about Susannah and Kevin. And what were they to someone who'd covered—what a terrible verb—wars, murders, revolutions, earthquakes?

Ollie Fenchal wrote that Wursup was "calm as a clam."

48

* * *

The key to Wursup's reporting is the sympathy
Keats called "negative capability," the apparent
absence of personal force which helps one enter
other people or things and to contain opposite view-
points simultaneously. Without himself appearing
calm as a clam Wursup has the inner calm which
lets himself give way to an almost total sympathy
with others.

White-haired, red-cheeked Ollie chain-smoked; his hands
trembled; he often didn't hear, or at least understand, what
was said. "What was that, Fred? I didn't quite get it."
Wursup's line with him had been that "whatever success"
he'd had came from "the bottle of skepticism I carry around.
Every story gets the treatment, you know what I mean, Ollie?
Every positive is negatived, every assertion turned inside out.
Give or take a little. You don't go far wrong exaggerating the
mendacity of public men."
"Could you give me that again, Fred? That sounded good."
Ollie's tragic, remote gray eyes were shot with smoke; a cigarette shook jags of it over the room.
Wursup knew how taking down other people's opinions
stirred resentment. Only when reporters were worked over by
great soft-soapers—charmers who pretended to share the professional mix of cynicism and instant tragedy—was the resentment subdued enough to get even the quotations right. (And
these were often the falsest stories of all.)
The profile was headed "Story-Trapping."

Fred Wursup himself looks harmless as a clam.
Dark, hefty, balding, brown-eyed, he's the sort of
man you know for years without remembering. Like
a con man or a great photographer, he blends into
scenery. His real existence is at his Smith-Corona.

Those who've felt Wursup's bite can hardly relate it
to the genial mollusc who interviewed them.

Wursup hit the ceiling. He called Spilotto. "That fellow
shouldn't be allowed within a mile of living men. My eyes are
not brown, they're black. Small, maybe, but clearly, definitely
black. And I'm not bald. He was smoking so damn much he
couldn't see his pencil. He even got the typewriter wrong. It's
a Remington Correcto. God help the dead. If Fenchal covered the Pyramids, people'd be hunting for them in Ceylon."

"You know the game, Fred. It always looks different on the
other side of the pencil. You'll survive Ollie."

"Two more like him, and the *Times* won't. Never again,
Tony."

It did surprise Wursup that he cared so much. He wasn't
making a case.

"It's the penalty for being a sage," Will Eddy told him.
"People come to collect wisdom, so you begin to think you've
got some to give them. You stop doing what you're good at
and sound like everyone else. Even Fenchals know when fish
begin to stink. The moment you agree to talk, they know
you're selling."

"What have I got to sell?"

"You don't have a new book out, you're not writing pieces,
you're dying not seeing yourself read. You're pushing *you*.
Like every other huckster."

"Ugly," said Wursup. "I don't like it. Is that really it? Isn't it
just killing boredom? I sit here day after day, nothing happening. The world's not spinning. At least when I shoot off my
mouth, I know I'm alive."

"Come have supper with us. Ellen and Mil are home."

Wursup loved Eddy's daughters; there were five of them,
the three oldest in college, Mil and Ellen at the Riverdale Day
School. It was the only family table which brought back to
him the pleasures of the one he'd had.

"Soon, Will, thank you. I'm just mouthing. The trouble with me is I'm not used to being on top."

"You don't have to give interviews," said Sookie. Her violet eyes, weighty with peculiar secrets, and her lips, which could foam with Lamartine and Shelley as well as hydrographical constants, transformed the slightest gesture into wisdom. "You don't like it, run. But don't moan."

"But they ask me. I've been promoted to sage. When they get a spare niche, they have to fill it. There are two thousand sages' niches a year in this country."

"Save yours for the typewriter. Some people are meant to speak off the cuff, some aren't. You're no Churchill or De Gaulle. 'Some chicken, some neck.' 'Vichy holds France by the wrists while the enemy cuts her throat.'"

"You got those from me."

"I get lots from you. But in the apartment, not off a stump, or the tube. Quit piling up material for the *Wursupiad*."

"Am I pretending to be anything? People ask me, I say yes. Is that so bad? It's *noblesse oblige*. Especially to newsmen. Which is why Fenchal upset me. Not that I'm deluded about the ability of my colleagues. I'm not trying to be Trotsky or De Gaulle. I don't go around dribbling laconic poetry over crowds. Or to my hangers-on. You act like I put on the buskins every morning. You're the one who's led around by the tongue. Dry up."

Tears. The Titian colors ran, the jauntiness folded.

"Oh Sook, sweetheart, forgive me. I got away from myself."

"No." Sob. "You showed your real"—sob—"self."

"I know. I'm treating myself like a monument. You're—"

"Your pigeon." Sob, sniffle.

"No. You're *right*." Tears soaked his shirt. "You're right as rain, and I'm a horse's ass."

* * *

Once, Will Eddy told him he acted as if he were a little guy. "You tell stories in which you're always getting the short end of the stick. Here you are, a beefy bruiser, and you act like Caspar Milquetoast."

"I feel like a little guy," he told Will.

Five-ten or -eleven, heavy, thick veined, Wursup had a tank-trap appearance which saved him from many a brawl. His face was heavy and broad. Perhaps his eyes showed the small animal hiding within the heaviness. They were black, set deep, and had an absorbtive power which picked up light with especial ease. (An ophthalmologist had once shown a colleague the unusual "snowdrop configurations" in Wursup's cataracts.) People sometimes said his eyes were yellow. "Like Stalin's," a Bulgarian correspondent had told him. "Really black or dark brown, but yellow to those scared of him."

Wursup felt neither handsome nor ugly. It didn't matter. Women had praised his looks, at least responded to them. Who could figure out what desire perceived? Women had told him many things about his face, his body, his character. Sometimes they were just trying out English. (In any case, a person will get much information about himself which is best forgotten.) If Wursup had vanity, it came out as theatrical humility. "I don't know anything," he thought often and said sometimes. No math, no science, a few fragments of many languages, never enough to appreciate when they were well spoken or written. He'd made a bad record as a student, and except for his poor mother (her brain softening in a Chicago nursing home), he'd had a bad press in his own family. Sometimes he wondered if anyone really cared for him. Even Billy and Petey, now that they were growing big enough to need to top him—"It won't be hard," he'd told them—made fun of him. He was awkward, partly color-blind. He tripped, bumped his head, spilled on the table . It was a joke when he was growing; it was a joke to his boys. The worst part of the vanity of self-reproach is the reproach itself: was one worth all the groveling?

"To be decent," thought Wursup sometimes. "Just to be a decent person." So small a thing, and not difficult. (If, in a way, impossible.) Rochefoucauld said the biggest obstacle to being natural was desiring to be; so an obstacle to being decent was working on it. And becoming a character in other people's lives made it harder. Spelling oneself out to the Fenchals of the world uncovered unsuspected parts of oneself. There seemed to be no end to self-discovery. Perhaps decency was getting as much of oneself on the record as possible, then letting other people figure out the results.

He himself was a part of millions of lives. Every time he appeared on a show, published an article or was the subject of one, some of these lives surfaced, and sometimes became part of his. He was used to letters and—until he got an unlisted number, after *Drain*—telephone calls from strangers. Until the mail got too heavy, he'd answered every half-decent one and was polite to all callers. The Fenchal profile ("profile with busted nose and teeth" was his last word to Sookie about it) brought in a new catch of epistolary fish: three appeals for help; four crazies ("Who you think you are, you Greaseball Yiddle Snoop? For the ovens, YOU!"); a "Digest of Universal Wisdom Based on New Evidence"; and four letters, one of which, from Millicent Sollinckas, a nurse in the gastrointestinal ward at St. Vincent's Hospital, went,

> I see from the story in today's paper that you are writing an article on death which you say is becoming "dangerously abstract" for you. I have spoken with Mrs. Schneewind, our Chief Nurse, and she agrees that it would be all right if I wrote to invite you to come on rounds with me and, if you like, talk with some of our terminal patients whose permission I would secure. I am sure that talking with a famous writer would cheer them. Mrs. Schneewind agrees. If you think it would help *you* in your work, please feel free to call (JK5–6181) or write me here.

It would be a pleasure for me to be of assistance to you.

This letter was so well written, so active, so to the point, that Wursup knew immediately he would follow it up. The typing was flawless, the signature square, unlovely, clear—an honest signature—and behind it there was, surely, a decent person. a *necessary connection.* It was about time anyway that he stopped hiding behind other people's wisdom. He started to telephone, pumping the little buttons, J–K–5–6, then stopped, thinking, "She's a nurse; the call will take her away from someone who needs her." Also, he hated waiting on the phone, and she'd surely have to be paged. Anyway, a literary man *wrote.*

DEAR MS. SOLLINCKAS,

I have felt insulated by much of what I've been reading. (I suppose that's what technology and its vocabulary are meant to do.) And what needs insulation more than death? Thank you for helping me get away from the typewriter. I will be as careful as I can not to upset anyone. If I don't hear to the contrary from you, I'll turn up at your door next Thursday afternoon about two p.m. You were good to write me.

Yours,
FRED WURSUP

4

Abby Schlosserberg's money was not her only contribution to the salvation of the *News Letter.* The money, in fact, was little more than a foot in the door, and when more of Abby came through, *Chouinard's* lost a few wrinkles, and the Chouinardians acquired some.

Piecing stories out of the shreds of European newspapers was not Abby's idea of journalism. Her model journalists were sleuths and prosecutors, the Woodwards and Bernsteins of Watergate, the Hersh of My Lai, the—younger—Wursup of Japanese economic scandals, Common Market infighting, the Pentagon fog machinery. Journalism was not a coroner's report. Journalists defined the questions and assessed answers; they were as much the makers of event as presidents and killers. When toilets flushed, journalists asked themselves, "Why?" They took nothing for granted. Every truth concealed as well as revealed; every lie was as telling as a truth. As for high-mindedness, it was the most banal of all covers. The essence of the best journalism was the revelation of hypocrisy. Every man covered his tracks—some primitively, like Nixon; some subtly. Her ambition was the exposure of subtle hypocrites. Journalism wasn't for those who fainted at whiffs of grapeshot.

Abby had been raised demurely behind walls of money which concealed the musky, genital odor of its origins. When she discovered the source of her fine clothes, good teeth and genteel manners, shame was overcome by a sense that discovery itself was the most precious of all human events. What could be more exciting, in a world which had outgrown geographical discovery, than to be a discoverer of secrets?

More and more, Abby thirsted to know what public events and personalities concealed. And then she wanted to—as she put it—*democratize* knowledge. Why shouldn't the familiar gossip of great houses, clubs and board rooms go to the millions who were being manipulated by pompous falsity? The ideal perch for a modern journalist was that of Doris Kearns, the pretty political scientist who sat in a rocking chair while, under her sheets, Lyndon Johnson warbled Texas arias about Daddy-fear and Momma-fury. Intimacy without contact; mutual, passionless manipulation. Didn't such psychic dirty drawers reveal more about Vietnam than the Pentagon Papers? The Richard Nixons and Anthony Edens who developed their life strategies of evasion by dodging terrible-tempered fathers began their Watergates and Suez failures at age ten. You could learn more from their old schoolmates, cousins, diaries and other leftovers than from mountains of parliamentary questions and judicial inquiries. It was a journalist's job to document the Wordsworth insight that the child was the father of his adult deeds.

"Mr. Miyako," she said a few weeks after Peggy Miyako's funeral, "do you have a minute?"

Kevin certainly had minutes for this exemplary little "almost-Rockefeller." From the beginning, before he knew of Abby's money, he'd sensed in her the aristocracy of possession. She was not the sporty, snooty Katherine Hepburn elegant but a darker, more bookish, more reserved inhabitant of the possessing class. She had the looks which wealth rescues from plainness: buck teeth had been braced back, sparse hair enriched, excess of cheek, forehead and nose diminished by the right stains and powders. To the casual eye, Abby looked like a haphazard, natural beauty—subdivision Wistful-Shy— the bloom of a spare but opulent root. Her voice was a whisper with sensuous shadows, as if under the timid speech there were giggle rollers ready for the right push. *Just shove a little,* said Abby's voice.

"I've tried"—it went now—"a different sort of piece. Not our usual thing, but I wondered if you won't think it might be something we could try every once in a while. I sort of happened on it." A little packet of pages was held by two soft, nail-bitten fingers just out of Kevin's reach. Abby's dark eyes were under lashes so thick they almost gave away their un-Abbyan source. For Kevin they were as compelling as headlights to an animal on a country road. What a wonderful piece of American prosperity. "I know *Chouinard's* isn't really in the news business, but this is a kind of story behind the story."

The warding-off-refusal concluded, Abby handed over the pages (flawlessly typed in an electrically feminine script), and Kevin speed-read them. "Whew." The pages consisted of Abby's interview with the wife of a cabinet officer. It began with easy talk about the woman's work with Trauma Centers and then slid into the ways Husband arranged contracts—and, consequently, national policy—to slake his monetary and sexual appetites. An enormous grain sale had been made— according to Mrs. Officer—so that Mr. Officer could "work himself in and out of Annabelle Peer," the wife of a grain shipper. Abby then cited the grain prices pre- and post–Mr. Officer's insertions: they made Annabelle Peer look more expensive than Cleopatra. "We just got talking," whispered Abby over Kevin's desk. "You know how that happens." No,

Kevin didn't, but Abby's whisper was itself a taste of it. "She knew I wrote, but she didn't say anything about talking off the record. It seems legitimate to me."

The slightly askew Latinism dispersed some of the seductive fragrance: "legitimate" brought a whiff of law and reminded Kevin of the traditions of *Chouinard's.* "It's fascinating material. And important, if true. But is it the sort of thing our bunch expects from us?"

Abby wished she could have retracted the word, but she was not going to relinquish a career for it. Demure suggestion was beefed up with a hint of the large *quid* for which she expected suitable *quo.* "My idea was that this sort of piece would attract a somewhat wider audience. I know how much you want us to be self-sustaining."

"Yes," he said. "I know you can't keep pulling us out of the drink. Well, why don't we try it out on Dame Mae and Susannah?"

"I guess that would be the thing to do. I just wonder, though, if older women would be tuned in to the sort of piece this is. Fine as they are, do they understand the openness this generation looks for? Watergate was a kind of political *Kinsey Report* for us. You know, it sort of opened politics the way that opened sex. I'm not sure too many older journalists should even be expected to alter their practice because of it."

This was the longest Abby speech heard around the office, and Kevin knew basic policy was at stake. Abby invested more of herself in stories than Kevin thought journalistically proper, but he also saw that she was the expression of readers who discharged their resentments on the heads of public figures. All right, maybe it was time for that. The *Letter* wasn't getting very far with lofty surveys. What was the point of resistance to the death if no one noticed either resistance or death? Why shouldn't this little heiress be the one to pull *Chouinard's* out of the journalistic, as well as the financial, drink?

So, to the surprise of the other staffers, *"Abby's Corner"* began on an inside page of their next issue. And every month thereafter, it offered what Kevin described to staffers and others as "its Stracheyan analysis of a newsmaker."

By its third appearance, it was clear that it altered *Chouinard's* quiet waters: there were several newsstand inquiries about the publication. (The newsstand representative pronounced it *"Swineherd's."*) After the fourth *"Corner,"* there were more than a thousand subscription inquiries. The Washington *Post* rephrased one story—with acknowledgment to Abby and the *Letter*—and other stories were picked up without acknowledgment, two by local television commentators.

Within six months, Abby was an insider's celebrity, and insiders gave her stories. Resentment, envy, indolent hatred and indolent inventiveness, all supplied material for the *"Corner."*

Her seventh story was fed to her from Illinois. The father of James Doyle, one of the candidates for the Democratic senatorial nomination, was found in a Madison Street flophouse. Abby was fed the story—as she was fed many—in a letter from a source which dissolved when she tried tracing it. But old Doyle did not dissolve. Abby flew to Chicago and interviewed him.

A perfect story: here was the father of the father of a hundred welfare programs, on the social junk heap. The story—she'd call it "Doyle on Troubled Waters"—was pure gold.

From the roof, Wursup cased Susannah's apartment. A cold night, snow hopping around the air, unwilling to kill itself on the sidewalks. In the living room Susannah and Kevin—dressed like a mugger—were having a hot discussion, maybe an argument. She held a manuscript with photographs in her lap. Kevin was a shrugger, a hand spreader. His neck bent from his black turtleneck in a servile bow; Wursup imagined him saying "So sorry." Susannah said little, but he knew the power of her silence, her stare, the lower lip rubbing against the upper. She raised a photograph toward Kevin. What a surprise: Jim Doyle. What could that be about? Jim was trying to get slated for the Senate in Illinois; perhaps *Chouinard's* was giving him a boost. He was the sort of public servant they admired: more or less apolitical—he'd worked for Republican and Democratic administrations—a social scientist who spent half his time in research institutes and think tanks. But why photographs? The only place *Chouinard's* used photographs was in their new gossip feature, *"Abby's Corner."* He'd known Jim Doyle thirty years; there couldn't be much scandal there.

The next day he called Susannah.

"What's on your mind?"

"Someone at the Press Club said he heard *Chouinard's* had dug something up on Jim Doyle."

"I didn't know the Press Club had heard of *Chouinard's.*"

"You rate very well down there. And of course that little girl who does your Jack Anderson stuff hangs around."

Silence. Susannah's energy went more into repression than expression, but even over the phone, Wursup felt that something more than journalism was bothering her.

There was. After the camaraderie which followed *Chouinard's'* salvation, things hadn't gone easily for Kevin and Susannah. What other people regarded as simple and natural was not simple for them. The first night their desires became explicit, Petey was around, and Susannah could not think how to deal with that. The next night, stirred again, Susannah thought of her ugly room and narrow bed. "Tomorrow, at your place," she'd said; but tomorrow wasn't *now,* and the chemistry of planning didn't do well by them. Years before, Susannah's peace of mind had been shattered by sexual planning. Now delay became caution, then awkwardness. Kevin thought it meant Susannah was looking back at what he imagined were the great times of life with Wursup, and he spent himself in imaginary comparisons. What was he besides the famous, beefy, confident ex-husband? Still, they managed to get into bed, and the excitement of seeing each other's hidden parts brought them through. But between their need and affection for each other and the clumsiness of their approach to the simple insertions and withdrawals, there was the history of their mute self-doubts. Kevin trailed an imaginary Wurs-up to bed with him, and Susannah found a mostly imaginary Abby there. She'd seen Kevin light up when Abby uriah-heeped into his office, so demurely instructable, and loaded, too. She knew Kevin was a patsy for the rich.

Susannah's economy of loyalty was flexible enough to let her hope that Abby's column would fail. It didn't belong in the *Letter*. She felt no loyalty to it. In fact, if Fred, with his mastodon connections, could somehow undermine it, it would be better for everybody.

"She's found out Jim Doyle's father's been on skid row for years and years. While Jim's been working up all those poverty programs for everyone. They think it makes a pretty sensational story."

"Where did she get it? I thought Jim's father died years ago. It sounds like baloney to me."

"I don't know where she got it. She gets tips from all over. The story sounds authentic."

"Maybe so. I may even remember something about his father running out on them. When Jim was ten or eleven. The guy was half dead then. It's hard to believe he's survived. Very strange. I wonder if she was tipped by someone who wanted to do Jim in before the election. Sounds like it. I mean, *Chouinard's* isn't NBC. It wasn't picked for its circulation. Someone just wanted it in print. Somewhere. They can bring out a clipping in a caucus room. Jim is not exactly Daley's cup of tea. He's a little tough for the machine to digest. Yet they don't want to make too big a thing of it. They'll take a chance the story will slide away. Lots do. Meanwhile, they've unloaded a guy who might not understand the little transmission system from precinct to Washington. I mean, Jim *understands*, but *that's it*. He *understands*. And may get a bee in his bonnet."

"I have nothing to do with it. I probably shouldn't have said anything to you."

"I'm not sure it's anything to me either. I've done my bit for Jim." Doyle had been one of the few heroes in *Down the American Drain*. "Still, I suppose I could do a piece for the *Times*. Temper the wind a bit. When are you printing?"

"There's some disagreement about that."

"I could do a quickie, get Jim to talk about his papa. That might take the sting out of it."

"Sounds as if it might make it a big story. Still, he's an old friend. Do you want me to call Adele? I guess she's in Washington."

"Thanks, Susannah. If I think it'll mean anything, I'll get hold of Jim. Probably, the best thing's to ignore it. Maybe no one'll notice it."

"Maybe," said Susannah. "But it seems as if it's the only thing that's noticed."

For her, "it's" meant "Abby."

5

"Mr. Wuship." Constance never got his name right. No point in correction. He never got hers right either; at least he didn't collapse Constance into one syllable as she did: Consss.

"What's up, Constance? I hope nothing much. I've had a bad scene in the street with my aunt."

"That frienda yours, the one that speak so rough, he call."

There was no point in asking Constance to take down names. And since he wouldn't use an answering service, human or electric, he had no right to get after her for murdering his messages. "Which one? You know I got a rough bunch of friends."

"Hee, hee, hee. This one's the rougherest of all. You know, way down here," and she fetched up a basso rumble.

He called Mike Schilp.

"What's up Michael?"

"I'm not pushing you, Freddy, but what's with our little graveyard piece?"

"I've got three hundred pages of notes. And I've just started."

"Crazy. Are you writing a dissertation? We're not filling the issue with all human wisdom on the subject. Relax. Just a few pearls. Hazlitt would have had it in overnight."

"Maybe you better get him. It's a nervous time for me. And the subject doesn't ease one."

"You always come through. Relax. I'll send you more stuff. Curl up with it. Then sleep. And you'll write it off in the morning. Listen to these titles. I got 'em on a sheet somewhere. Here. Listen to these: *Dying at Home; Immortality or Bust.* Can you imagine? *Grief.* That's straight enough. Here's a lulu: *How to Die.* That should move. *American Suttee.* Suttee would prolong a lot of husbands' lives. I'll send 'em over."

"Why not, Michael? I might as well drown in print."

"Speaking of which, didya see about Hamish Blick?"

Wursup had done a piece for *Life* on the playwright in 'sixty-nine or 'seventy. It was 'seventy—he'd flown back from California for Sookie's graduation in Chicago.

"No. He died? I didn't see it. I save the *Times* for bed."

"You spelled it out. That was a good piece. I remember it. A strange fellow. They found his rowboat out by Santa Barbara Island. Empty. Except for a razor and a pillbox and a few rocks he couldn't fit in his pockets. They fished him up yesterday."

"Terrible," said Wursup. "Poor old Blick. I'm surprised he lasted that long. But he hated the water. Why did he go that way?"

"That's why."

"I guess so, Michael. I remember that old Karen Horney book on suicide. Horrible. People wrapping themselves around steampipes, biting their wrists, sticking hot pokers into their guts. I guess when you hate yourself, it's anything goes. Unbearable."

"That's the ticket," boomed the phone. "Now you're into it again."

When the books arrived, Constance was put out. "Where'm I gonna fit'm all? This keep on, there gonna be no room for

64

you. Evah since your girl got all this furniture you wants me to wax."

Constance came to Wursup after Sookie, yet resented her as the intruder. "Just shove 'em anywhere, Constance. And why don't you ease off on the waxing? It smells like a lemon grove here anyway."

"Don't rile me. I wiv you too long for you to be telling me my bidness. Three years Febry fourteen."

"Valentine's Day. Why didn't you bring me a box of chocolate?"

"Hee-hee." And then, musing, shaking the black horsehair—she claimed was her own—as she steamed with Machiavellian schemes. "Whyn't you give me some? You *knows* what I have for chocolate."

There was much he was supposed to know about Constance. "You *know* how I hates this cold." "You *know* mah doctor says I can't do no scrubbin'. You tell your girl she gotta clean her own dirt. Looka that tub. You just got to *know* yellow like that come from oil she uses. Your skin don't need no oil."

That was some of what she knew. What he knew about Constance was that she was a great cleaner and tyrant, and that she only worked for single men. "I don't need no woman messing around wiv my bidness. 'Clean here, clean there.' Nobody tell me what I cleans. Let your girl fix her own messes." "Whyn't your girl iron that tablecloth?" "Can't your girl sew none? She's so smart."

The girl was pretty; that, she granted. "She sure is a pretty thing. What kind of blood she have?"

"Red."

"Don't sass me. You know what I mean. What's her nationality?"

"American."

"I mean is she Eyetalian or Porto Rican, or Jew or what? You *know* what I mean."

Sookie tanned easily; he said she was part Indian. Something rumbled under the horsehair. "That make her like me. I got me lots of Indian blood."

"Maybe you're cousins."

"Don't be so smart. Lots of cousins between whites and coloreds, you better believe it."

She warmed up early for Christmas, came in with a box in a paper bag and, before she went into the closet to change clothes, said from the door, "Lookit here; I want you to see something beautiful." Out of the box a string of red glass knobs. "That necklace cost Mr. Smoot fifty dollars. Isn't they somepin bee-yu-tiful?"

"You are one lucky woman, Constance. I wish I had Smoot's money."

"Huh. You got a perfession, ain't you? You a news *pa*per man or somepin, ain't you? He wuk for a living."

Since she'd admired a panel of embroidered flowers his father's girl, Mona, had sent for his birthday, he wrapped them up and gave them to her for Christmas. The next Tuesday she stormed in fierce-lipped and, for an hour, said nothing to him. When he came out of the study for coffee, she glared at him.

"I'm a little surprised you didn't thank me for the present, Constance."

Her opening. Five feet two inches and a hundred and fifty pounds opened up. "I'm glad you bring that up. What kinda walls you think I got me at home? Don't you *know* I have every inch of my walls covered with paintings? From Yurp. You give me something's been hangin' on *your* wall."

"You said you liked it."

"I said I 'mired it. I didn't mean I wanted it. If I wanted everything I 'mired, I wouldn't have me no room to sleep."

"Bring it back; I'll give it to Sookie. She likes it. How about a bottle of perfume?"

"Don't you *know* I sold perfume five years? I got every type of perfume they is."

She wanted money or jewelry, Smoot-variety. Last year he'd given her two weeks' salary at Christmas. She'd thanked him, mildly. She surely trumpeted the gift to Smoot—whose necklace had not cost more than three-fifty, unless Woolworth's prices had gone through the roof. "Will a check be all right, then?"

"You don't have to give me nothin'; I ain't askin'."

She'd left him twice. Just didn't show up, and when he called her, she said she couldn't stand working for a man who was being "taken over by a woman. Don't you *know* she don't like me? She stuck gum under the bed to see if I be cleaning right; she move the chairs every time after I fix them. And who bought all that new furniture I got to wax? Not you. I don't wuk where there's a woman. When I fuhst come, I felt kinda sorry for you; you was all down and all, but now you changed. She's the rooning of you."

"I'm sorry, Constance. I'll miss you." He'd be damned if he was going to throw out Sookie to please this Stalin.

But the agency who'd sent her had folded; at least, the woman—who was the agency—said she'd gone out of business. ("I sold my cards to a lady wuks the West Side. She don't supply East.")

Wursup was off to Southeast Asia for a month; he'd look when he came back. When he did, he first called Constance. "Want to think about coming back?"

She'd think about it. She'd given away his Tuesdays, but she didn't like the new man. "He's a dope fiend. They's guns in the closet. I'm scared for my life. So maybe you see me Tuesday. Evahbody 'titled to a chance."

He was surprised how pleased he was.

"Sookie, you better keep clear Tuesdays. You heat up Constance's paranoia."

"You're wrong. She likes me."

"Roasted."

Sookie bought a five-pound box of Schrafft's chocolate for

Constance and told Wursup to make sure she knew where it came from. Constance melted. "Though she oughta *know* I oughtn't eat no chocolate. Doctor says my heart's like a bubble. But I 'preciates it. You tell her. Whyn't you have her come for supper Tuesday wiv your son?"

So it was peaches and cream *chez* Wursup. The two women treated each other like sisterly queens, and the peace and courtesy flowed over him.

Like most, though, he had an appetite for disorder as well as peace. Across from Blick's obituary was an Izzie Shenker feature on Robert Fitzgerald, the Homer translator. Fitzgerald said he'd sent Ezra Pound an early version of some lines of the *Iliad,* and the old poet had written back from the loony bin that too much iambic pentameter would do in the best subject. Order for its own sake was ruinous. (At Auschwitz, the motto was *zauber machen*—"clean up.") Madness tried to cover itself with order. He'd gone to see mad Strindberg's apartment in Stockholm. Every pencil in its place, every india rubber. The genius, chaos inside, craved orderliness. Look at the money-mad Gettys, Gulbenkians and Howard Hugheses. They were all anal obsessives, terrified of disorder and filth. Billionaires, lunatics, poets. The world dirtied up their visions of it. They hid behind walls or—the poets—words. Like poor old Blick. He'd shrunk everything to a controllable minimum. It wasn't enough. Every year another poet killed himself: Sexton, Berryman, Plath, Jarrell, Kees, Pavese, Hemingway, and now Blick. The world didn't live up to their poems.

Blick's face gloomed over Ollie Fenchal's obituary prose.

The American Beckett said, "Early getting a whiff of life through the kitchen transom, I decided to shut it tight." Blick critics have wondered how tightly

shut the playwright was able to keep it in the plush
arroyos of Hollywood.

Tania had told him to go out and do the piece. He'd been
working on the middle chapters of *Drain*, and there was very
little money coming in. "I can't get another nickel for you.
Even from Will. Besides, you need to see your name on a
magazine cover." In the wire-backed chairs, her authors felt
like bread in a toaster. Tania buttered and Tania ate. "You're
going to break for Sookie's graduation anyway. So there you
are. Instead of forking out airfare to Chicago, go out to Hollywood on *Life* and stop off on the way back."

The beautiful tokay eyes held every soft promise. *You, you,
only you,* they said, though behind them was Tania's Plan:
This is where you belong now; this is where you will be later.
"You're the only writer in New York who'd close up shop to
see his girl friend graduate."

"This isn't high school. It's a doctorate. That's nothing to
sneeze at. And I promised her. Besides, I'll see the old man,
too. It's been a year and a half." (He'd given up seeing his
mother in the home. She hadn't recognized him in years.)

"I love these brilliant little girls. Comes Mother's Day or
graduation, there they are in their pretty dresses. Okay. Go
watch your Madonna of the Rocks wiggle her ass up the aisle,
but bring me back something to pay the rent. Anyway, it'll be
a relief for you to stop writing about politicians for a few
days."

So in the middle of a chapter about Dr. Dooley, Cardinal
Spellman, Joseph Kennedy and the Knights of Malta, Wursup had flown to O'Hare with Sookie and left her to pass on the
geopoetic word from the Lamont Lab to her old profs. "On to
L.A. while it's still there," he said to her (full of geologic hand-
outs on plate tectonics, fault creep, Los Angeles snuggling
into the arms of San Francisco).

Sookie had told him to watch himself. "I find any molten

starlet on your parts, I'll make you read my dissertation. See you Friday." (Their amorous creed was *No Chains*, but something deeper demanded sexual strictness. Once, she explained what she called a "little go-round" while he was off for six weeks in Asia by saying it was a way of forestalling an earthquake, setting off small explosions along a fault to relieve the pressure. But when he, fired with pain, rattled off his own list of relief operations, she wept and said humans weren't rocks; every part of their relationship touched every other part; they must try to do better. She was right. He did; he would.)

Wursup drove out to Hamish Blick's Mandeville Canyon house in a red Sting-Ray from Avis. (He'd changed to a sportshirt in the plane's bathroom, a Houdini triumph.)

He hadn't been in Los Angeles since 'sixty-five when he'd done a shaky piece, "Ovid on the Coast, or Metamorphosis as Con," about what he'd called the "Illusion Factories—Disneyland, Movieland, Nixon-Knight-and-Know-Nothing Land." (It had tried to explain the Watts riot as an assertion against such illusions.)

The Canyon was another illusion, a sort of Potemkin village of domestic architecture, Burgundy farmhouse here, Danish castle there. Brassy shrubs concealed most of these Xanadus. (Less perhaps for concealment than for advertisement of something to conceal.) In back, soft, mammary hills showed the saffron scars of new growth (after the last canyon fire).

Blick's house was unconcealed, a one-story gold-and-glass affair that could have been a post office or mortuary. Wursup pulled his little red ship alongside a silver Bentley and walked to the house. Blick came to the door. "Let's sit out" were his first words.

Blick was quite a sight. "A Grünewald Christ, just down from the Cross," wrote Wursup in *Life*. Except for his outfit, which was Beverly Hills pizzazz: a scarlet sport shirt, deeply woven, studded with gold buttons and monogram, and even more extravagant pants (on emerald serge, expensive fingers had stitched buttercups, dandelions, marigolds). From the sport shirt hung wiry, speckled arms. The feet were equally wicked.

"No Movieland tourist should be allowed the sight of Blick's feet," Wursup had written. The toes, knobby with calluses and armored with grim nails, snaked from open sandals.

Blick's face was of a piece with his extremities. It pushed toward verticality, was deeply grooved, Giacometti thin. The features bulked and jutted—a great venous nose, heavy lips, and eyes "which," wrote Wursup, "have the peculiar opacity of a leopard's, black and dusted with gold."

The interview had been arranged by the producer of Blick's last movie, *Weekly Rates.* Blick himself had played its central role, Morton Frahm, the owner of a Southern California motel which specialized in accommodating the handicapped. The motel had sections for the blind, deaf, and crippled. There were areas for dwarfs, great beds and tubs for giants. The film centered around Frahm's creation of a zoo whose cages were filled with "ordinary people," cooking, sleeping, watching television, making love. The final scene showed a fully clothed Frahm being shot through a flaming hoop in the motel's marineland. The film won prizes in Cannes and New York, and Blick won Academy Awards for Best Original Screenplay and Best Supporting Actor. (The awards were collected for him by the film's leading dwarf.)

He and Wursup sat at opposite ends of a park bench outside the glassed-in patio. There was no small talk, no offer of drinks. Wursup asked why Blick had acted in the movie. "As far as I knew, you hadn't acted since walk-ons with the Group Theater."

"Correct." Blick's voice was gruff, throaty, as if it were making its way through a gutteral avalanche. "Actors were having

71

trouble with the part. Couldn't tell if it should be played for laughs or not."

"How did you understand it?"

"You saw the film?"

"I did. Still, I'm not sure how to take Frahm. He could be anything. A loony, a champion of the oppressed, a perverse melancholic. Is there an ideology behind him?"

Blick ran fingers—unlovely as his toes—up and down his cheek grooves. "Let's say he's a more accurate expression of his feelings than most of us. Since he's made of film, not flesh, he has fewer feelings. I suppose several ideologies could be geared to him. To what he does, anyway."

"Jumping through the hoop? Starting the zoo?"

"The way he walks, drinks water, gets out of bed. I blank out at ideology. It's a word I've looked up many times in the dictionary. I can't hold on to it."

"You're a visual," said Wursup. "Or a cinematic, I guess. Which brings up this place. The setting. You yourself. Those slacks are unexpected." Blick looked at them as if they were being knit on his legs. "Are they . . . is all this"—Wursup pointed at the hills—"significant for you in some way? Beyond the pleasure of living in a lovely place? I mean, is it a diversion from another Blick?"

Blick had nodded—Wursup was afraid he was going to sleep—then said in a voice which made his words seem the survivors of a tough battle with silence, "Mr. Wursup, you're in the questioning business. You stir things up. I spend much of my time making things I've seen. Something comes to me—answers without questions, you could say. I think it would be nice to see it on the stage, or on film, that's my work. Then there's eating, sleeping, my so-called life. I have to live somewhere. I buy a house. I need to wear something. I wear what pleases me. If this is more complicated, I try hard not to know about it."

Wursup had often heard people famous for their complexity insist they were simpler than they appeared. Of course, everyone kept much of himself back. Wursup's job—which he'd never much liked—was to force out what had been held back. Blick was helpful—he tried to express what he felt—but his personal life seemed like new snow to him: he didn't know if he should ruffle it. There had been very few interviews with him; these questions seem to have been asked for the first time.

Wursup's next question was the sort he usually hated asking, but the act of interviewing simplified, even brutalized, him. He became his readers, became the machinery of the medium: the presses needed ink, the air needed sound waves. Readers needed the diversion of other people's troubles. "Mr. Blick, as far as I can find out, you never married. And no one I've asked knows anyone, male or female, who's lived with you. Your parents died thirty years ago, and your sister told me on the phone that though you've never been anything but friendly, she hasn't heard from you in five years. Is there anyone in the world—man, woman, child, animal—to whom you're close or have ever been close? It is the sort of thing people want very much to know."

For the first time, Blick looked at Wursup. The leopard eyes were reproachful. (What did I do? thought Wursup.) So many years he'd intruded meanly into other lives. Journalists praised his roughness, his technique. It was only insensitivity, rudeness. Blick wanted to talk, had probably always wanted to talk, but to a friend. Wursup was not a friend. Sympathy wasn't friendship. And in Wursup, it was just a come-on. It went with the notebook. *Forget it*, Wursup was about to say. *Don't answer. Why should you answer me? Forgive my nosiness.*

But Blick was answering. Gutteral and gentle, a flux of mud. "I've always been ugly. Not only on the surface. I was different; I felt different. I'm the child of old people, and I was their curiosity. I was raised as a specimen. I became one. I

73

was let alone a great deal as a boy. I hated it. I grew accustomed to it. At fifteen, I tried again. I wanted others. But I was clumsy, timid; my being was unattractive. I was resisted, ignored."

"How hard for you."

Blick seemed puzzled, but it was the discharge which mattered, not its recipient. "For a long time, I did without. I felt privation. I *was* without. Then that odd human change began. Before you know, it happens. What was pain became need. I didn't look for solitude; it found me. Since then, I can only be alone. There is no one, never has been, nor will be."

Dry-lipped, agitated, breathing in the heavy air, Wursup wrote and wrote. It was too much feeling to take. Confessors had screens; he only had his notebook, his profession. He was aware Blick had got up, was aware of a door's opening, but when he stopped writing, he felt an unusual barrenness. He waited five, ten minutes, then knocked at the glass door. No response. He walked around the house, knocking, peering, ringing a cowbell at the front door. No answer. And despite the seemingly ubiquitous transparency of the house, there was nothing visible inside. After a few minutes, Wursup realized that Blick had staged his solitude.

"Wow, what an exit," Poppa Wursup said the next day in Chicago.

Wursup had written a draft of his piece on the plane to Chicago and was trying it out on his father before going off to Sookie's graduation. He wanted him to hear it, but it was more important to fill the time which otherwise was filled with his father's philosophizing and doggerel. "Is there such a thing as retroactive heredity?" he'd asked Sookie after an afternoon of listening to his father's poetry. (Poppa Wursup had made a rare visit to New York "to find a publisher.") "The minute I published a poem in the Hyde Park High literary magazine, Poppa became aware *he* was a poet."

74

"Submit it to *Scientific American*," said Sookie. "I like him."

And Poppa Wursup liked her. It was partly her beauty which tamed the bellicosity anyone with advanced degrees excited in him. He regarded academic authority as a plot against self-tutored genius.

In the university neighborhood in which he'd lived for fifty years, there were many such plotters. Poppa Wursup had read the gas meters in many Hyde Park homes and was wise to scholars. "These little bald guys who shoot their mouths off around the earth but can't press the right elevator button." (Twenty years before, one such villain had ridden in the elevator with Poppa Wursup and had pressed EMERGENCY instead of LOBBY.) "Misguided measles," Poppa called such helpless types. "Bald little disease-launchers."

Poppa Wursup himself was only five feet four. "You'd think he'd feel comfortable with these little fellows," said Sookie.

"No," said Wursup. "He thinks he's a giant. Look at the way he stoops. You don't see many small men stooping. Poppa doesn't have to strut or stretch. He's fifteen feet high. God forbid you were a poet. He'd have your head. He was thrown out of Mandel Hall when Eliot read there. He booed 'Prufrock.' Eliot said he agreed with his 'critic.' Poppa went on to heckle 'Gerontion,' and the ushers hustled him out. It was just after Momma went into the home. I guess she was undone trying to handle him. Mona doesn't try."

Mona Kloster was Poppa's companion. For fifteen years—since Wursup's mother had begun fading out of her body—she'd taken care of him. That is, in return for *la dolce vita* of watching soap operas and attending the free cultural events of Chicago (Grant Park concerts, library slide shows, museum exhibits, and Poppa's lectures), she endured his abuse and managed to get a meal or two on the table. Poppa complained that Mona didn't understand him.

"You're lucky," his son said, adding, for pacification, "It keeps you mysterious."

"Nobody ever understands him," he said to Sookie. "He worked forty-six years for People's Gas. At retirement they gave him a stereo. Forty-six years, and they didn't know the man was tone deaf."

"You said he played the opera full blast every Saturday afternoon."

"He was making points. He couldn't tell *Pagliacci* from Horace Heidt. He opened all the windows to let the world know there was an opera lover inside. A man of culture. In the thirties, that apparently went a long way. He traded the stereo for an electric typewriter. So he doesn't have to think, just type. He's written more poetry in two years than Homer. If they gave Nobels for literary tonnage, there'd be no contest."

Poppa Wursup was as severe a critic of his son's work. He didn't like the Blick piece. "No human poetry, Carlo." Only his father and mother called Wursup 'Carlo'—after his middle name, Charles. Wursup's mother had thought it beautiful—she too had listened to the operas. Occasionally Mona tried to use it, but that angered Poppa; she was trespassing on family property. "Now I want *you* to hear something."

"Poppa, I've got to get to Sookie's ceremony."

"Five minutes. You got plenty of time. I use some of that stuff you bought me from Russia."

"?"

"That pamphlet on that old poet."

On his last trip to the Soviet Union, Wursup had spent hours in bookstores looking for anything readable in English (or in any language he could read); he'd had enough of ten-day-old copies of *L'Humanité* or the free pamphlets on Soviet marvels available at the book racks in Intourist lounges. The only English book he'd found in Baku was an illiterate pamphlet on a fourteenth-century Azerbaijani poet. He'd brought it back for his father. "To broaden your knowledge of world poetry." (And to divert him—briefly—from contributing to it.)

Poppa pulled his green Barca-Lounger into the upright position and read from the long sheets of pink mimeo paper (which a friend at the gas company got for him).

> "The world, they say, will be made for the old.
> Whose virtue isn't the possession of gold.
> Keep them—chemically—up to snuff.
> And they won't slice themselves into the rough.

"That's from golf," explained Poppa.

> "What they've seen of the earth,
> Its sorrows and mirth,
> They will pass on, and, as living temples,
> Show their grandkids the best of samples.

"Off-rhyme," said Poppa.
"Very pretty," said Wursup.

> "An old Russian doctrine teaches that God
> Is inscribed on the faces of men of the sod,
> Cosmic mysteries are in the face,
> The secret sermon for the human race."

"That's okay, Poppa. There's rich stuff there."
"There's more, Carlo. You'll love it." Poppa Wursup shone under his son's praise. "Mona," he called. "Carlo loves the new poem."

Mona, great-bottomed and beagle nosed, was bewigged like the Sun King. She came into the Poet's Corner, which, at Poppa Wursup's, was a swollen angle behind the television set. *"Pour moi,"* said Mona grandly, *"questa roba significa nada."* Mona's secret revenge on Poppa was a peculiar gift for languages. The languages were mixed up, but Mona rolled them out without difficulty. Wursup, who made his way around the world with a few hundred linguistic handles—*Qui est là? Wer ist da? Kon hai?* (Hindi)—had used her for interviews in Spanish, Italian, Greek, and Polish precincts in Chicago. Mona hadn't spent a month of her forty-five years out of the city, but no human speech was long alien to her. The ·responses to Poppa's guff, suppressed in English, came out in the linguistic stew. She translated them for him into semicompliments, but meanwhile she'd blown her steam.

Poppa slid back in the big lounger. He looked like a bean seed in its pod. "I stole that stuff about God on faces from the pamphlet. Except it said God comes out in the faces of handsome guys, not old ones. But that's stupid. It's experience, not looks; that counts. Besides, you and me would be bum texts if it was based on looks, eh, Carlo?"

"I guess so, Poppa. Me, anyway. You do all right."

"*Avec son nez du perroquet,*" said Mona.

"*Do, screw, flew.* Women aren't pounding the doors here."

Wursup, who regressed into household syntax at home, said, "Uglier than you is called beauty today."

Some Polish sweetness came from Mona. Poppa, darkening, said, "Dry up, moron. *Ugly* goes too far, Carlo. Anyway, you told me to broaden myself. So I read. But I figure if you just take old stuff, and don't convert it, you're nothing. That's where you reporters go wrong. You're little hash machines. I mean, you're as good as they come, Carlo, but this guy Blick should have just been raw material for you. All you do is act like his tape recorder."

"Poppa, I'm going to miss Sookie marching. She'll be miserable."

"See," said Poppa. "Once again, you're just somebody's footprint. Do your own stuff once in a while. That's what poetry's about. That's when God sits on the face."

"Oh, *Scheiss, alors, stamateesteh,*" said Mona gently.

Wursup arrived panting at Rockefeller Chapel, just in time to see the academic procession. He spotted Sookie in the black spine moving over the glittering lawn, in the loose black robe with maroon stripes. The silky tassel bounced on her shoulder-long rust-gold hair. She herself was a pageant.

Dr. Sisley Dyce Gumpert. Ph.D. in the Department of the Geophysical Sciences. In the thick program, her dissertation title was printed beside her name: MELTING CURVES OF BASALT WATER IN THE MAGMA.

Wursup stood in back of the enormous nave. Organ and trumpets poured terrific sound into the gray limestone vault; the great window light churned wonderful colors out of spring hats, dresses, the velvet pews, the rose and purple academic robes.

Wursup hadn't been here since his own graduation. In a similar outfit, he'd walked up the same aisle, past his mother and father. The graduation was a peak of his mother's happiness. How much he'd loved and how little he'd noticed her. Her words were the neatness of the house, the comfort of meals, the good sense which leveled Poppa's outrage. Her forgetfulness was their house joke. She was their patsy. Wursup could hardly bear to think of the way she shrank when he blew up because she'd forgotten the kind of sandwich he wanted. Yet he knew she knew how much Poppa loved her. She was almost never ill, but when she was in bed for a half day, his resentment at having to get the groceries was subdued by terror that something would happen to her. And then, three or four years after that graduation day, her forgetfulness became dangerous. Gas jets were left open; she went shopping and couldn't remember her way home; she let the bathwater overflow. Wursup persuaded Poppa to hire a companion-housekeeper. That eased the logistics of the household, but removed Momma even further from the routines which kept most of what mental orderliness survived. Then it was the home, and he helped Poppa get her into it, and stayed with him the first days in the empty house. After that, he tried to come back once a year to see her. He'd drive up to Winnetka and make his way through the sad drifters to her room, take lunch and a walk with her. She looked scarcely older, her hair even now was as much dark as gray, but she would forget to lift her spoon to her mouth; he would do it for her—hadn't she done it for him? She smiled, she kissed him, but it was clearer and clearer that he was little more than some vague benevolence in the general darkness of things. It was terrible to see her; yet once, walking in the garden, holding her arm, he'd heard her say, "Carlo, dear," and for eight years he had gone up to the home in hopes of hearing it again. Two years before Sookie's graduation, he'd stopped going, and when Sookie asked him if he was going to visit her, he said there was no time, he'd already broken his routine for the graduation. As Sookie came back up the aisle, his refusal and his memory of Momma in her blue dress at his graduation came together, his heart rocked, and Sookie, walking by, proudly, winking and smiling at him, saw him crying, and thought, "Oh, that dear sap of mine, what a softie."

Two weeks after Wursup's piece appeared in *Life* with old photos of Blick juxtaposed with a Grünewald Christ and a Giacometti head, the magazine printed a letter from him.

SIRS:

Every law-abiding human has the right to keep his features—however amusing or repellent they may be—to himself and those he visits. You have not only abused my right, but compounded the abuse by treating me as if I were an artificial creature, worked up like an artist's painting. Your magazine calls itself by a name which mocks its attempts to send everything into its morgue. I'll handle my own undoing if it's all right with you.

H. BLICK

* * *

To which *Life*'s italicized subscript was, *"Feel free."*

Wursup was enraged at *Life*'s response, and then furious at himself for doing the piece. The description of Blick's feet and clothes, the reporting of Blick's answers, even the sympathy which showed through them, disgusted him. What right did he have to dig up the fellow? The old answer—Blick didn't have to see him—didn't matter now. No one but an experienced public man knew how he could be made to look by a skillful reporter. Wursup wrote Blick apologizing for his piece, for the illustrations and for the meanness of *Life*'s response.

To his surprise, Blick answered him.

DEAR WURSUP,

I owe you the apology. Our talk was too much for me that day. I didn't have the courage to stick it out and couldn't even face you again to tell you that. As for your piece, you did what you had to do. If it hadn't been about me, I would have liked it. As it is, I can't say anything about it. I stay back from it the way I stay away from the ocean (because I can't swim and fear it). But I came as close to enjoying the afternoon with you as I have any moment but those when we make the films. So I'm glad you came, despite the frightening publicity—we asked for it, we got it—and it might be that you will have another hour sometime, and I might have the courage to enjoy it with you.

Yrs.
HAMISH B.

* * *

81

Wursup felt grand, and the wonderful letter went into the file of special ones he'd received. (He saved almost everything for the Collected Wursup Papers. What would history be without them?) Now, six years later, looking at Blick's obituary, he felt the loss as he hadn't when Schilp had mentioned it. It was not just another vacancy above ground, but within him. He'd seen so many people, drawn them out of their versions of themselves and written them down. Almost every one of them who died gave him a twinge or two, but usually he took it less hard than he took the breaking of his coffee mug. Sometimes there was even the deliciousness of a death, the thrill of an extinction. Death enriched thought; it was an excitement, it deepened life. And Wursup's portrait of a man might be most of what was left of him; the man could no longer contradict it. In the way an aristocrat owns his family portraits, Wursup owned the man. So death, for Wursup, had often been more acquisition than loss. Blick's death, though, was just loss, a sadness, a piece of space in the world—no benefit.

Sookie bent over his shoulder and looked at the picture in the paper. "Was there a suicide note?"

"No. Just the rocks, the razor and the pillbox."

"Quite a farewell address."

"His last picture show. He must have gone over it a thousand times. Maybe even when I was with him. I smelled death all over Blick—anybody could—but God knows I don't want praise for my acuteness. I wish he were still here. Old Macfarlane used to demonstrate the unreality of death. He got it out of Spinoza. The idea was death could only be real to the dead, and since the dead couldn't feel, it was an unreality, and thought should only be reserved for reality. QED, death wasn't worth thinking about."

"I like that," said Sookie. "That's not foolish."

"It's another cushion. Blick didn't use them. He took care of himself. The rowboat would have floated back. And his body would have stayed down if they hadn't bothered going after it."

It was a bad day for the old and broken. On the way back from the Forty-second Street library (where he'd been reading about the instability of male chromosomes), he saw his mother's oldest sister, Rachel, making a scene outside D'Agostino's Market with Anna, the lady who'd cooked and cleaned for her for half a century. Around the geriatric agon, a ring of Lexington Avenue gawkers assembled. His little aunt, in apron, sweaters and unlatched galoshes, was stomping snowy muck on the heavy legs of the eighty-year-old Westphalian "girl" who was trying to pry her hands off a metal shopping cart, meanwhile telling the crowd she was responsible for Mrs. Schiff, she wasn't supposed to take the carts home, Mr. D'Agostino had warned her he wouldn't let her shop there anymore, not that she was fit to shop anyway, she, Anna, being the only thing between her and the mental asylum. When Wursup came up, Anna said, "*Denks Gott*, Mister Fred." Wursup managed to let his aunt know who he was, got the cart away from her fierce grip and told the spectators the show was over.

Three of his old aunts lived within blocks of one another. As with Wursup's mother, their hearts were deathless, but their circulatory systems worked well only as far as the neck. Their limbs were powerful; they resisted their incapacities with fury. Each of them had gone through two husbands; their present ones were on crutches. The forgetful aunts abandoned their helpless spouses in barber shops or forgot them in the park. Robust vacancies, they walked through the East Side, marketed, ate at Schrafft's, shopped and forgot things. Now and then, though, there were odd clearances in the mental night; other ancient Jewish ladies would be saluted and identified: "There's Rose Fuld, she must be ninety-four, she was at Quakerridge" (or Century, or one of the other clubs of their old bridge, Mah-Jongg and golf days). The aunts had a village view of New York and the world. The secretary of state's mother had catered a party for one of their friends; the U.N. ambassador's mother had been another's trained nurse. One of them lived in the apartment house of a president's widow and exchanged the time of day with her sweet children. The world's notables were notable for their placeability in their network. A good-morning in an elevator was more memorable than the settling of a war. "He is such a fine man, so courteous, always says good-morning so nicely." Now and then corridors to the past opened in the old brains, and Wursup would hear stories of pre-electric New York (the installation of lights or the first telephone on the block). Mostly, though, conversation with his old relatives was cyclical and erosive: "You're getting along well? I believe you're a newspaperman. With the *Times*? Poppa was a dear friend of Mr. Ochs. And you work for his newspaper. Is it the *Times*? Mr. Ochs was a good friend of Poppa's." Grandpa Schneckler had stayed in Wursup's room when he visited Chicago. He was a tall, white-haired, white-mustached man and wore a long white nightgown; he kept a water bottle by his bed and snored. His daughter had married beneath her. This was conveyed in hundreds of ways to Wursup, who had never before felt such protective affection for his little father. In his aunts' recollections, Grandpa Schneckler had been a friend of all the significant great—Lehmanns, Seligmans, Loebs, Wertheims, Otto Kahn. There was no evidence of these friendships—they were probably transformations of good-mornings in elevators—but for the grandson of Adolf Schneckler, there was a pleasure in these links with old New York that compensated for the terrible repetitiveness. "You're getting along? You work for a paper, don't you? The *Times*, isn't it? Poppa was a friend of Mr. Ochs."

"Do me in, Sook, if it happens to me. You should see the scene at Rachel's. Three people, the combined age over two hundred and sixty years, and not ten grains of rationality in the household. They bump around like drunks, sometimes furious, sometimes merry. Rachel's husband knows five stories; he tells them over and over and over."

"But she doesn't remember, so they're always fresh to her."

"That's right. She's like a goldfish thinking every trip around the bowl is just terrific. But I won't have that luck. I'll sit like Momma, wondering what that silver thing is, and that hot stuff someone's putting into my face."

But it wasn't real to him. Rachel was real and his mother was still real, but they were not of his species. If it came down to it, he would handle it like Blick, work it out, and do the job himself. But it wasn't worth the thought. Now. To that degree, Macfarlane—Spinoza—had something.

6

Thursday, Wursup walked the four miles from his apartment to St. Vincent's. It was a brilliant day. The light was powerful, heavy, an African light. Wursup had a cold—caught on the roof the night he spotted Doyle's picture in Susannah's hands. "You should be in bed, dosing," said Sookie, who peddled the pill gospel for everything short of cancer and broken legs.

"All your capsules have is adrenalin. Which is what I get walking. The only good that portable pharmacy"—her purse—"has done is when it clobbered the mugger." (Sookie had driven off a Central Park marauder.)

"When you don't have a bug, you're glued to the desk. That's when you should be exercising."

"What your heart's in does your heart good. That's medicine, not Confucius." He was fortified with his research. "It's called 'appropriate expenditure.' I burn as many calories typing as a drill presser drilling. The work on stress—"

"—doesn't tell you to exchange bacteria with the dying. I'd

rather have you flying off to Rome." (Wursup had found out Doyle was there.) "And don't talk exercise to me." Fingering her way through his clothes to his belly. "No one's mistaking this for anthracite."

Against the chill, Wursup piled on fur, an Australian sheep-herder's jacket, a silver karakul he'd bought in a Kabul bazaar, muskrat earmuffs from a Moscow dollar shop. Sookie said he looked like Bigfoot. "No one gives me a second look when we're out. Except to warn me about the creature beside me."

New York–walking was Wursup's passion as well as his therapy: galleries; florists, discos, bars; sooty high rises; the hung-over polygons of new museums; little churches looking older than Rome's; the surprises, the fossils, the crystalline se-ductions; fur, lace, jewelry, silver, meat, wine, vegetables; the quick shift from luxury to porno seediness, from mob and noise to the bleak forts of the twenties; the old Armory, like a forgotten chunk of Ferrara, waiting for the wrecking ball—nothing stirred up dreams of civic splendor in Wursup like a few miles of Manhattan.

St. Vincent's was something else. An old hospital with old odors, corridors colored like squash meat, the white drift of medics, sheeted patients, the huge elevators rising at mortu-ary pace.

Millie Sollinckas waited for him in the Gastrio-Intestinal corridor. She was sturdy, small, apple cheeked; her peach-colored hair was balled on a powerful neck. An icon of health, she shook hands like a Prussian cadet—one large pump. But with a blush: encounters with nonmedical males were rarer than death in her twenty-one years.

The blush was for the outside world. In the regions of the sick, Millie was as authoritative as Vergil. She led Wursup in and out of wards, care units, operating rooms, laboratories—pointing, explaining. Machines and people fused into thera-peutic chimeras; plastic tubes emptied and filled human ones; on heart screens, purple balls bounced and exited like chorus girls. "He's getting glucose." "She's getting plasma." "Coronary Care Unit." (Metallic ranges of screen and dial registering human time bombs.) "Kidney dialysis." This for a ten-year-old black girl leashed to a hose, studying an ancient copy of *Fortune.* "Hi," said Wursup. No response: too many greetings had washed over her.

The first patient he had any time with was a seventeen-year-old boy who lay on his side in a curtained bubble off the corridor. "This is George," said Millie. "He was shot last November. He won't-or can't-say by who. The police think it was his mother. Nobody knows why he's alive. They took everything out. There's nothing left inside him. And there's nothing to do for him." She bent to the gaunt black handsome face. "How are you today?" Some grunting negative came through George's fine lips. "I've brought that famous reporter I told you about. Feel like talking?"

A spur of window light shone on the lump George's rear made in the sheets. Something like "Mahtswill" came out of the lips.

"He doesn't mind," said Millie.

"Are you in pain?" asked Wursup. Leaning over this eviscerated agonizer, he felt like a statue, the weight inside his coat and pants accused by George's emptied flesh.

Another negative grunt on the thin lips. (Had some Portuguese midshipman gone wild over George's great-great-great-grandmother on the terrible Atlantic crossing?)

"Is there anything you'd like, George?" How could one ask this boy anything? What contact was possible? Anyway, his salon had closed for the day. George's eyes were great, black Picasso eyes, but now the current was off.

"Maybe another day," said Millie. She tugged the blankets a half inch so George could sense there was still some care in the world for the body that some other human had wrecked.

Down the hall was a G-I patient, Mrs. Simms, an eighty-two-year-old black lady whose daughter, gray, pert and bespectacled, sat beside the bed. Mrs. Simms held a Bible in a hand that would have served an anatomy class. Wursup shook and was held by it. "Where are you from, Mrs. Simms?"

The daughter said, "Alabama."

"No, I'm not," said the old lady. She explained that Beautown was in Mississippi, two miles from Alabama. She *shopped* in Alabama. It was an old skirmish.

"Would you rather be back home?" Wursup's professional life was, as Blick had said, largely interrogatory, but here it felt as awkward as his weight had felt leaning over George. Touch and eyes counted here. Mrs. Simms and he made connection. Apparently dying was a trip on which one made friends quickly.

"This is home," she said, moving their hands to the Bible.

"She reads it all the time," said Millie. "She is a very fine lady." Wursup leaned over and—mostly for want of something to do—kissed the crosshatched forehead.

"Thank you," said Mrs. Simms.

In the mustard-colored corridor—relief from the intensity of the little death rooms—Millie said, "I've saved the best for last. Francesca Buell. Everyone calls her Cheechya. Spelled C-I-C-I-A." Millie was like a good curator—ambitious, learned, proud. "I'm glad you came today, 'cause she'll be going home soon."

"She isn't very sick?"

"Oh, yes, but we like them home if they can manage. She's just here for some treatment now. I think you'll like her. She's young, educated; she knows what's happening to her. She reads up on the disease, asks questions. She's anxious to talk to you. She knows who you are."

"How long does she have, Millie?"

"To live? Hard to say. Melanoma's strange. Six months. A year. Two. Sometimes there are amazing remissions. I had a man last year—Mr. Scherbaum. They'd closed the book on him. Nothing to do. The stuff was all over the lungs. He went home. One day he took a walk and a squirrel bit him. It was probably rabid, but they decided, what the heck, why inflict rabies shots on him—they're not pleasant. So what happened? His immunity system lit up for some reason, and on the way, it stopped the melanoma. Or that's the way Dr. Giessen tells it. No"—looking at Wursup—"we can't bring in a squirrel that's got the right bite."

An hour later, walking up Seventh Avenue from St. Vincent's (the air so brilliant it was as if some power had sliced up New York and was regarding it through a powerful lens), Wursup realized that he had been gripped by what he'd come to recognize as a love seizure. Every now and then these seizures occurred. It was an odd, unpredictable business. He thought it might be an early sign of the mental decay of his mother's family, the dissolution of a piece of his brain. His seizures weren't reserved for women. They could start up at an old picture of his sons or at a glimpse of an old man on a bus. And he sometimes felt premonitions before he'd fixed on the object of the seizure. So before he saw Francesca Buell, he'd felt something trembling when he'd bent over Mrs. Simms; perhaps it had begun when the little girl reading *Fortune* looked blankly into his eyes. In fact, he'd been in a susceptible state for days. On Monday, he'd noticed the portrait of his mother's mother leaning on the wall of the closet. It was a miserable oil squiggle painted fifty years before by an admirer of Aunt Rachel's, a gambler named Flaxmeir whom his grandfather had thrown out of the house. There it sat, a few square feet of paint in a gold, curlicued frame. He'd lifted it up and looked at the old face. "Grandma, darling." His grandmother had been dead since 1935. "How much Momma looks like you. I never noticed your eyes were black. And those glasses. Didn't they have frames in nineteen twenty-five? How beautiful you were." (The old lady had his own thick features, but in the grip of sentiment, alone in the apartment, Wursup

was enchanted by his grandmother's beauty.) "You were a little girl, you wagged your little bottom, you fell for Grampy,
you went to bed, you and Grandpa made love. Why didn't I
know him? What were you like? Dear, sweet lady who dunked
sugar cubes in your coffee and gave them to me, who took me
to the zoo."

Even a week ago he'd felt a spurt of love for Billy; ten years
and inches fell off the six basketball-playing feet of his son,
and Wursup remembered an argument with the little boy during a football game on television. "Billy, darling, why did I
scare you?" (He'd threatened to dump the boy in the bathtub
if the Packers scored again.) "You know I'd give my arms and
legs for you. Bless you. Bless your life."

These goofy storms of feeling could come anytime: staring
at margarine tears on the toasted wheat of the English muffin
en route to his mouth; soaping his great knees in the tub on
whose bottom Sookie had glued pink and blue florets; standing before a painting in a gallery. (Once, in Amsterdam, he'd
started sobbing before a Vermeer; passersby had skirted him
as he groaned into the fleece of his coat.)

What were these fits? Some passage of soul? Wursup believed in nothing immaterially based, but might there be
some quarkish particulate foaming between grosser sub-
stances? *Esquire* reported that a Swede had discovered the
weight of the soul: he'd put the beds of terminal patients on
scales and weighed them before and after the last heartbeat.
Average weight loss: twenty-one grams. (A twine of mist between breath and human meat?)

Francesca Buell was not even his type. Though, as he
thought later, that night up on the roof, staring vacantly at
Susannah reading in the green armchair, neither were Sookie
and Susannah. Odd. All his life he'd itched for small, slender,
fine-breasted black-haired girls. How was it that he'd spent
most of his life with the tall, the fair, and the light-eyed?

Francesca was square faced; her hair was dark blond and

thick, her face radiated country health. But there were violent grains in the milky flesh; vascular battles were being fought there. She was tall—her feet made little peaks far down the bed—and the hospital smock did not keep her breasts a secret. A pretty girl with a fine, subtle smile that showed as much in cheeks and chin as in the lips.

"It's good of you to talk with me," he said.

"That's what *I* want to say," she said. "I've never met anyone really—excuse this—famous, in or out of the hospital." Her voice was full of feeling, quiet, but lovely. It wound Wursup around her. "I only hope I'll be able to help you. Concentration's a problem here. I often can't read or watch the tube." A glassy box hung in the air like a space station. "You lie here, and before you know it, your mind's leaking all over the universe." Her eyes were peculiar, the iris a thick, iron gray set in a mottled white. Another trouble sign, thought Wursup. Did she feel the war beneath? The voice gave no sign.

She'd read his work. "Lots of articles. Not the books, I'm afraid. I remember seeing the *American Dream* one all over Brentano's window."

"The *Drain* one?"

"Sure. There you have it. I get nothing right. I did read the *Times* review and came as close to buying it as I'd ever come to a political book. 'An American epic.' It's something. Did you like that?"

"Sure. There's a period when they can call you Dante and Homer and you're so crazy you wonder why they left out Shakespeare and Goethe. 'What did I do wrong?' you ask yourself. 'They must be blind.' It's an insanity. Which especially hits ex-reporters who go from knowing they've produced nothing but background print for doughnuts and coffee to thinking they're performing open-heart surgery on the earth."

"News used to be such a diversion. I don't know why it was one of the first things I lost interest in. I just couldn't concentrate on it. Even last year, everyone was high on all the impeachment stuff, and I just couldn't stay with it. I was in here when Nixon made his resignation speech. Millie turned it on, and I could only think, 'Poor dope. Look at the sweat on his lip. He's like a kid with the jam on his face.' I fell asleep during it, and it was short, wasn't it? I thought about being a reporter once. I don't know why. Why did you? Oh, you're sweating, too. Not from guilt, I know. They don't recognize the oil crisis in here. Take off your coat. Please. Tie, too."

"Thanks," said Wursup. "Why did I? I wasn't good at anything, that's why. I have fancier reasons for journalism classes."

"I heard you on Dick Cavett once. You said something about Mohammedan news. I can't remember, exactly."

"That's one reason to be a reporter. Stuff you read stays with you longer."

"Not me. I'm aural. If I hear it, that's it. It was just that what you said was a little remote. But it was grand."

"I remember. I'd prepared a lecture the week before. The Mohammedan stuff had to do with the Arabic word for 'news,' which became the word for the tradition of stories about Mohammed. Like 'gospel,' the good news about Jesus."

"I remember now, too. Your idea was they used to collect every scrap of news about sacred figures; now we collect it about anyone we can. News replaces gospel. There's no one center of interest. Just everything personal about anyone to whom anything happens is absorbing."

"A gospel a day. 'Hadith'—that's the Arabic word. In Mohammed's lifetime, when you asked, 'What's the news?' you only meant, What did you hear about Mohammed? Did he eat fish, drive someone away, kick a camel, or what? You needed material to govern behavior. My idea was, it's much better now. Instead of relying on a few remarkable men, you have many more people to tell about, lots more—I guess the word today is—'life-styles.'"

Wursup felt the talker's joyous passion for his listener. What a lovely girl. So responsive, so alert.

"Without anything being sacred?"

"Exactly. A reporter was part of Gospel, Incorporated. The Associated Gospels. Then it turned out, most of what we were doing was finding out what Ike ate for lunch and what he thought about what so-and-so thought about him. Still, I'm all for it. It's spreading the wealth. It's easy to become sacred for a day or a year now, a little harder to stick around for ten. The trouble is, some of the old-fashioned authority is gone. And then, anybody can dress up like a hero or saint long enough to fool the press for a few hours or months."

"Less and less about more and more?"

"Something like that. But then I can come and talk to you and try to tell people about your feelings. You don't have to be a princess or prime minister to be important."

"Just being here," she said, moving her head around the tiny yellow room with the lunar tube and the orange armchair. "Not exactly an accomplishment." Her hair flew around like a skirt. "Tell me what I can tell you."

A kind of inertness had come into her face, a bit like the abstraction he'd seen in the faces of street people in Calcutta, a shrinking into self as if to occupy as little space in the world as possible. She'd been all out talking about his trade; he'd brought her back to herself, to his story, and there she abandoned him. Perhaps the best thing was to go on.

"Do you ever feel you've been cheated?" She put her hands to her face. *Oh, God,* he thought. *Please.* But she just rubbed her temples with the tips of her fingers. A way of thinking, calming herself. "Never mind," he said. "We'll talk of something else."

"Of course not. It's what you came for. I wish I'd thought things out as well as you did your reporting. I'm not too smart. I haven't worked out a new way to act. I'm sick, but I don't think sick. Mostly. I'm still here, still part of everything."

"Yes," thought Wursup. "Part of this lousy armchair and that lousy tube and the hospital bed." Still, he must try to get her to spell things out. "I mean, why should things go wrong for you?"

Her right hand rubbed at the right temple; she was going into herself, but then came out. "Not cheated. Puzzled a little, maybe. It's not so much *me* and *them*, me versus the healthy. There is a big difference between being sick this way and not being sick, but my guess is it's more like being blind. I mean, you know there are things you don't know, can't do, and some you try to find ways of doing. You get messages by more roundabout ways, usually more slowly. Yet there's more intensity, too, things counting more, being clearer. Your coat on the bed. I'll think of that—the sleeves, the lining, the blue stripes. Your face, the eyes, the fleshiness of the face, its—what?—concern, the words you use. They may not come at once or together; I drift; but they'll pop in sharply. I have a friend who lives upstairs in my house. She's a poet, a wonderful one. I feel as if I'm closer now to the way she must think, isolating things, putting a bright light on them. Not the verbal part, I don't have that, just the concentration."

"My guess is, you've always been especially lively. Most people walk the streets like zombies."

"I'm a bit of a zombie now. I mean, as long as you want to know, lots of things just go by me now. I told you I can't follow the news. I just don't get it. And lots of things. My dad writes me about his doings; he's one of these terrific autodidacts and health freaks, the most worldly person I know. And I was a little like that, but now his letters just go through me. And he's someone I know. But I feel, underneath, he's just whirling around his confusion about me. I mean, why should he have produced these damaged goods? Has he done something wrong? As if there's any blame in it. He doesn't understand; he still thinks a few weeks in Bermuda'll do the trick. Or just going around with him in L.A., being part of life. I can't even concentrate on his letters."

"What does hold you, Cicia?"

"I dunno. Dreaming. Pulling myself together for one thing or another. Cancer's so nutty. Even the hardest heads around here say they don't know what to make of some remissions. They don't know exactly what the will is, but Dr. Giessen—who's the hardest of the hardheads—says he's sure patients who will to live and hate their cancers, which I do—I want to live and I hate the thing like the devil—do better. So I've got these crazy hope dreams. And I sometimes concentrate everything I can into aiming a kind of psychic X-ray at some place a tumor might be. I go up and down myself with it. It's batty, but I believe in it. And then, their part, the technical part, holds me. The possibility part." She was all lit up now, an intense, charming girl talking important things at a garden party, in a seminar, a board room. With perhaps a special concentration that showed in the depth of the eyes, the small movements around the mouth. "They learn new things every day. They may even have the answer in some computer system in Bulgaria. The immunologists are particularly hot now. I get transfusions from blacks who've got white blotches. It's got to do with their immunity to some disease involving melanin. If you know any, send them up. I dreamed the other day I was the blond werewolf of Harlem. Mugging blacks on a Hundred Twenty-fifth Street. The body's so damn complicated. And the head. Part of me's checking out of things, the other's building a house in the woods somewhere. Of course there are bad times too. Really bad ones when I'm probably crazy."

"What are they like?"

"I don't know. I'll tell you sometime. They're bad. I don't want to think of them. One thing that gets me a lot: it's not crazy, it's just vanity, I guess, but I've done nothing. I haven't made anything. No children, no poems, never even made a person very happy. The guy I was with for two years got scared when this started, so I helped him get off the hook. That's not much of an accomplishment. A couple of years ago, we—I—had a garden in the country. I did most of it. Hibiscus, Queen Anne's lace, strawberries. Not much. But I made something grow. And that's it. Not too good a score, is it?"

It was four o'clock, icy, granular and sad; New York was getting ready for the evening. Traffic picked up, salesmen added up accounts, cooks poured staples into iron pots, waiters set the evening tables, people thought of subways, drinks, supper, the night's TV programs. The terrific African light had gone to the Poconos; the snow seemed on the lookout for dusk.

Wursup walked out of the angled streets of the Upper Village, up Seventh Avenue into the small-business world of candy stores, diners, bars, novelty shops. He wanted to buy something for Francesca. Some terrific necklace or fur, or a picture. For whatever room she'd be in. What kind? Some Pollock calligraph, indecipherably beautiful, a gorgeous tangle into which she could dip for whatever she needed. Or maybe some confident Renaissance beauty, a Titian portrait of a doge, or a Piero della Francesca encounter—the Queen of Sheba and Solomon (souvenir of their own meeting). Or something clear and remote: a Hopper gas station in the woods, isolated, empty, the lights fuzzy. He'd give her his postcards; at least he'd pick out a hundred beautiful ones from all over, make her a little museum. Or would that make her see how much she'd never see?

Home, he went through the boxes of cards with an absorption that deflected what was coming over him, a kind of pressure, a warmth, an intensity which, strangely, foolishly, was amorous.

7

When he was in Rome for official business—which had not been the case for years—James Doyle stayed at the Excelsior, but when there, as he was now, for breath, for ease, for nostalgia, to think things out, and to see his old pal Henry Knoblauch, he stayed where he'd first stayed a quarter of a century ago, the Albergo Bologna, on Via Santa Chiara, around the corner from the Pantheon.

Though he was doing little in Rome but hiding out—"getting his mental sea legs "—it was not a vacation. Vacation in the sense of a mental and physical spring cleaning was not an operable notion for Doyle, whose mental furniture was a little too heavy to move. He was in Rome for a few days to get ready for politics. And it was here he heard from Fred Wursup about the mean story that was going to break in the next weeks. Fred was coming over to help with that. Till then, Doyle read Italian newspapers, walked the streets, went to galleries and churches, and saw Knoblauch.

Twenty years ago, he and Adele had bought a family vaca-

tion place in northwest Connecticut. There he did some of
his best work. They'd drive up from Arlington in July, the car
trunk stuffed with boxes of reports, position papers, legislative
history and presidential directives (plus twenty or thirty new
novels "for taking the world's temperature"). On the section
of the wraparound porch reserved for him, Doyle carved legislative actuality out of executive intention. "Sculpture out of
conative foam," he'd put it to Wursup in the interview which
made him what Scotty Reston called "one of the few uncol-
lapsed stars of *Down the American Drain.*" (Reston also noticed the "amiable intimacy" of the portrait.) On the porch,
bare feet up on the barkless railing, the piny hillside rising in
front of him like a reminder of a more durable, if not higher,
process than what went on inside him, half aware too of the
country music—the humming, buzzing, clicking, soughing,
the kids' racket muted by the quarter mile to the lake—Doyle
worked out the delicate paragraphs that would hold up under
staff-agency-budget and congressional pressures. The per-
suading, trading, squeezing and counting, the almost eroti-
cally compulsive life of Washington, seemed not just miles
but dimensions away.

Doyle had worked for the federal government off and on
since the Kennedy days. Before, after, and in between, he
worked for foundations and institutes, writing reports and
analyses (many of which he described and defended in journals like *Public Interest* and *Foreign Affairs*). These were not
his favorite times: between analysis and legislation there was
too much space; despite the racket, he liked working in the
engine room.

Now, though, on the edge of getting back, or trying to get
back by the door he'd never entered—politics—he felt something new, a doubt, small as the movement in a bird's throat
but definite and recurrent. Did he have the energy, the tenac-
ity, the optimistic fury, which formed political nerve and
muscle?

Many had lost them in these last years.

Doyle himself had early sensed the accumulation of petty fear, vulgarity and meanness in the capital. Men of worth had sunk back into the worst part of their natures, retreating to what they'd spent their lives escaping. They spent their days working out the foulest, stupidest, wildest attacks and defenses. Flair, toughness, braininess and decency looked like scraps of phony behavior pasted over old fears by men acting as if they were little boys dodging big ones. Yet Doyle had also seen mean, selfish and egocentric people turn around and act like Arthurian knights. Doyle knew himself well enough to know he was capable of almost anything short of treason and martyrdom (and who knew if these couldn't be boiled out under certain pressures).

Another part of his doubt was his ambition. Whatever it was, did he have enough of it? He knew he had energy and knowledge, and that he took terrific pleasure in large—national and international—arrangements. Nothing else appeased him for long, but was it ambition enough to be stripped and whipped in public? He could talk it out with Knoblauch.

He and Knoblauch had known each other thirty years. Knoblauch was dumpy, gimpy—he had a clubfoot. He'd come to Chicago in 'thirty-seven as a refugee from Frankfurt am Main, had done a brush-up year in English, gotten a fellowship, then a lectureship, at the University of Chicago. Doyle had been in his seminar on international trade; he was living off a small fellowship and jobs in the student laundry and dining rooms. Knoblauch helped get him a bigger fellowship, which gave him enough to finish his doctorate. By that time, Knoblauch had gone to work for a cable-and-wire company which, after the war, sent him to Rome to rebuild its Italian corporation. Doyle went into the Army for eighteen months and returned to an instructorship at the University of Illinois. There he'd written his three books—one an economics text that had been obliterated by Samuelson's—married Adele Rumson, who'd been in the Macfarlane survey with him, and met Thomas Cochrane, an old Harvard friend of Kennedy's who'd given him a push, first into the Brookings Institution, later into the administration.

Knoblauch, meanwhile, lived on a survivor's plateau. The relief of that early escape from Germany led not to the isolation of some refugees but to the life-hunger of those amazed to be alive. All right, disaster could be anywhere—one had a third eye that never slept—but the strain of perpetual alert was too great, one had to live in the present. The return to Europe was a brief menace; he had to remember he returned not as fugitive but as American executive. Expatriate life was not exile, and in the postwar world, Rome was its most alluring American site, the city of the sweet life. With useful work to keep his conscience clean and pockets filled, Dr. Knoblauch—he was called that by the Italian staff—invested his energy not in accomplishment but in possessions, growing children (a boy and a girl), after-work leisure, delight in the sheer motion of business and public events. His marble-floored apartment on the Via Cassia Vecchia was filled with the artwork and artifacts of two millennia: clay pepper pots from the first century, tropic-color squashes from the day before yesterday. At the American Club, he played gin rummy with diplomats, correspondents, businessmen stationed in Rome. Through the club blew men who shaped the world's business, leaving story fragments of negotiations over ammonia plants in Algeria, pipelines in Kuwait, palm oiling in the ministries of the world. Like his possessions, these fragments accumulated, so that Knoblauch felt he had some notion of the structures of power which operated those events described in newspapers. Such knowledge was another possession. At his own desk, he figured he himself was a small part of the scheme of furnishing and movement which made up most of the western world's business. Okay, he was insignificant himself, but as part of the immense structure, he counted.

When the structure discarded him, he should have been less surprised than he was. (Hadn't old catastrophes—his clubfoot, Hitler—wised him up? By no means.)

Standard Cable d'Italia lost enough money two years running to become valuable as a tax shelter; it was picked up by California's Bechtel Corporation (then engaged in its vast service operations for the Occidential Oil Company in Libya). Knoblauch's old friend and boss at Standard, Franky Cadetto, assured him that there'd be a place for him in the reorganized company, and he helped Franky reorganize the company so it would be both more complex and less profitable. Then Franky called from Cleveland. "It breaks my heart, Henry; they won't let me keep you." Knoblauch knew the unmysterious power behind "they." (Many times, he'd used that pronoun as his holy agency.)

He took to his bed, and then to the floor. A stroke. At breakfast, he was reading *Il Messaggero*'s account of "the merger"—actually reading his own name—when he realized the groups of letters meant nothing. "I can't understand the words," he said to his wife, and fell over his scrambled eggs to the floor. Two days later, he was carted off to the hills behind Lausanne, where, among the dysfunctional rich of Europe, he slowly learned to talk, read and write again.

Three years later, he still could not write script. The note Doyle had from him at the Bologna was printed in a shaky, child's hand: DEAR JIM, MEET YOU USUAL PLACE, TUESDAY, FIVE-THIRTY, HENRY.

The usual place was Rosati's, in the Piazza del Popolo. Doyle had prepared himself to see a shrunken Knoblauch; but no, limping to the sidewalk table, fifteen minutes late, was his old pal more or less unchanged, a little fatter, a little grayer, but clearly chipper in a white suit, his grand smile a fan of small fish teeth spread into his cheeks.

Doyle was almost half again as big as his pal; standing, he bent to him like a courtier, took both his hands in one of his own and patted them with the other, the hello-and-good-bye sign of a friendship which had never known a harshness. "You're rosy as a cherub."

"You are looking at a man who heard his doctor say, 'I have a dying man on my hands.'" Knoblauch sat down to the Frascati Doyle had poured when he saw him limping out of Via del Babuino. "I am a kind of spider. Not pretty, but tough."

The piazza was streaked with the closing day's gold fuzz (Roman sun in Roman dust). To their right were the two plump churches which made this the most maternal of Roman piazzas, or, with the obelisk in the center, the most hermaphrodite. Traffic swung crazily around the old pillar; cars flaked off patrons for the cafés. The gorgeous egomaniacal theater of Rome. It was balm, bliss, a wonderful human place. Knoblauch asked his news—they hadn't talked or written for two years. Doyle made a papal gesture over the piazza. "The great thing here is it makes your troubles insignificant." Not exactly an answer. Knoblauch knew Doyle disliked talking about any but public troubles. He was an activist, and he was a listener, but he was weak in self-analysis, or, at least, in confession. "When my news isn't in the newspaper, I don't have any. For now, I'm more or less the same. Ditto Adele and the boys. You're the one with a private life."

Knoblauch was also its chronicler; the chronicle was more enjoyable than its contents, at least when such pals as Doyle or Wursup were there to hear it. "Financially," he said, "I am, I don't know why, A-one." The company had made him a good settlement: two hundred thousand 1968 dollars, half in lire, and the company lawyers helped him shave the taxes. In addition, he received six hundred dollars a month in lire under Italy's retired-executives plan.

"They know more ways to bleed themselves to death than we do," Doyle said.

"You want them to throw their old men away like grape skins? The *paese del umanismo?*"

"Of course, you've paid Italian taxes all these years."

Knoblauch's hand covered his mouth in burlesque of the Italian gesture of concealment from the crowd. "Theoretically. There's still more. Fifty a month when Jennifer and Benno were in school here. Plus American Social Security—don't forget, I've got fourteen years on you. Then, I wasn't an economist for nothing. Knight and Viner would have been proud of me. I felt the money crunch coming, and went into gold. So, *mon vieux,* you are looking at a gentleman of some means." He moved the glass of Frascati into the light so that it looked like a liquid version of his happy investment. "I'd forgotten how easy making money was. When there was nothing to do but make it."

"We—*they*—ought to bring you in to run the Treasury."

"You know me. Knoblauch works good only in a dark pantry, off the kitchen." The sharky grin opened and closed. "But, Jim, things are not all roses and gold. *La vie privée* is wearing a little thin."

Knoblauch and his wife had barely spoken in years. Doyle knew a few such couples, could never understand what kept them together. There were always more reasons for inaction than action. Great systems of intellect could be traced to the rationalization of evasion, drift, fatigue, or laziness. Doyle had seen how many large decisions came unexpectedly, as much from fatigue as resolution. Decision was more often sheer relief from the strains of debate than anything else. Yet in the West it was usually stamped prime grade. Socrates to Jesus to Sartre, doing was sweeter than not. Doyle had written his own last letter of resignation the day the House voted against what everyone had told him for a year would be the first measure passed in the session. (He'd kept the letter for a month so as not to leave looking whipped. No one was fooled.) As for the Knoblauchs, both children had suggested, urged—in the confident dramatics of the intelligent young— divorce; instead Henry and Doris made arrangements. Doyle thought even Kant's view of marriage—the contractual exchange of genitalia—was a warmer view than theirs. The arrangement was that Doris supervised the house and called the doctor in return for being Henry's legatee. The doctor came often; it seemed to promise early inheritance. Doris was twelve years younger, pert and elegant. There was the appearance of constant wit in her little pouting lips, but it was a heavy gaiety struggling against the gravity of unhappiness. She dressed beautifully, played cards at the American Club, shopped, gossiped, rode horseback, read new books, and kept in shape, waiting, almost surely celibate, tense, life just outside the doctor's door.

But watched pots don't boil; Knoblauch lived. And didn't wait. He had women. "I cannot be without."

His erotic saga was one of Doyle's chief Roman pleasures. Doyle himself had trimmed down desire very small. Sexual boredom was seldom relieved, but he cared deeply for Adele: she was attractive to him; they answered each other's diminished needs. When, a few years ago, she had put on forty pounds, he'd wondered if she was turning in her sexual papers, but then, prodded by friends, she lost most of the weight. Now again she was slim, an autumn-colored Anglo-Celtic woman, intelligent, forceful, surer of herself than he of himself. Early she had fought, at least to a draw, what Doyle thought of as the sexual terror of the Celts. He himself hadn't—for a decade—known days like those Knoblauch described, days which were little but sexual mouths (teeth in the body, mind unable to focus on anything but the breasts, knees and soft apertures of women). Tall, puffy, soft, rosy, old carrot head already whitening, blue eyes bulging in strained corneal fuzz, Doyle looked like an ex-alcoholic employed annually as a street-corner Santa Claus. There was something in his looks, his dress—nutty hats, slop in the decent pants—that remained as boyish as his head. A father, a head of missions and departments, supervising a hundred thousand men and women, an authority, he still felt and played a boy's role. He treasured astonishment, and treasured folly, the bizarre, gags; and he did not ignore what rattled his heart.

But he could not flirt. He stammered, he drank, he joked, blushed, swallowed and looked high and away when sexual beauty approached.

Not Knoblauch, who, two heart attacks nearer the grave than he'd been at their last meeting, was still palpitant. Though finished now with his five-years-long affair with the classical historian Rosalba Cirinulla, niece of a Roman cardinal. This was the "thinning" of his *vie privée*. He drew an old newspaper clipping from his wallet. *Il Messaggero*, SEPT. 21. Doyle took the little tissue of private history and translated the headline: *Suicide Attempt of Cardinal's Niece*.

"What a business, Jim, you cannot imagine." The dark eyes were dense with recollected affliction. "Twenty-five years here, and except for Present Also's at art shows, I've never been on any page but the financial." Brought by a movement of Doyle's wineglass to the discrepant coldness of this sentence, he shook his head. "I know it's terrible to think of that. It's just that there was something private and lovely, and it ends in this public stupidity, as if we were a show in the circus—it's too much." (Doyle shivered at a flash of the story about him in *Chouinard's*.)

What had happened was that Knoblauch had been making love with Rosalba when he'd doubled up with angina. "She'd never seen anything like it. She thought I was going to die on her body. She crouched under me, shaking like a mouse. I was in unbelievable agony. I thought, 'It's all over.' Somehow I got my pills; I made it through. While she shrank like a wet chicken and cried. Such crying. So, enough. She says she loves me, will always love me, but never, never can she make love with me again. I say, 'Rosalba, *carissima*. That's impossible for a man like me. I must have a woman. That's the way I am made.' Is it so unusual? For a month we have these terrible sad talks, tears—trickles, little rains. Three words, and her eyes fill up, trying to smile, tears pouring. Four years together. It was lovely. I have never been so long with anyone but Doris. Twice, three times a week, we met. Down near your hotel, across from the Pantheon. A little apartment. That's right, you were there. We had lunch, supper; we talked, played music, went to bed. There must be bed. There must be. And for her, there couldn't be. Nevermore. So I said, 'Dear Rosalba, it's over,' and the next day, I called the first listing in the *Messaggero*—the *relazioni sociali*, you know?" Doyle didn't. "The girls—or whoever—put in ads: 'Conversation and delicate relations with young *—giovanissima—*well-educated girl, speaks German,' or English or whatever, with a phone number. I didn't need to speak German; my Italian was good enough to pass myself off as a South African. 'Jan Smuts.' Good? I didn't think 'well-educated' included knowledge of much beside the business at hand."

"How much does it cost?" Doyle questioned from economic, not sexual, curiosity. "Fourastière used barbers' prices as cross-cultural indices, didn't he? These are better."

"Fifteen dollars. Ten thousand lire. *Molto ragionevole.* Very reasonable. Italians regulate these things well. The girl is extremely nice. Very beautiful."

"You still see her?"

The sweet shark smile spread, a bit of pride. "Why do you think I was late just now?"

"How old is she?"

"She says twenty-three, admits to twenty-seven. Maybe thirty-four."

"How long do you get?"

"Same as an analyst. Fifty minutes. Not quite so strict, but she must be businesslike. She needs a hundred thousand a month for rent, another hundred for her clothes. I could give you all the figures. Jim, she is very agreeable. If things don't go well, she says it doesn't matter; we have tea; she talks with me. Very *simpatica*. She says if I'm having difficulty anytime, I should just come up and talk. No charge."

"Nifty."

"My only condition is that I don't run into anyone. When I come or when I leave. Everything's arranged by phone."

Doyle held up the clipping.

"Yes. So I told Rosalba, 'I'm sorry. We're finished. It's over. I know how bad it was for you. I understand.' She'd shrunk away; she was paralyzed. There I was, in unbelievable pain, and I had to comfort *her*. Please God you'll never know the pain. It is like a leopard tearing your insides apart. So that was that. I couldn't help it. Next day, I get a call at home. Rosalba has never called me there. In four years. She tells me she has just cut her wrists." Knoblauch was sweating; moisture formed in the furrows of black and gray knots on his great head. Staring at his old friend, Doyle wondered how many men and women at these tables, in the streets, in every city and town in the world, were suffering erotic pain. What networks of feeling under those of commerce. No wonder you couldn't calculate the votes of five hundred congressmen. It was a miracle any legislation passed.

"But what got it into the paper," said Knoblauch, "was the wildness of her answer to the reporter."

Doyle looked at the little clipping. *"Non ho potuto superare lo choc della morte de Allende."*

> "I couldn't overcome the shock of Allende's death," said the *nobildonna*, her arm covered with blood, while her friend, Dr. Henry Knoblauch, former managing director of Standard Cable d'Italia, prepared to accompany her to Ospedale San Giacomo, where, later, the doctors declared her out of mortal danger. The niece of Cardinal Cirinulla is at present completing a monograph on the antifeminist policy of the elder Cato for Editore Laterza.

"Everything in Rome ends in a monograph or a statue," said Knoblauch. "The Rome *Daily News* just translated the story. Except *amico* came out 'fiend.' Thank God Jennifer and Benny were in the States."

"Where could she have gotten that business about Allende?"

"If you aren't agitated about politics in Italy, you don't get invited to dinner. Though, I know the only politics Rosalba cares about are pre-Christian. She recites Cato's antifemale laws in Latin."

Doyle watched the obelisk light up for the night show. Untouched by all the histrionics around it. "I'm so sorry, Henry."

Knoblauch knew his pal. "I know personal crises look like bubbles to you, Jim. You deal with such big problems."

"It's not that. In Rome, I see everything at the small end of the telescope. But I know it must be a misery for you."

"No longer. Now it's a story. Here you need a new story every night. The key word in this old place is *new*. 'What's new?' That's the great question here."

"The more past there is, the more you have to pump just to keep up."

"I've grown used to doing nothing, Jim. And not only *used to*. I love it. I love cleaning out a hairbrush, getting the scissors blade into the bristles, pulling out the tangles. I read when I want. I garden. I enjoy knowing I earned the money to do what I want. Picking flowers—I can't stoop over too much. Arranging books—I love that: histories ancient, modern, European, Oriental, novels by century and country, philosophy. That's the small life I lead. Plus my sessions on the Via del Babuino, the street where Gogol wrote *Dead Souls*."

For Doyle, such a life would have been prison. His domestic service was on the scale of billions. It wasn't so long ago that his mother came home after ten hours of cleaning other people's houses to hold their house together while his father drank himself into the charity ward and then where no one knew until the girl from Susannah Wursup's newsletter flushed him up. For years Doyle had a recurrent dream about getting out of a presidential limousine to see a hand coming from a pile of rags in the gutter. "Gotta dime for your old man, Jimmy?" Doyle tried never to think, let alone talk, about those times, though much of his life was spent working out ways to prevent such humiliation in other lives. God knows what had gotten him out of it. His mother? The newspapers he read as well as sold? The public library (his church, his heaven)? The gift of pacifying his brothers and appeasing his father? James-Jimmy-Doyle, comic Irish name stuck on an awkward, clowning, pacifying ragamuffin, a statesman at age seven, at thirteen, mad for books, poems, ideas. He worked seven hours after school and got home to the wild household where his regal little mother somehow made sense of the noise, the bareness, the monotony. The facts of what he had never felt as "poverty" were so intimate a part of him it was only their statistics that could affect him now. Only to Adele, Henry Knoblauch and Fred Wursup had he ever talked of it. What was the point? This swapping of personal histories was a sport you gave up with stickball. Most of the histories were alike: some went up, some down. Were human beings only their histories?

Knoblauch's picaresque was something else. That's what he did, what he was. He was the salt of the earth, yes, but not its bread and butter. A life cleaning hairbrushes and banging whores. The men Doyle spent his life among also had hairbrushes; they slept, ate, itched and scratched, but this didn't fill their heads or consume their force. In his book, Fred Wursup had made a case against the problem-solvers. It was too easy. For Fred, problem-solvers were problem-makers. He'd let Doyle off that hook because he was a court jester. Not quite. He believed in the grandeur of great decisions. The limousines and jets were regal hangovers, but they'd been earned. There were no greater star-lovers than stars. This fellowship of celebrity was more than expert appraisal of expertise: it was the sediment of the old need for authentic power and grace. Loss of office was a terrible form of the bends. Doyle had suffered it: "Driven out from bliss, condemned in this abhorred deep to utter woe"—that was the absolute Miltonic version of it.

The difference between such lives and Knoblauch's was a difference of species. His life was motion, not existence. Then there was the life Doyle's father led, if you could say one "led" such a life. It was more like falling. Or was that verb too grand? It was more like jouncing in a no-gravity world. Doyle hadn't let himself think more than a few times in his life of this gene dispenser (he saw more of him in the shaving mirror than he wanted). The few memories which surfaced were unbearable—the silent red-faced man with a bottle of beer, listening to the White Sox games, borrowing dimes, stumbling in the street while he and his brothers looked away or crossed to the other side. A few others that were easier—a ring (some Crackerjack giveaway), a pocket knife, a pile of sadness in the corner.

Anyway, his life was basically different. He'd worked—and he mostly worked now—with relish. He'd learned, from a column, that the German Mafia in the White House called him "the Bolivian Goat," the creature, quoted the columnist, "which climbs the highest and feeds on the lichen no one else can stomach. Doyle gobbles this demographic data ten hours a day and out come statutes." There was praise as well as resentment in that.

The amount of resentment in gifted men always astonished him. He was disliked for wisecracks, for working for anybody who asked, maybe for working the way he did. Who knew? People adored trivia. From stained-glass windows to *the National Enquirer* and the girl on *Chouinard's*, the media traded on this passion for trivia. And a great career could be smashed for a few minutes' amusement.

"I've been a court jester too long," he told Knoblauch.

Knoblauch saw that his pal was worked up. The puffy hands flew over the table, the high voice was full of throaty rumbles and pitches, the blue eyes dilated as if they'd spotted some Helen of Troy stripping on the obelisk. "My motor's been overhauled, I've put gas in the tank, and now, I'm hardly out of the garage when this little gossip shitter puts a nail in the tires. Digs up someone who says he's my father. Fred telephoned me about it. It's coming out in that newsletter Susannah works for. Fred's coming over here to write some sort of piece that'll take the stink out of it. I wonder who can have it in for me. I suppose I ought to find out, but I'm a babe in that wood. It's stranger to me than those hieroglyphs out there."

"I have no wisdom for you, Jim. Yesterday, I get a letter from my son and heir, dear Benny. He says he's just learned 'Knoblauch' means 'garlic,' how could I have abandoned him to such a fate? 'Would you have kept the name Henry Turd, or Henri Merde?' So I seem to have done him in, getting born in Germany with such a name. That's as much trouble as I can handle. Your troubles are national. They're too big for me. Politics. People having it in for you. Writing up stories in the papers. Look what two words in the paper do to me. The garbage of other lives is so delightful. And one's own, so lousy."

8

Wursup went to Rome more for his own relief than Doyle's. Cicia Buell was the most obvious pit east of the Grand Canyon. To follow her into what some of the books called "the death trajectory" would be the living end of journalistic commitment. Good actors fall in love on location, and good reporters sometimes fall for their stories. To understand all was not only to forgive, but to love it. The professional code of toughness and surgical cool existed to shield the skin-off readiness of the nerves. One temptation of journalism was to lose yourself in other people's troubles. (The windows of New York were jammed with field-glassed amateurs sneaking peeks at other lives and bodies.) Wursup had known war correspondents who finally needed to be blown up. (Like bullfighters who have to be gored, gamblers who have to be wiped out.)

For Wursup, there was a Koufax Elbow: the closer he got to Cicia, the better material he'd get; the more material he got, the closer he felt to her, the less willing to use it. He baptized this subset of the Elbow "the Strether virus," after the Henry James hero who wouldn't let himself profit from his mission. *There* was charming Maria Gostrey ready to cheer his awakened heart, but Strether backed off in a cloud of scruples.

Sookie's colleague, Torsten Rimmel, had a geophysical explanation for such—and most other—behavior. Torsten made mathematical models in Sookie's lab. He was a merry, dwarfish redhead with eyeglasses so thick you couldn't tell the color of his irises. Now and then, she brought him back to cheer Wursup with his manic explanations of culture and society. For Torsten, "the Platonic stain" on Western culture derived from the volcanic destruction of the island of Santorin. "Minoan survivors fled to the mainland. They saw the destruction as punishment for their pleasures. Thus, Platonism." Torsten's corrugated forehead had a terrific crop of freckles which in expostulatory excitement glittered with sweat.

"From fear of pleasure to St. Paul and asceticism it's a hop and jump. Then New England witches, Hawthorne and your prissy Henry James." Torsten gleamed redly over Sookie's goulash. His full lips were dabbled with flecks of beef. Under his red hair and wrinkled forehead, vague chips of blue, green, and pale brown broke and floated behind the lenses. "Puritans harvest punishments. As if flesh weren't heir to sufficient natural shocks."

"You'd think transcendence of the flesh would appeal to him," Wursup said to Sookie. "Can he really have any luck with his own?" (Torsten was a great sexual boaster.) "I guess he gets his mind off his body doing math. But the rest of the time, he's cruising, dreaming, paying whores, or talking about it."

Torsten claimed to be writing a treatise on the geophysics of behavior. "Sexual Puritanism comes from those who live near rocks and deserts. They envy the inorganic. The death wish. Freud was a rock person. Most Teutons are. We try and break loose, go south, sing about Sicilian lemons and dream of big tits."

Sang Wursup, "'It was written by a Latin / A gondolier who sat in / His home out in Brooklyn / And gazed at the stars.'"

"Wagner couldn't finish *Tristan* up north. He had to go to Venice. It should be called *Dead End.*"

Of Cicia—*his* dead end—Wursup said no more to Sookie than that he'd sent some of his postcards to a dying girl at St. Vincent's.

"I don't get it. 'Having wonderful time, too bad you're not'?"

"No. Some pretty cards. I thought she'd enjoy looking at something nice. I don't even know if she got them. When I called up, the nurse said she'd gone home."

"I thought she was terminal."

"Not immediately. You'd never know to see her."

"Poor girl. How old is she?"

"Twenty-two or -three."

"Pretty?"

"In a country way. Kind of blond and rosy. Healthy-looking, till you sense there's something not quite kosher. A little pallor in the meat."

"No more," said Sookie. "Don't tell me anymore."

He wasn't planning to, certainly not about his sentimental confusion. You didn't make trouble for trouble's sake. The sexual subway shuttled between farce and torture. There was Sookie, opulent and rosy, all systems chugging, and—as the scruple formulator James would say—"deliciously there." Yet what wound in and out of Wursup's head but the cheer, the sadness and the sick beauty of Cicia Buell. *Am I necrophiliac?* He had flashes of Cicia lifting the hospital smock over her breasts, her body coming out of the sheets. The fervor of the dying coal. Crazy. He forced himself toward Sookie. Dear Sookie: his pal, his beautiful *copine*, with whom he shared ten thousand signals, his wife without portfolio, who had the key to his car, his apartment, who went around with him in the couple society of New York, his twin star. Not that it mattered what spout you let your steam off in. But it did matter, and the oldest aphrodisiac of old relationships poured in: pity. (There were so many varieties.) Fifteen or twenty years ago, he and Sookie would have married. In Wursup's marriage days, the fifties, marriage was often the consequence of a limited vocabulary: after you'd said "I love you" as many ways as you could, "Will you marry me?" was left. He'd proposed to Susannah on the Paris Metro while they held on to the white pole and the train rattled between Concorde and Châtelet. So noisy, Susannah didn't get what he said. For a second, he didn't repeat it, but there she was, with her wonderful green eyes and lovely smile, holding on to the white pole while the train swung her this side and that. The sign in the Metro read, ANYONE WITHOUT A TICKET IS IN AN IRREGULAR SITUATION AND MUST PAY AN INDEMNIFYING FORFEIT. That old language covered his situation. Marriage was the ticket.

He trotted his Cicia confusion across the river to Brooklyn Heights.

Will Eddy's house was one of the happy places on earth for him. He and Will sat in deep chairs in front of the East River, south of the Brooklyn Bridge, looking at the darkening, piquant, melancholy fishing-village tip of Manhattan. Behind them, the girls' record players cooked up a crazy sonic macaroni—Handel sonatas, rock complaints, amplified dolphin cries. Will drank Scotch, Wursup whatever white wine was cooling. Behind them, Frances and one or more of the girls made the small, happy noises of dinner. (That old system had not altered here.)

For years, they had sat here, usually at this hour and after, watching the human lights take over slowly from the sun. The soft chairs, the sugar-restoring liquid, mutual tolerance—not without its formality and reticence—the marvelous view of river, bridge, Wall Street, and the tiny, unmarked extrusion of the old island, all this and the long years behind them made these cherished hours.

They differed essentially, at least ideologically. Will was a serious Catholic convert, a needling conservative, a man who relished the notion of sin and his own capacity for it. Wursup thought him one of the pillars of the earth. Sure, Will was troubled occasionally by a sense of failure—but then who wasn't? Will had the Church, and though that was—for Wursup—an unimaginable, crazy reliance, he was glad Will and anybody else had it. The same was true of Will's analysis. What counted was that Will had been miserable and now wasn't. Or so Wursup thought.

Will was certainly less unhappy now than he had been, but he still suffered from a situation that was too comfortable for him to abandon. His job was absorbing, sometimes enchanting, but it was also grueling, narrowing. There was no progress, only accumulation. As for Frances, she was intelligent, sympathetic, beautiful and well off, but she functioned best as the jailer of his feelings and his life.

Will had the official goods on himself. The doctor who supplied them had pulled him out of a paralysis. One evening he was found on the bridge, unable to move. He was taken to Payne Whitney. In ten minutes, Dr. Steubenstein had untied the knots. "Only temporary relief," he said. "A contingent parole."

"Contingent on my starting with you?"

"On your starting to help yourself. With me or someone else."

Will knew many variations of therapeutic beginnings, but secondhand. Steubenstein had actually taken nails out of his hide.

Four years of analysis told him much and helped him live with what he called "failure." And it freed him for at least some of the sexual feast of his time. No more the quick, angry relief inside his official sex mate's cold beef; streets, offices, parties, swam in offers of bed and tenderness. After a life of frigid temptations—he and Steubenstein were getting to that—he felt he'd suddenly been given the directions to his body.

Not that things were clear. Was there anything in the world for which he couldn't feel both love and hatred, sometimes simultaneously?

Will accepted Steubenstein's results without his ideology. What counted was the relationship. It wasn't that he didn't pose for Steubenstein; it was that he didn't worry about changing poses or showing that he knew he posed. Steubenstein was his stage. For two hundred minutes a week, he was free as he could be. Which meant terrific encounters with the doctor. "I was great today," he might tell Wursup. He raked Stuebenstein's "mystic German guff." "Your *love stuff*," he'd said to the bald ex-halfback. "The phlogiston left over from debased Christianity and boredom. The psychological equivalent of ether."

As a boy, Will's mother had told him he would be a poet, and in high school, he'd been inducted into the art by a beautiful priestess, his teacher Angela Stuberloch. (The similarity of his doctor's name was not, in Will's mind, accidental. Perhaps he wouldn't have been helped by a doctor named Jones.) Angela walked with Will after school and brought him to her apartment in Lincoln Park. On the victrola were one-sided Chopin platters; on a tray, crème de menthe and vanilla ice cream. Nocturnes poured from the breasts of the priestess of poetry. "You're going to be the laureate of a town that's had little more than 'Hog Butcher' Sandburg. Chicago is nothing more than that until it's been sung by something higher." Bending for the plate, Angela was dazzling. All but the nipples of the beautiful breasts were there for the extended boy. Who, one day, leaned over and kissed them. His head was shoved away. "I'm the transformer of your gift. It would die if

I became its diversion. Do we want to be like everyone else?" Millennia into poetic celebration of sexual passion, and Will Eddy's tutor transformed him not into a poet but a mute of word and love.

Though within two years and ten miles of this parlor he was fornicating with Frances Bricker, convinced that this was what poets meant by love. In thirty years with Frances, he never got much beyond sexual relief. The affection, trust, pride and loyalty which were also there for ten years were subverted by contempt, disgust and—gradually—hatred for her. Yet he remained dependent on her approval and services.

There was one love affair in Will's pre-Steubenstein life, but it, too, was savaged not by disgust but by shame and farce.

Shame, first and lastingly, because the woman was Susannah Wursup, and because he loved as well as envied Fred Wursup and cared for Susannah as person and confidante as well as conquest. It was a French-farce affair of plants in windows, drawn shades, grocery-store rendezvous, and tricks with the telephone. It began when the Wursups first settled in New York. Wursup was off on assignment, and Susannah, terrified of New York solitude, called Will for crises—blown fuses, accidents, a theft. It was after he'd taken little Billy to Lenox Hill for a broken leg that they'd kissed in a new way, and, after a week of holding off, made love. It had gone on for two years, when Susannah said she couldn't bear it any longer, and, since she could not bear losing him either, begged him to find a way to go off. It turned out—even as he was arranging with the firm to work a year with the London office— that the Wursups went off to Japan.

By the time they returned, Will could not believe that he'd ever felt anything for Susannah. As he was installed on Steubenstein's couch, he "realized" that he never had. "You haven't been able to love anyone. That will be one of our little jobs," said the halfback. "To restore you to love and work doesn't mean the love and work your sickness imagined.

You'll never have immaculate intercourse. And you may have to settle for less than mother Angela wanted. Your publishing work counts. Every word you suggest to an author, every concept you spell out, every book you sketch—and Will, I know from others how many—breaks your silence. You are not exactly an unknown quality."

"Nor a household word."

"Nor a household word. Not Lucy or Brillo or Himmler."

"Or—"

"That's right, nor Joyce nor Homer. We'll have to face up to that."

This tax-deductible understanding and sympathy helped, though later Will believed that his trouble had only shifted into his circulatory and digestive systems.

Of Will's emotional confusion, Wursup knew very little. There are confessors and confessors, those who confess and those who receive confession. It was Wursup who opened up, who spelled out his groans, who threw to Tania, Will or Sookie whatever gathered up in him enough to call a mood. Oh, he knew Will wasn't made of concrete—he'd had a few laughs about Miss Stuberloch; he saw the extra heartiness in Will when his parents were around, guessed some of the emotional mess beneath it—but his own feelings seemed so clear to. him, clear blocks of pleasure, annoyance, affection, amusement, tolerance, scorn, pity, or even clear confusion; that he did not guess the wildness beneath Will's wonderful laugh. Sure, Will had done what almost everyone did, carted off his bafflement to a shrink, well and good, and Will had told him marvelous dreams and new sensations, and also some of the labor of analysis, but this was simply another fascination. Not that Will was someone to write about. Will was an atmosphere in his life, a state he could visit for its temperate climate and old-time amusements. In more than twenty-five years, Will had never failed to give Wursup a hearing. They'd never quarreled, hardly even argued. Sure, once or twice he'd been piqued that Susannah clearly enjoyed Will and relied on him—there'd been a small shiver of sexual jealousy there—but it was so remote, so distant, so basically unlikely, it never became a part of his feeling toward him. If anything, it was just a way of bringing a little excitement into his own feeling for Susannah and a form of charity to Will.

"What am I going to do about this girl, William? Or myself? I can't stop thinking about her. I don't like it. Am I some kind of necrophiliac?"

"I doubt that. Isn't it the oldest feeling in the world? Loving what's not going to be around. The deepest feeling, anyway. You're no different from anyone else."

"The girl wants to be a story. You know, to make something out of what's happening to her. But I can't write about her, feeling the way I do. When I write about it, I get rid of it. And there I am. I don't want to be rid of it."

"We're all nuts," said Will. "The more we suffer, the better we think we are. Some of the meanest men alive go around boasting how they suffer. I don't mean you, Freddy. You're not boasting."

"I guess I'm not suffering much either." Sunk cosily in the armchair, tipping his head to sip Chablis, looking at the bridge, its loops strung with light.

"How else show you count? Who has a worse press than the insensitive? Some of the toughest nuts alive develop the most fascinating vocabularies to describe their despair. The only thing that ever moved them was greed, envy, rage and hatred. They can be moaning and groaning about their misery, but let them get one sniff of a rival, no matter how distant, and whammo, their heart contracts with the closest thing they'll ever know to real suffering. They want to murder. Sometimes they work up some marvelous stuff to cover the wounds. *King Lear.* Or at least *Timon.*"

It was such an aria that Wursup, looking at his white-beard-ed pal, wondered for one of the few times in his life if Will could possibly be talking about his feelings for him. No. Why mess up so good a thing? All this repellent analysis.

Wursup felt he stood with the world's cynics, but life had treated him easily, and his cynicism died at the surface. He would not let himself think that any of Will's white hairs grew in resentment of him. If Will didn't care deeply for him, what the hell, no one could care for anyone. The wine was buzzing now; lights popped along the bridge; the roast-beef smell floated in on oboes and flute. It was hard to be faithful to trouble in such conditions. He managed to get back to his, but didn't feel it. "The girl goes to bed between Sookie and me. That's not right. All this love-death confusion isn't right."

"You have a great out for dilemmas," said Will. "Take off. The world's full of almost-stories waiting to be Wursupped."

Another small twist, yet true enough. And there was a story he could do. "Jim Doyle's in Rome. I'm thinking of giving him a little boost. A few words in the *Times* couldn't hurt him."

"There you are. Give him my best. And go see St. Clement's for me. Isn't that the church with all the layers?" Will had never been to Rome.

"I think so," said Wursup. "Trust you to smell it out. Such a deep fellow. Come along. You must have things to get away from."

"Me? Driven-snow Willie? You must be nuts. And how am I going to get along without my dinners? My girls?"

It was partly so. Like an old prisoner, Will couldn't make it outside.

9

Wursup loved Rome. Age seven, after he said he loved brown Betty, his mother told him, "You can't love what can't love you. You *like* brown Betty; you don't love it. That hard sauce isn't melting for love of you." But he did love those hot apple lumps in their sugary coats, and now he loved cities, he loved Italy and England and Kyoto, he loved Bach—what Bach wrote and what he was—and, in fact, loved many more things than he did people. He thought of old Macfarlane. Like most great haters, Macfarlane was a great love booster, and like Wursup—not a great hater—he had an impressive love list. "I love thousands of unresponsive things: moonlight, halibut, virtue. I love *virtue!*" (Shouted like "fire!") "I do not necessarily adore the organic matter which fills the seats, but the seats themselves, the classrooms—what the classroom stands for. That, I love. The *idea* of the university. Not skulking Newman's idea but *the idea* of it."

Since his first assignment in Rome, Wursup usually stayed in the Pensione Orazio-Moche on Via Nazionale, three blocks down from Piazza Esedra. The *pensione* had been recommended by Knoblauch, who, several times a refugee himself, sympathized with the owners, a tiny octogenarian Chinese couple, Signor and Signore Moche (pronounced Mush), who'd made their way to Rome from Shanghai in 1950 with twenty-five wagonloads of furniture. The signora's daughter had married an Italian—Signor Orazio—who'd worked in the Chinese customs service. There was a close connection between his position, their marriage and the safe arrival of the roomfuls of silk chairs and dragon-toed tables. Signor Orazio himself was not in evidence. His deposits were his classical name and corpulent four-year-old daughter, Loretta.

The Moches understood but preferred not to speak Italian. Indeed, they did not speak Chinese with each other. Their *lingua franca* was English. Old Signor Moche had never learned to read or write Chinese; he'd gone to English-language schools and worked forty years for a German dye company. He spoke the Shanghai dialect; Signora Moche, only Mandarin. Their English too was special. It was bare of articles and full of a peculiar if unintended harshness, derived, Wursup thought, from Shanghai viewings of old American gangster movies. Signora Moche greeted him every morning with, "Good morning, big shot," and when Billy made more racket than usual, she said, "Shut yap, punk." Over the marble floors, she padded in her little felt slippers, pinching the Italian maids, bowing to the guests, slipping the weekly bills— made out by her husband during long nights—under their breakfast plates.

The bills were memorable, handwritten in English and unfolded into lengths Wursup was used to tearing off Teletype machines: column after column of "One Egg: Baby; One Orange Squash: Lady; One Choc. Surprise-Extra: Mister."

In the early years, the most conspicuous pensioner was Sigora Orazio's paramour, Major Boschetto, an ex-official in the Bureau of Mines and Fortifications. A large, phlegmatic man, he sat in the white front room in his brown suit, shirt collar open, string tie loose, talking of his life in war and peace in a slow Italian which enabled Wursup to make the transition from his grammar book and dictionary to the small Italian he still spoke. The major was proud of his having descended from one of Napoleon's officers. French cropped up in his conversation. "I was the eighth *soldat italien* captured in *l'Afrique du Nord,* stood number eight in my class at school. The name of *mon père* is Ottavio, and I adore oysters. Ho, ho, *voyez-vous? Huîtres. Huit et huîtres.*"

In a life of travel, familiarity is precious, so in Rome, Wursup continued to stay in the *pensione,* though it was no longer well run. Old Signor Moche was dead and the major was in the hospital. "Too big heart," explained the almost-centenarian Signora Moche (who was now about the size and stability of a cigarette ash). Loretta too had gone off. "Flown coop," said the Signora. " 'Merican gob." Replacing the major in Signora Orazio's bed was a tubby Egyptian, who also replaced him in the front room, where he told his life story to the *pensione* guests. These were still mostly foreigners, secretaries in the Food and Agricultural Organization, students, and newsmen (Wursup's recommendation was still on file at the Press Club). Signora Orazio had let the pension run down. "Sheets clean, eye peeled, foot moving" was the old Signora's prescription for "good house," but the sheets were no longer clean, the prices had tripled, the Egyptian wasn't as pleasant as the major, and she had slowed down. Still Wursup returned.

He called Doyle as soon as he settled in. Nothing should have been easier than getting together, but they made it difficult for each other. Which was foolish, since Doyle was the ostensible reason Wursup was here, and Doyle had been waiting for him.

Their relationship was not simple. Old friends who enjoyed each other's company, they had a competitiveness between them that led to—and was reinforced by—frequent arguments and finicky detours from what they both wanted. Knoblauch said they were like Versailles courtiers disputing over whose cushion should be closer to the king's. "Americans think they don't need rules to govern human relations," he said. "But look how Emily Post sells. No wonder it took eight months to agree on the shape of the table at the Vietnam negotiations. It wasn't in Emily." This to Doyle while they waited for Wursup in Rosati's after Knoblauch finally arranged the meeting. "Tocqueville predicted Americans would become more Spanish than the Spaniards about etiquette."

Doyle said, "Fred's always edgy with me. He offers to help and then thinks I'm using him. He comes to me for stories, and resents it when I give them to him. He's kept me off the record much more than I asked to be there. He didn't want newspaper people thinking he had to butter his way into inside dope. How else do they get it? You don't see Cy Sulzberger apologizing for his connections. Fred's a Puritan. He hates gossip—which is his profession—and thinks he has to work everything out like a philosopher. A true Macfarlanite."

Actually, it was largely Doyle's fault there'd been the delay. He could not bring himself to think about his father, let alone talk about him for an article. For decades, he'd hardly thought of him at all. If one of his children asked about him, he said he'd hardly known him, he'd been a man with a liquor problem, and that was that. Even now, when his father had been dug up like a dog's bone, he couldn't bring himself to concentrate on him. A swatch of colorless color surrounded the thought of him, yet he knew he'd have to buckle down when Wursup questioned him. Still, it had been good to hear Fred's voice. He was lying on the bed at the Bologna, sighting the ornamental lantern of the church across the street between his red-socked feet. "It's terrific of you to come," he had told him over the phone.

"I wish I'd taken longer. I gave myself two days."

"That should be plenty for what you want, Fred." The

"what you want" was the carelessness that altered the tone; he knew it as soon as he'd said it, yet kept from making the easy turn away from it.

"I'm not sure what I want. I got the impression you thought it might be a good idea to get a few things straight in print."

"That's as good a version as any," said Doyle, following the shift he himself had started. "It's stupid to let a half-assed account stand by itself. I was hoping you'd make sense of it. You've done so well by me before." It was a bit of peacemaking, but both of them knew that Doyle had resented as well as taken advantage of the portrait Wursup had drawn of him in *Drain*. Favorable as it was, he'd felt himself confined by it, as if he had to maintain the portrait and was nothing more than what Wursup had noticed and written about. It was—he knew—the danger in all portraits, but this one had the currency of international success and, in his own case, the supposed authenticity of old acquaintance. Old acquaintance, even old friendship, could be more limiting than ignorance.

"I mean to try again. It's why I came." Believing it as he said it. Jim was an old pal, he was a decent public servant, he deserved to have the job he wanted. Wursup had come to help him. A wasted trip. On his own dough. Jim had too much to fall back on. He didn't give a damn about Congress. He was a technician. Here he was, doing Jim's worrying for him, turning himself upside down so Jim could have what he probably .didn't want.

But he *had* come, he *was* here. "How about an early dinner? Maybe we can see Henry later."

"It's an idea," said Jim. "The only thing is, I'd sort of planned to just walk around Trastevere. I haven't had time to myself. But we could meet in front of Santa Maria in Cosmedin. There are a couple of good places there."

"No point in rushing it. Maybe you need more time to think things over by yourself. We can meet tomorrow. I'll go see Henry."

"Whatever you say, Fred. Maybe you could leave word for me if you change your mind. I'll call in to the hotel. Or we could use Henry as our drop."

"Right-o. Have a good walk, Jim."

Wursup was furious, yet relieved. Signora Moche padded in as he sat by the phone—you used a house phone at the *pensione.* "Bad news, mister, eh? Tough. Mug all red."

Wursup said no, he was okay, it was nice to be back among his old Roman friends. "Especially good to see you, Signora. It's been too long."

The tiny woman was little more than a stack of wrinkles, but one of the upper ones was surely a smile. "Thank you, pal," she said.

Wursup had got up, but sat down again to call Knoblauch: Signora Moche stayed by. "Always on wire. I remember." Tapping her head with a finger not much thicker than a comma. "Big shot."

There was no point in waving her off. It didn't matter what she heard, though for a foolish reason, this was a difficult call. The reason was that he frequently forgot Doris Knoblauch's first name, and he couldn't remember it now. He didn't know why he forgot it. He'd known her since his Chicago days, he liked her, and when he'd first come to Rome, she'd been wonderful to Susannah and Billy. His embarrassment was doubled now because of another small bone in his social throat. Doris was a great reader—they always exchanged recommendations—and the last time he was in Rome, she'd recommended a novel which he then bought at the English Bookstore on Via Sistina. He flipped through it, disliked it and told her so. A few nights later, he picked it up again, was gripped by it and read it through on the plane to New York. He meant to write her immediately to apologize, but once again couldn't remember her name. He called to ask Susannah, but she was out and he forgot about it. Now, remembering the apology but not her name, he hesitated over the phone.

131

"What's up, mister?" He shook his head. What would he do if *she* answered the phone. He could "Hi sweetheart" it out, but that wasn't his style.

Still, he called, prepared to alter his voice—despite the Signora's antique alertness—and announce, "Mr. Wursup to speak to Mr. Knoblauch." An Italian maid answered, and he told her to please ask Signor Knoblauch to telephone il Signor W-U-R-S-U-P at the Pensione Orazio-Moche.

At the name of her establishment there was a shift in the oval pile of wrinkles. One surely detached itself as a smile. "That's ticket, mister. Give plug."

What to do now? A quiet evening with the Signora, her daughter and the major's replacement? That was not the ticket. He knew all sorts of people in Rome; there was only a question of deciding whether to see them, or which one.

Or should he, like Doyle, just wander around, gawk and eat? No, he wasn't hungry for food or sights, but there was another hunger. And one not as easy to satisfy in the *pensione* as in Roman hotels. (He'd played hookey from the Signora.) The elevator man or the concierge, seeing a man by himself, would let him know there was a beautiful girl just down from the mountains, eighteen if she was a day, a true blonde, and if one said "Maybe," there'd be a knock on the door and a soft "Monsieur" would be the invitation to relieve himself. Part of traveler's aid, like brushing film from the teeth and emptying the bowels. Hotel life looked good now. Whore hunting was humiliating, and whore finding wasn't often much better. Usually he took care of himself, and felt virtuous, if cheated. A few times, he'd called in the pure blondes from the mountains, and once—his marriage ragged—he spent a few nights with Elizabeth Farr, who had worked here for *Time*. In fact, she might still live here. Elizabeth was one of those sexual scorekeepers, but there had been one marvelous night with her, which made for a kind of loyalty. Just remembering it made him perspire. "Need towel?" asked the adherent Signora. He shook his head. It hadn't been in Rome, but Rangoon. Elizabeth was a chatterer, pest and busybody. She had a little blond avian head topped by a blond cockade. They'd flown in on the plane from Bangkok, to cover a trade conference. The porter at the Strand Hotel told them it was Krishna's birthday, a good night to visit the Shewe Dagon, so at midnight they'd gone up to the temple.

It was beautiful, an immense golden turnip which wound out of the dead city as if all the life of Burma were in it. Bells tinkled in the soft air, bonzes in saffron robes swished brooms on the pavement, there were old women praying at the gold and cinnamon shrines surrounding the great stupa. It was remote and spectral. He and Elizabeth had walked barefoot, and said nothing. Walking down the mud steps lined with beggars, old bonzes, filthy chickens, children and bony dogs, they were so charged with the ghostly beauty of it all, they drove back to the hotel and went to her room without a word. Under the bat-wing fan, Elizabeth took off her clothes. In them, she seemed dumpy, a fat pigeon, but naked, she was beautiful. Her flesh had a special translucence he'd seen only in a few women film stars. It was as unexpected as a killer's good manners. A week later, Kirpal Singh, the *Time* stringer in Delhi, told him Elizabeth had said they'd had a wild night in Rangoon. Wursup thought he'd never speak to her again. Yet now, he was so wound up that if Elizabeth were at hand, he would have fallen to the floor with her by Signora Moche's slippers.

The Signora regarded him from some upper line in the facial manuscript. "Sick, mister? What's up?"

Could the woman perceive, guess, remember what need was, what its signs were? "Is there a copy of the *Messaggero* around, Signora?"

Henry Knoblauch had told him about the *relazioni sociali* columns.

The message took a second getting through the clotted

wires, the Signora raised the wide, soft funnel of kimona sleeve and flicked her minute forefinger toward the front salon. Wursup managed to straighten up. He found the columns, and took them past the Signora—limp now, as her internal puppet master dreamed—into his room to study. He didn't want to get Knoblauch's girl.

"It took some negotiating to get him here," said Knoblauch. It was noon. He and Doyle sat outside Rosati's drinking punt y mes.

"He's late."

"Twenty minutes. What is it makes you such prima donnas?"

"Stupidity. Nothing's worse than thinking an old friend is taking advantage of you. I suppose billionaires and tyrants feel this way about everybody." Waiters had to step over Doyle's legs, which stretched into the street. Despite the easy slump, he was nervous.

Wursup saw them as his cab rounded the obelisk, saw them a second or two before he identified them, and there was the small shock of reconciling what he saw and what he remembered. He hadn't seen Knoblauch for eighteen months, Doyle, for two years. Posture, puffiness, slump, and coloring were altered. They looked like a couple of ex-conspirators: Doyle fat-cheeked, graying, in a seedy green polo coat that was probably ten years old; Knoblauch plumper, sturdier, more clownish, though, with his rimless eyeglasses and great forehead, still professorial. He was also nattier, Roman, in an ivory sport shirt and grassy leisure jacket.

Wursup himself felt terrific. Set up. Last night had been lucky. The girl, Liselotte, was a charmer, an Austrian who made an annual Roman pilgrimage and returned to Linz to invest her considerable earnings—he got her whole financial history—in property. She had a diffuse, lewd, rather ugly face, spoon shaped and blotched, but her rapid intelligence and beautiful small body made it a wonderful evening, not just the pulling of an agonizing tooth. There was a kind of sublimity of acquaintance which subdued his uneasiness about Sookie. Liselotte had agreed—against her habit and for only ten thousand lire—to come to his *pensione* at eight o'clock. (He had captivated her with celebrity stories.)

The sun caught on the brass buttons of his maroon blazer. "What a dazzler," said Doyle, coming to the curb. They put their arms—awkwardly—around each other. "What dopes we are."

"I know," said Wursup, melting. "It's so good to see you, Jimmy."

Knoblauch's fifty-yard grin marked the success of his production. His pals were not no-apology, no-explanation Etonians, but men who'd come way up from far down by spelling out what silver-spoon types took for granted.

For an hour they stayed at Rosati's, exchanging news and gossip. (When Knoblauch mentioned Doris, Wursup, flooded with relief, broke in with, "While I remember, Henry, tell Doris that novel I called drivel was beautiful; I hope she'll forgive me." Puzzled, Henry said he'd pass it on.)

They taxied to Knoblauch's favorite restaurant, up on the Via Cassia Vecchia, near his house, and sat among lattices filled with fig vines (from which they plucked the dense, subtle fruits ad lib). There was a grand view of Rome: domes, squares, the river-colored palaces and apartments, the cat's-eye-yellow muck of the slow river. Knoblauch had ordered the house pasta, thin veal, peas—"fresh every noon from the country"—salad, Gorgonzola, apples, wine from the Campagna. There was a luxurious, intense detachment from the old urban tangle below, but as the sun thickened over it and filled the poplars and cypresses around the restaurant, Wursup drew Doyle into the older tangle that was behind their reunion.

Knoblauch stayed out of it. He became background; he

managed the waiters, said nothing, only listened and watched. He watched Wursup draw Doyle out, first on the strategy of refutation, then, slowly, deeper and deeper into the life behind the story. There were laughs, a few about the gang of brothers and sisters and even about the helpless father—"His only talent was making us"—then stories of money panic, juggled funds, the endless crises of rent, food, shoes, the humiliating logistics of the poor. Doyle's blue-eyed ease burned off. Knoblauch watched Wursup remove it, then remove irony, until Doyle was back, a terrified, angry kid. Even as spectator, Knoblauch was exhausted by the tension of it. Four hours passed, and it was over. Knoblauch surfaced first and brought his friends back toward ease, toward the occasion, their reunion. He paid the bill and ordered cabs. Outside the restaurant, they said good-bye, Wursup and Doyle telling each other it was nuts to follow each other only through newspapers, they were getting on, what was life about anyway, wasn't friendship the best of it.

Yet Knoblauch guessed that Doyle's revelations and what Wursup would do with them would estrange them. The exchange had gone one way, there was an imbalance; the intimacies would be converted into publicity, benevolently but beyond recall. All but the hardest or deepest people would find that unbearable.

10

Cicia lived near the Hudson in the nape of Manhattan, just north of its financial skull, in one of the few houses which hadn't been ground into lots for truck cabs or turned into a warehouse. The three-story Federal house belonged to Jimmy De Witt, whose family had built it when Madison was president. Jimmy had enough money to refuse the offers of the port tycoons and the grit to face down the deposits of garbage and dead rats or—what arrived without apparent corporate subsidy—the drunks, heads and stray gays from the West Street bars who slept, or left their curdled innards, on the doorsill. Jimmy dealt with the abuse, the threats, the uninvited, and did well by his tenants—Cicia on the second, Tina Rhome on the third floor.

For Cicia, he could do little now but see that she had food, wasn't uncomfortable and knew she could talk to him whenever she wanted. As for Tina, he listened to her poems and kept an eye on her roommate, Gopal Datta.

Gopal was in a bad way. He'd been due back in Calcutta

139

months ago. His mother, his uncles and brothers had all written him to come—it was time for another brother to have a shot at the world. He'd bought a ticket, packed his bag, and then missed his flight. Since then, he had scarcely left the house. He hardly spoke to Tina, who paid the rent, made their supper and shared her mattress with him; he didn't study—his textbooks were either sold or packed—and he was ashamed to ask Tina for money (for porno flicks, for the newspaper, for chewing gum). Mostly he sat in front of the television set and stared through its soap operas to a running one of his own featuring the small, powerful, dark, handsome prince of East and West, Gopal Datta. So: Prince Gopal walks with his monkey retinue to the family compound; the greedy creatures beg for more rice cakes; Gopal meets the giant, challenges him to a race. Gopal flies so fast the air whips into twine. With it, Prince Gopal ties the giant to the magic bo tree, where he is transformed into a maiden fair as ghee and mild as Chablis. They exchange the *shura drishti*—the "significant look"—of the Brahmin couple and sink into an epic of pleasure.

When Tina returned from the shipping office in which she typed and filed invoices, Gopal turned off both soap operas and lay on the mattress until she put his plate of fried eggplant-and-onion or mushroom-and-chopped-spinach at the door. He ate in the bedroom. Tina washed up and did the laundry in the cellar machines. She also shopped, though if she left a list and money on the television set in the morning, Gopal would do it.

When Cicia came back from the hospital, Gopal talked to her when they passed on the stairs. If she came to talk with Tina, he went into the bedroom.

Gopal loved Tina, loved her oddly, for though they slept beside—and sometimes held—each other, they had no sexual intercourse. Tina loved him also, and when they first began living together two years ago, she forced herself against her

140

disposition to try to have sexual relations with him. It didn't work. They slept together almost as Gandhi did with his niece—in sexless intimacy. Unlike Gandhi, however, Gopal did not have the passion for *brahmacharya*; and, unlike Tina, he was not homosexual, so the intimacy was a strange trial for him. Several times a month, he stayed with one of the girls in his classes at Columbia, but Tina was the only one in his life who touched his soul. He didn't know how to handle this affection. "If I were a meat eater," he told Cicia, "it would have been impossible. But then I would have missed the intoxication and clarity of my nights with her."

Tina was unlike anyone Gopal knew, and he'd known hundreds in Calcutta, London and Rome, as well as in New York. She was simple, straightforward, modest, and yet absolute. Since she was sixteen, five years ago, she had supported herself with boring jobs. Sometimes she felt she would not survive another hour typing shipping codes or filing invoices. Every day she dreamed of an inheritance, or of finding a wallet at the door. But her center was poetry, ever since she discovered that poems did not have to clip-clop along in high-school meters. The Beatles were her textbook. Her poems were neither descriptions nor emotional trips; they were more like the debris of an accident, their centers as difficult to locate as the victims of midair collisions. The poetic smithereens were made out of the idioms of New York, out of hit tunes, Gopal's pyschopharmacological texts, horoscopes, encyclopedias, fortune cookies, television commercials; yet they adhered to each other in the most unexpected, rattling way. James De Witt and Cicia were the first to say she should publish them, and Gopal's friend (from his high-school days in Rome), Benny Knoblauch, an instructor in physics at Columbia, sent them to a friend who published poems on his own press. With almost no public notice, Tina's book accumulated readers. She got midnight calls from troubled girls and addicts, fan letters from professors and poets. Organizers of gay and feminist groups tried to conscript her, begged to meet her, to sleep with her. She developed an icy telephone voice which refused all applicants.

A few months ago, Tina had stopped writing. She got awful headaches, her mind felt watery; she couldn't concentrate, often couldn't get out of bed. Gopal told her she was having a schizophrenic episode; on his own, he gave her dopamine inhibitors. They did some good, but her suffering was sometimes unbearable. She believed it was the attempt of her subconscious to share Cicia's illness.

Her feeling for Cicia was profound and tragic. She did not want to figure out its mixture of hunger, love, abstinence, pity and despair. The week Cicia returned from St. Vincent's, the feeling burst out like a firestorm into a poem; since Cicia's return, she'd written three more. (And her headaches had stopped.) The poems had to do with clairvoyant anticipation of loss and with what Tina called "premature recollection." The titles were "Never Seeing Paris," "It Didn't Bloom Next Year," and "Leaving Before Coming." She didn't show them to anyone but James, couldn't show them to Cicia.

When Cicia told her about Wursup's visit, Tina said, "I don't like you turning into a journalist's story," but her own Cicia poems were folded up in her corduroys. Did she have any more right to cannibalize her friend?

Now, two weeks later, Wursup was coming back for more, and Cicia's excitement went beyond the small vanity of being the subject matter of an article. "It's the closest I come to making poems," she told Tina (who'd taken the day off from work). "I describe what I didn't even know I thought. Otherwise, it's just drift, and, you know, being scared, or drugged. He's a very nice fellow. Kind of klutzy. He looks like a shaved bear, but he's smart and sensitive. I haven't figured him out. Maybe a writer's supposed to be unfigurable, part of the scenery. Not that you're that way."

"Poets are different," said Tina, who opened the door when Wursup rang, pointed him upstairs and took off.

She was a quick study, though, and envious curiosity sharpened her view of him, which, as rapid impressions went, was positive. She liked the little eyes "way back in his head as if trying to get closer to his brains," as she told Cicia later. "They weren't just little showcases of feeling." And she liked "the blocky, unrehearsed kind of awkwardness. You don't feel as if you're with someone who's working on his diet. He's just there, take it or leave it. Nice. That cubic yard of head, with that nutty salt-and-pepper cap. And that neck. They put up statues on smaller pedestals. I'd watch out for a guy with a neck like that. Still, he isn't showing off. I like that. He looks like he's saying, 'Here's what they gave me,' like a guy getting out of prison in the forty-dollar suit."

Wursup too was a quick study, and he was taken with the stumpy, black-eyed girl with a soft voice who introduced herself as "Tina" and pointed him to Cicia's. "I've met dictators who gave off fewer human ergs," he told Cicia, who told him who Tina was. "Yet she said next to nothing and said it quietly. I think it's those great, big, take-in-everything eyes trying to hide under the little-girl bangs."

"She asserts herself without trying. When you know her, you just feel her intelligence, her funniness. She's got the sweetness of very smart people, which doesn't mean she can't be tougher than anyone. She's the best. She loved those gorgeous postcards you sent, too. I meant to write you, but I couldn't find a pretty-enough card. And didn't have the words to make up for it. If I were Tina, I'd have written a poem. No. She doesn't work that way. What'll I give you now? I have anything instant: soup, oatmeal, coffee. There might even be a bottle of Chianti under the sink. I guess that's instant enough to be here."

"Do you have tea?"

"Sure."

"I've got my Russian cabbie's cap on, so I drink tea. My hats determine my day. You'll see." (Though the instant the future tense came out on the pronoun, Wursup felt a soft thump behind his eyes.) Standing, Cicia looked smaller than she had in the hospital bed. It was partly the great white room which diminished her. The ceilings were twelve feet high, the cornices grand with their plaster egg and darts. The room had plenty of chairs, tables, a desk, a sofa bed, bookcases, and, in a corner, a sink, a stove and an icebox (everything but a toilet was here), but it was still big enough to seem uncluttered. Cicia, her hair heavy on her shoulders, primly easy in a high white blouse and loose bluejeans, looked lost as an ashtray here. Her face was rosy, her smile was grand, but Wursup felt a shrinkage. "How's it going?"

The kettle fumed. Cicia poured water into two silver-rimmed cups, shifted a tea bag from one to the other. "I don't know about *it. I* don't go. Very much. Out. Around. I've been a house bum."

Cicia's voice pleased him even more than he remembered its pleasing him in the hospital. Not just the uncasualness of response to the casualness of his question but its weight, not heaviness or slowness, but the weight of consideration. On a stage, it could have stood for seductiveness. Not here. Here it just seemed to inflect everything around it, to make it count: the steam from the silver-curled cups, the peacock-tail colors in the rug, the Motherwell and Rothko posters, the tiny clunks of a plate-sized alarm clock, the grand, rather gloomy room, and Cicia herself, the blue eyes, the long legs too thin in the loose jeans. Like the clock noise, the voice made a sense of passage in the room.

"I got up for your visit. I've mostly just laid around. When Tina's here, we talk. And James—he's my landlord, and friend—he comes up and talks. I heat skim milk for instant oatmeal—I'm so lazy. Tina cooks me vegetables. I give her a

144

raspberry Twinkie. I *have* been out to get the groceries, but mostly James and Tina get them for me. I watch the soaps—I hid the tube behind that screen there—I listen to records, maybe one the whole day. Laura Nyro, Melissa Manchester. Do you know them?" Wursup didn't. "All girls. Kind of white blues. Not too heavy a schedule."

"You're not rehabilitating addicts, no, but then you're not making any."

"I spend lots of time looking at those cards. It was really a great idea. *The Return of the Hunters.* Is it Brueghel? I can't remember which one. Just those little birds hung in the air, the dogs, the little skaters, the snow. And none of the faces showing. I love it so. And that Chinese—I guess it's a scroll or a silkscreen or something. Do you remember?"

"No."

"A tiny brown boat floating on a green nowhere, and a tiny man on the side like a white bean. The card says he's the painter saying—there are words—'At moments like this, I forget my name.' The card says he has one name as a painter, another in 'real life.' Isn't that grand? To have a different name for everything you do. Cicia, the Tea Maker; Veronica, the Lover; Melissa, the Singer; Chrissie, the Tennis Player; Tillie Schnook, the No Good. Imagine the phone book you'd have to have. Maybe that's what a computer bank is, your ninety different selves attached to your social-security number. Can anybody stand just one version of himself? I mean, who wants to be just described as Patient B? Or the rich Miss Creep?"

The talk made a rosiness in her face, it was richer, and there didn't seem to be war bulletins coming into it from beneath. The eyes were still edged with rust, but almost anyone would say here was a healthy, energetic, very pretty girl. She felt it, too, for she asked him if he'd like to go out; she wouldn't at all mind going for a walk.

They passed Tina on her way back from the store, carrying

a grocery sack out of which poked the purple backside of an eggplant. "Where you heading?"

"Central Park," said Cicia. "Want a lift?" She wore a fuzzy pink hat tied like an infant's under the chin and a sleek like-beaver fur (her father's last Christmas present). Tina saw her all lit up like a Forties Movie Daughter on a big date.

"No," Tina said. "I want to turn on with Felicia, here." (Ogling the purple backside.)

They taxied to Fifty-seventh and Sixth and walked into the park, around the lake, toward the zoo. It was three o'clock, the warmest part of an anemic, first-of-spring day. Only a few old people sat around the lake; it was like having the beautiful, complicated park to themselves. Only in the zoo were there more people—nurses, mothers, small children, a few bums sitting on the sunnier benches, amusing themselves around the seal pool at the fleshy creatures, like themselves easier in an element other than the one they breathed in. Cicia held Wursup's topcoated arm, he slowed his usual park pace, and since she needed her breath for walking, talked and talked.

His talk generated itself. Incidents in Tashkent led to others in Lagos: Mr. Sunday Omega smashing the pots his father had used in hexing him (Wursup had reported the trial.) He talked about interviews in the Quirinal and the Groote Schuur; anecdotes of guzzling Azerbaijani technocrats, eaten Congolese senators, Cypriot spies; the opinions of Malaysian barbers, Venezuelan poets; the flowers of Java, the crêpes of *La Vefour*; packets of spiced fire in Bombay chowks; jokes from Poland ("What's green, hangs in your room and hums?" "A herring, painted green, hung in your room and humming to make it hard to guess"); the boasts of Arabian kings (Ibn Saud, wounded in his parts at the siege of Riyadh, summoning a girl while the bullets buzzed to show his aide he had not lost something more precious than the city); the queues of Liverpool and Moscow, the traffic of São Paulo and Hong Kong; ballet dancers, thimble merchants, officials of GOS-

146

BEK and GATT; car accidents, skirmishes, heroism, disasters. A few mouthfuls—from the hundreds of thousands of file cards—slanted for Cicia with nostalgia, self-mockery and the simplifications needed for anecdotal point. "My life's my file system. Burn that, I'm no more than ashes. My only originality is the cross-index system—names, places, topics. The Wursup Decimal System, my chief claim to being a practical, inventing American. A little like this"—touching the metal plaque on the cage of the striped hyena: HYAENA STRIATA FROM HYS, HOG, INDIA, ASIA MINOR, NORTH AND EAST AFRICA, NOCTURNAL; EXCITED; ITS HOWL BECOMES THE DEMONIC LAUGHTER WHICH GIVES IT THE NAME 'LAUGHING-HYENA'—"a sliver of life here, another there, all sorted into types, species shading into species. The big thing is deciding when there's a big enough jump to change stupidity into malice, like dogs into wolves."

Excited but exhausted by the Niagara of gruff, fluent, allusive chatter, Cicia leaned more and more on Wursup's bulky arm. She watched his heavy face in motion, the deep black eyes, the small mouth under a swatch of black bristles his razor missed, the great, blocky head itself growing down from the foolish pepper-and-salt cap. It made small pumping motions as it fetched out story after story, reflection after reflection. Would he index this afternoon? "Cicia, Sick Girls, A Day in the Park, Parks and Leisure: American." For her, staring at a postcard or listening to a song filled an afternoon. Almost none of her afternoons could be indexed, let alone preserved. Only loss made them precious. But for this dear, clumsy galoot steering her past the caged animals and the hundreds of people, drifting, schmoosing, waiting out the day, filling it, letting it fill them, whatever, the afternoon might already be split fifty ways, indexed, half written up.

The park was a little green basin scooped into the great stone apartments of Fifth and Central Park South and West— north it went toward perilous parts she'd never visited. It was

like the afternoon itself, a precious storage, a condenser of
endless life. And it was wonderful, a wonderful afternoon, the
stuff to make a thousand others rich and happy, if, yes, if—
feeling suddenly little piles of heaviness, hives in her stomach, her head. All right. Whatever number there would be.
Maybe there'd be as many as anyone else here had. But now
she really felt worn out. "I think I better get home."

Wursup half carried her to a cab, and she said absolutely he
should not come with her, they would see each other very
soon, it was a wonderful afternoon, one of the very best, ever,
thank you, and he said thank *you*, and gave the driver directions and money and kissed her on the mouth.

11

Cicia's father, Tommy Buell—founder and president of Excello Glass and Aluminaire, Los Angeles—was in one of those fine states in which everything heard and seen recalls something else. He looked through the front window (ten by twelve, two inches thick, single-glazed, hinged to a one-inch aluminum sash, gold anodized) of his Beverly Glen bungalow, regarded the elephant-eared leaves of he-didn't-know-what tropic shrub and tuned into his recollections. A lovely, undemanding morning, Sunday, and he hadn't read—or yet picked up—the L.A. *Times*, would not pick it up from the mailbox at the end of the driveway until the inside parade had gone by. He did not care who the men of the week were; he treated himself—as he did more and more frequently—to his own covers and centerfolds. He was on most (Man of the Week), and why not? What Tommy had seen, done, been done to, and what held everything together—his own lucky, now-easy life—was what counted. Outside, the yolk-yellow flop-eared leaves glowed with their vegetable intelligence. If they neither spun nor wove, neither did they fret. A lesson for a man in a splendid red kimona (from Maru-Maru's, on the Ginza), sipping brandied mocha coffee between bites of his own blueberry buckwheat cakes doused with diet margarine and (why should he stint where it counts?) pure syrup carried across the continent from Vermont sugar maples.

For years now, when Tommy had wanted to take off somewhere, he went, and where he went, he went not as a ransacker (stuff grabber, picture snapper, sight counter) but to see the way things worked. His glass business was an entrée: he wrote to Ministers of Trade, Bureaus of Tourism and Chambers of Commerce, letting them know what he thought of their sash-and-door work, suggesting how they could improve the quality of their glass and insulation. Glass was only his foot in the door. In Tokyo or Lagos, Leningrad or Caracas, Tommy took to the streets and offices; he inquired, took notes and pictures, drew diagrams and charts, and, home, wrote up his impressions and had them printed. (A business write-off: the pamphlets promoted good will.) The day Cicia called to tell him she was leaving the hospital, he was finishing the pamphlet on his six-week African trip (*A Businessman's Survey of Bush and City: The New Africa, Dakar to Nairobi*). It would go to the employees, customers and business peers of Excello Glass, to the Africans to whom he had promised it and to several hundred friends and acquaintances around L.A. and the world. He himself would take one to Cicia when he went to extract her from the awful sink she lived in to bring her back to California for sun, good food and cheer; to get her on her feet once and for all.

The only flies in Tommy's life had been his wife—long since exiled to Florida—and Cicia's health. Tommy had survived Dolly, and he had lived a full life for many years seeing his daughter only once or twice a year, but the thought of her as an invalid was something else. Like him, she was independent. He had not interfered with her choices, bad as many were. She had lived two years with a fool, and had since lived alone in grim isolation, her chief friends—as far as he knew—a kooky poet, her Indian lover, and a derelict landlord who spent the rent money keeping off the scum that washed in from the port and Greenwich Village. Taxi drivers couldn't believe it when Tommy directed them to Cicia's place. "Nothing but warehouses down there." And cleared lots full of decabbed trucks, unhoused door frames, and enough rubble for a small planet. A terrible place for his daughter, and Tommy meant to get her out. She had nothing more to prove to him; she'd earned her spurs on those night streets off the Hudson, dodging the bums, junkies, drunks, faggots and rapists.

Tommy had many mottos, one of which was Nietzsche's *amor fati*, which the note in his philosophy book translates as "love what is." Got a lemon? Squeeze it for juice. This was not the same as Hindu passivity, or turning cheeks. That's for saints. Tommy read it as "love the brains God gives you, and what you've done with them." Centuries of Italian (Buell was once Abbaglio) farmers underwrote both Tommy's confidence and his ducal strut on the great avenues of the world. The solid little frame, the bathtub-white hair, Mountbatten nose, and eyes impenetrable as handled coin said, "Here is a handsome man, sure of his looks and what's behind them, but giving nothing away." Not that Tommy withheld from avarice or caution. "Better be robbed than surround yourself with scarecrows" was another of his Nietzschean mottos. (He hadn't often been robbed.)

For many years, Tommy thought of himself as just a little smarter than others in his trade. (What geniuses do you meet in plate glass? Or in the reclamation—junk—business, in which he'd started?) Now, though, the little autodidact and world traveler wondered what he might not have done given a different push here and there. His pamphlets might have been books, his insights not local and limited but applicable everywhere and always.

Hundreds on the Corso, the Ginza, the Rue de Rivoli, Fifth Avenue and Piccadilly, passing the solid little fellow in the gorgeous topcoat—with its flaps and belts and blue and gray squares, an eaglet's feather jaunting from the gold twist cord of his soft maroon fedora—"This is a man on top of more than the pavement." The white hair, the creases in the long head, the unblemished rich skin—how it would have been pinched on the slave block—the face colors subtle as a Turner seascape, speak of deeper decisions than those behind the terrific outfit. Tommy had the look of a survivor, not of some epic endurance in the ocean or the Andes but of many difficulties, many problems. His splendor had been purchased by himself, not inherited.

Tommy's most grueling endurance was Cicia's mother, Dolly. Eight years ago, when Cicia was fourteen, he bought her out of their life. She lived in Florida, a rich woman, betting at the dog track, owning dogs herself, bribing companions to stay with her until they felt the insane bitterness which he and Cicia together had fought to a draw.

Dolly was a woman of rough intelligence, but the intelligence produced nothing but malice, like a machine which undoes at one end what it assembled at another. A deceptively comfortable-looking, plump woman who—people wrongly thought—must have been a beauty, Dolly Buell gave off poison as a toaster does heat. The poison was both pain and anesthetic. (Though the pain came out in nightmares.) She had a loud, sharp, English-pitched voice (her mother was English), and a witty English lady's charm. Much of her force worked through the mouth, which had a fishy extrusiveness. The wide eyes retreated, the internal fury worked its way through the throat—always scarfed—and pulled her lips into firing position. She almost never failed to hurt people. Her talk slithered destructively under a veneer of compliment. Lying beside her in the old days, Tommy heard in her night thrashing and screeching the fragments of whatever terror made her what she was; but awake, she expressed nothing of it. Dolly had no ties to anyone. It made the separation arrangement very easy. He proposed, she accepted. They did not bother to go through divorce. "You don't divorce a knife," said Dolly. "You extract it." In Sarasota, she ran a kennel of whippets with Amos Plitt, a smart black trainer who lived high in Coconut Grove on money diverted from the kennels. Dolly indulged and mocked Amos's "Jig-Jew" ways, his sports cars and girl friends, his Sulka sport shirts and electronic gear. Amos doped the dogs, bought off inspectors, and coined money at the track. For her, he placed phony bets which covered the inflated kennel bills. Each knew the other knew: there was a mutual swindle-and-malice society, with Tommy paying the bills. Two or three times a year, Dolly called for more money, and Tommy sent off ten or fifteen thousand dollars. (He knew what she could be like in court.) She never spoke to Cicia or about her.

Life bloomed for Tommy after this. Only a third of his time went to business; he could run it in his sleep. He bought, he traveled, he played, he read, he gave parties. He had girl friends as he had lunch, out of ordered need. (Usually two at a time: one that excited him, another that did his errands. Category One moved every few months into Category Two.)

Mostly, Tommy educated himself, which soon involved educating others. He had the didactic strain that had to supply as well as consume. From his plant, he recruited evening discussion groups—sash men, metal men, sanders and salesmen who rallied around with the Great Books they'd stoked up on during weekends that would otherwise have seen them bowling, sailing, polishing their cars, taking kids to the beach. "You want to bowl your brains down those gutters," said Tommy. "It's not pins you're knocking down, it's your humanity." Few resisted the boss's pitch. "Unprepared for life, you shatter your soul like half-inch plate" went a prepared recruitment handout. *"Chi ha la testa di vetro non vada a la battaglia di sassi.* That is, glass heads better not volunteer for rock wars. That is, empty skulls aren't ready for life's hard knocks."

So Tommy formed his Mind Groups (though some members thought life had no harder knock to offer). Then the groups and Tommy were written up in the "People" section of the L.A. *Times,* and Tommy was called in by the Los Angeles Educational Council and asked to start groups in other plants. He did his stuff, going from plant to plant, talking local professors into leading them.

Tommy's literary life had begun with his report to the Educational Council. Condensed and rewritten, it was printed in the "Education" section of the *Times.* The essential sentences were:

> Most people never think beyond "what's for dinner" or what kind of a car they're going to buy in April. Television opens them a little, but mostly they're afraid of the world beyond their nose. Fear cracks the mind the way alkali cracks glass. Being in the glass business, I think of people in terms of *opaque, semi-opaque, translucent* and *transparent.* The best are opaque inside, transparent outside; that is, the principles are firm, but they take in whatever is out there in the world. I can express it another way out of my business, on which I am somewhat of an authority (a kind of professor of windowology). Hundreds of years ago, the English taxed you by the

number of windows in the home (glass being precious before modern methods). Rather than pay, people bricked up their windows. Here's the point: there's a kind of penalty here in the USA for how much light and air you let into your head, so many people spend their lives bricking up the natural windows of intelligence God Almighty gave them.

The piece led indirectly to Tommy's second piece of literary work. He had received a letter from a Professor Walbank praising his "fine, neatly expressed educational philosophy." Walbank lived down the way, in Westwood. Tommy called to thank him and invited him for a drink.

It turned out they had a lot in common. They were the same age—to the year—both Midwesterners, their fathers had both worked for the Rock Island Railroad, though Walbank's was an office manager and Tommy's worked in the yards. Walbank played tennis, and Tommy had just taken up the game. Their first collaboration was on the courts.

Walbank, an awkward, bearded fellow, was delighted by Tommy. He himself had been raised narrowly; his great move had been leaving the mean religion of his parents. Every time he lit a cigarette or took a drink, he shivered with triumph. Tommy had the ease and inventiveness he admired, and what he regarded later as Tommy's crudity was compensated by his generosity. Tommy picked him up for their games, and after, took him back for wonderful lunches. He enjoyed Tommy's talk also. He wasn't used to such frank narcissism. Tommy said he only played at games at which he could improve. He'd given up softball with the Excello team when he saw he was swinging twice as hard for half the distance, and touch football when he broke his nose clearing a sashman half his age out of an end sweep. "The Clipper Woman has given us just so many years. Should I sharpen her blades?" Walbank quoted such imagery to his classes. Tommy had the natural gift his church assumed in the elect. The professor kept on losing sets to Tommy—despite his decades of play—in order to see more of it. As well as the enjoyment of Tommy's blue and silver Avanti, the seafood dishes Tommy's cook prepared, and the wine which cost fifteen times more than the bottles Mrs. Walbank bought at the supermart.

One day, over wine and cigars, Tommy proposed that they write a joint autobiography in alternate chapters. "After all," he said, "we're two Midwestern guys who worked our way up from not much, you in the education field, me in business. We could tell our parallel stories. It might be better than each of us doing a separate one. It's not as if we're Einsteins. And I don't know for a fact that I could write a whole book myself. Of course, you already have." Walbank's book, or rather his unpublished dissertation, was called "The Rhetorical Devices of Mayor Sam Yorty."

Walbank sniffed an interesting item for his smallish bibliography, and perhaps a small commercial success (for he could see Tommy hawking the book up and down the state, if not the country). It would be nice to turn his toothless Impala in for a Corvette, or to have a year of research in Oaxaca or Florence.

"It's worth a try," he said.

So Tommy spent his mornings at the typewriter and wrote chapters on Grandpa Abbaglio, who helped build the railroad, and on Poppa Abbaglio, who worked on it, on his old neighborhood and school, and on his time as a soldier ("From Georgia to Germany"). Walbank listened to them over glasses of Baron Rothschild's red wine, then took the pages home and riddled them with a red pencil. This was the extent of the collaboration. He didn't supply word one of his own.

"I told you he'd fink out, Daddy," said Cicia. "He just liked listening to you and drinking your wine. He's too scared to look at a mouse, let alone himself. And maybe he's right. Who needs to know that Grandpa could slice flies with a knife?"

At seventeen, Cicia was usually gentle and well mannered. Her revolutionary girl friends regarded washing as a concession to male tyranny, but Cicia was fastidious and never went out without perfume. Only now and then did little gusts of witchery rise in her, and he could hear Dolly in her tongue. The autobiography worked her into one of them. "You can't make Excello Glass into Rome. Or St. Louis into Corsica. What is it about the rich which makes them think they're entitled to inflict their stories on people? Is it fear they haven't got anything else that'll speak for them?"

"Walbank's not rich."

"He's worse. He kisses rich men's asses."

As if *he* had grown up sucking gold tits. She knew about his life: ten grades of school, working in the beer plant—stuffing bottles into the washer, getting cut by broken ones, his hands like bloody steak—working in Hammond, organizing for the union, putting together a pickup with the few bucks he'd saved in the war, going around the yards for junk, then taking the risk and buying the furnace, hiring ex-cons and scabs for half wages till he could pay them right, dodging the unions, getting forced out, coming to L.A. and starting again, and all the time—like his own product—trying to turn the muck and ash of his life into something clear and bright. Excello Glass and Aluminaire. A kind of miracle. And he'd become a sort of scholar of this ancient manufacture. He would speak to Cicia of the glass bottles in Egyptian murals, the windows in the Temple of Karnak, the stained glass of the cathedrals. He'd wanted her to feel her father was part of an old and honorable human enterprise. And, when she was small, she sat in his arms like a pearl in a shell, keeping away from her mother's tongue, taking in his stories.

Was her anger about his autobiography fear of remembering her mother? Maybe she wanted him to stop writing before her mother came into the story. She was so lovely a Jacobin, though, *l'Air du Temps* rising from her throat, that he sometimes baited her.

"She has the abstract fury of a poet," he told Walbank, who'd caught the edge of her scorn. "You can't take her criticism seriously. Just enjoy the way she says it. The words come, and she just nails them to whatever's at hand. Me, you. She's not like her mother; there's no real animosity. She's really gentle as a flower."

In his revolutionary's turtleneck and ferocious Lytton Strachey beard, timid Walbank did not think he should suffer even the spray of Tommy's daughter. What did father or daughter know of what it took to leave the Missouri Church of Christ, what it cost him to smoke a cigarette, to feel something for a woman without thinking of hellfire? To put any of that down beside the crude street stories of this Attila of plate glass was out of the question. "Francesca's right about something, Tommy. I think we went into deeper waters than we knew. A book like this has to be written with special care. Since we're not famous, the book has to live by its style."

"You mean my style is too straight? I give things away too cheaply?"

"I hadn't thought of it that way, but in a way, yes. You're too direct. There's enough intimacy-peddling around. Who needs to count the hairs in your nostrils?"

"What does that mean?"

"I mean your surface is genial. Why do you have to be a gutter rat on the page?"

Francesca had mocked the infancy concealed by Walbank's beard. "He's got everything that should make him good-looking. Yet he's a mess. His face has no point. I guess it's why he grew a beard, as soon as beards were in. He looks like someone made up to look wise and virile. He's so earnest and sincere, you just know he's tortured by deviousness. Look at his walk. I don't mind awkwardness—I'm no Olympic skater—but Walbank's too much. He's awkward by design as well as nature. As if he's ashamed of anything graceful."

Cicia convinced him about Walbank. "You're right, Cicia. Wallace used everything up when he left the church. The rest goes into putting up the show. He knows he doesn't have anything much, and maybe that's the best part of him. The worst is covering up. That business about style, when the real thing is he's too lazy to write himself. There are people who cross out and people who add. Not that I'm eager to take criticism. But I don't need a professor to give it. If my stuff's simpleminded, that's one thing, but if it's just a question of words and grammar, you can tell me that. And at least I did it. Like you do your papers. That honors paper you did at school about that beautiful Irish girl who ran that South American country with her lover. That was terrific."

"Eliza Lynch."

"Wonderful. I remember it today. Leading the women regiments against Brazil, going whoring in Paris after the lover—"

"Salano."

"Coming back to South America and watching a play about herself. That was a story, and you really told it. With feeling. You put yourself into it. Wallace would travel from here to Brazil just to dodge his feelings. And make the trip twice before he'd admit he was dodging."

"I'm just a bad-mouther, Daddy. Don't let me ruin your book for you."

"It's not you, Ceech. Wallace and you were right. I'm glad I wrote what I did, but it's not for other people. There's not enough there. But it gave me the habit. I'll do other things. More up my alley."

Even then, thought Tommy now, at the window, looking at the floppy yellow leaves, when she was still his red-cheeked, smart-mouthed Cicia, before anyone found anything at all going wrong with her, there was self-deflation in her, a back-tracking, as if she were punishing herself for his delight in her. It was what her mother had put in her, what he'd tried to knock out, telling her how grand she was, what a future she had, the world just waiting for her to tickle it. Brains, beauty, strength, industriousness. The paper on the Lynch woman was fifty pages long and got a rave from her professor. She had the world by the tail. Except for the poison Dolly put into her, trying to step on her whenever she did anything Tommy or anyone else praised, whenever she got a new dress or put on lipstick. "You look like a fishwife. Take that paint off your mouth." Or when she got all A's at school: "The school doesn't challenge you. They have no right to swell their pupils' heads."

And Dolly herself. How she had changed. They'd been in grade school together and even then she was the only girl who took no guff, and never got any. Clean and fine, as if turned out by a different system. Her father, Armbruster, a one-legged, walleyed building inspector, was as big a thief and liar as they had in Missouri, living high off slices from every piece of pipe or coal sold in west St. Louis. And there was Dolly, her mother's angel Latin student doing her declensions and practicing the "Minute Waltz," staring down bums like himself—till he squeezed the bum out of himself, and made his first money in the junk world. Reclamation, Inc. Which she called Resurrection, Inc. (Her tongue always knew its way around.) Armbruster lost everything but his fingernails in the market; she came to work for Tommy, writing letters and contracts, and then selling. And already souring, but not much, not so much that he didn't go wild when she flapped her skirts and talked French. Well, he wasn't the first to be fooled by boobs and refinement. From altar on, it grew darker. It was a disease. "The Golliwog's Cakewalk" and *doleo, dolere* couldn't hold it off.

And maybe Cicia's disease was another form of it. Who knew? It was beyond speculation. Something was happening in her, and it was time for him to do what he could. Here were his pamphlets, bound in blue leather, lined up in the bookshelf: *On the Trail of Vasco da Gama, From the Azores to Macao, On the Silk Route in Central Asia.* He gave them their money's worth. ("Silk from the Chinese *si*—the mulberry moth's larva—called *ser* by the Greeks, *sericum* by the Latins, *soie* in French, *Seiden* in German.") It cost him fourteen hundred bucks to have them printed and mailed. Let alone the cost of the trips. And there were no returns (except deductibility, and a little ego varnish). But he couldn't write up his daughter and stick her in blue leather. Three thousand miles away and fighting some cellular misery, and he was here sitting in the sun with his buckwheat cakes. For years, he hadn't "interfered." (Her instruction suited his needs.) When she'd lived in Connecticut with Framingham, the blond lamp designer, he'd said nothing. Her taste was hers; he'd said sure, the boy seemed a decent-enough fellow. Even that had rubbed her wrong, so he'd stayed farther away. She hadn't sent for him now either, but last year, she'd come out on her own and got her strength back in the sun (though not the sun, for the thing she had, had something to do with sunlight). It was time to go to her.

When Cicia got back from the park, Tina came from De Witt's apartment to meet her. "We've got a little salon going. First your dad—"

"No."

"Half an hour or so after you left. Gopal remembered he was alive and did the honors. James brought us downstairs for goodies, and then Benny showed up. Thank God. He's wowing your pa with his quarks."

"You'd think he'd have called. He's such— Doesn't matter." But there were tears in her eyes. Happiness and fear, both—fear not of seeing him but of his seeing her, and of breaking up if he guessed more had happened than he knew.

Luckily, Tommy had been spellbound by Benny. Who could tell where you'd strike oil? And Benny's gusher could be barreled by someone like Tommy for years and years.

As for Benny, he discharged himself on whoever was at hand. Passengers on the Princeton shuttle with barely enough time to look at the front page would feel the heat of his great-browed head and see the great, sharky mouth within opening up on the low light frequencies which enabled human beings to see each other as wholes. "The basis for our anthropomorphic provincialism." Even elevator passengers, staring away from each other, might not be exempt from a sudden gush of intelligence. The passenger, turning in fright, fury or annoyance, would see a bulk of intelligence so needful of radiating, so abstractly benevolent, so whitely harmless, that though he would separate quickly from it at Princeton Junction, would respond to it till then.

Benny looked like a combination of frog and apple. His rosiness was stippled with gold freckles, but from mouth down, he was froggy. Even when Benny was blowing full steam, the swelling nobility of the upper face was comically undercut, as if the marvelous wisdom were coming out of an enchanted frog. Yet it was one of life's excitements to hear Benny holding forth, especially on the gluons, hadrons, quarks and antiquarks that were his specialty. "At last, after twenty-five-hundred years of atom theory, we're going to *know* what's behind things."

Benny worked at the Institute of Advanced Study and occasionally lectured at Columbia (where he'd fastened on to Gopal). Now he'd "dropped by"—from his room seven miles north—to let Gopal and Tina in on his latest gatherings. Tommy was an unexpected addition, some new desert that wanted irrigation. In fact, Tommy was exceptionally thirsty, and Benny was giving a combination course in physics for beginners and his own most recent notions about those "peculiar special-delivery parcels we call particles."

Cicia was able to get to her father before he had time to break away and work up the feelings which would otherwise have overwhelmed her. "Daddy." Arms around him, holding then suppressing the force she felt transferring from Benny's particle visions.

"Ceech. Darling." Getting up in her arms, nose to nose—they were the same height—kissing the red cheeks, hugging her, and then feeling, somehow, somewhere, a slackness, which, for seconds, became a fright for him: something had happened, something was happening here. "Ceech, sweetheart." Almost in tears now, his little girl, his precious, whom his swirling, traveling, pamphleteering, exercising life had overlooked.

Even Benny, absorbed in aggregations of energy billions of times smaller than human beings, could feel in these seconds not just the meeting of an affectionate father and daughter but the recognition by both that they understood a terrible reversal was occurring, the younger breaking up while the older was intact.

James, for whom Cicia was a surrogate daughter, and Tina, for whom Cicia was more than what family could ever be, watched the few seconds in tears; and Gopal, who had put fifteen thousand miles between his will and his family, felt those miles now not as safety but as chains keeping him from what he had to do. (He made a reservation for Calcutta that night.) Benny acknowledged something local, something that affected people he liked—though he *liked* everyone—a king's acknowledgment that beggars had stomachs. Still, his comparative remoteness, his approximate humanity, saved the sociableness of things. He was in the middle of the couch (the only place in the room that had multiple seats), Cicia and Tommy had to sit apart, James brought tea in a silver pot glossed with silver leaves (the work of Paul Revere) and with Tina poured and passed scones and a local version of Devonshire cream from a midtown store that he and his peers and followers had kept afloat for a century.

This was but expansion of their usual Sundays: the ceremony familiar, and Gopal and Benny familiar parts of it. Tommy, unfazed in kraal or palace, relished the silver, the surprising, formal domesticity of this household, his daughter, her bright-eyed poet-pal, the delicate Bengali, the red-haired genius, and the thin, sweatered Wasp host in his fossilized world—gold-framed portraits, eighteenth-century silver, twelve-foot ceilings, wainscotting. It was sufficient deflection from the cloudy dread he would not let come to more now. Benny deflected it still further with what, to him, was appropriate family talk—the last letter he had sent his parents in Rome. "To my dad, really, who's borne the foolish label two-point-three times longer than I." The "label" was his surname. "Stuck on one of our ancestors by some Napoleonic sergeant, I suppose. They loved sticking comic names on Jews and other rabble. I only know German enough to read physics papers and newspaper headlines; I never came across my own name. 'Garlic. Benny Garlic.' Is that a name to trundle through passport lines? I asked my dad if he'd have let me go through life as 'Henry Turd.' He wrote back that garlic was probably the magic herb which saved Odysseus from Circe's power—that's dubious, I'm told—and that it's used for protection against the simoon in Afghanistan. But who's going to Afghanistan? With this name, I was turned into a comedian before I could talk."

"Our name was Abbaglio," said Tommy. "Did you remember that, Ceechie?"

"Yes."

"It means 'dazzle,' or 'mistake.' I guess the mistake from being dazzled. My father changed it when he worked on the line
at the Pontiac plant. There was bad feeling for Italians. He
made it 'Bull' but must have mispronounced it—he spoke like
an old Don Mustache—so it came out the way it is. People
think we're English. The name and the coloring. Cicia's
mother is English stock; her mother came from Surrey. My
mother was a Lombard. Fair-haired, blue-eyed; like Cicia.
You remember, Ceech?"

"Yes, Daddy."

"A name should be like a place," said Tina. "You should be
able to love it, even if you've suffered from it."

"Who can love a name?" asked Benny, who found it hard
enough to love a person.

"Almost anyone," said Tina. "And some of us love names
more than what they name."

"I wonder," said James, who among the portraits and furniture of the De Witts would not dream of admitting pride or
pleasure in his name. "It's not as intimate a part of you as
your arm, perhaps, but it is something given. I'd think it
would be some sort of amputation to change it. Of course, if it
seriously inconveniences you . . . "

"Names" said Benny, "are arbitrary conveniences. They
designate certain states of energy or areas of event or possible
event. If they interfere with the sort of event they demarcate,
they should be tossed out. That's all."

"At least you see names are powerful, Benny," said Tina.

"I don't."

"Look how you suffer from yours."

"Forgive me," said Cicia. "I walked hours in the park, and
I'm a little tired. I think I better lie down a few minutes."

Tommy, feeling chill spread from his belly to his eyes,
asked his daughter if she minded if he came up and sat a bit in
her room; he too was a little tired from the flight. "That's fine,

Daddy. Though you can lie down in Tina's room, if you want."

Tommy kept himself from helping her up the stairs. When she lay down on the sofa bed, he did take off her boots and cover her with a blanket, as she hadn't let him do for twenty years. He sat in a high-backed chair by the great window and watched her sleep. The tables, the art posters, the old chifferean, the piles of gloves, scarves, stockings, the little animal ashtrays, the shadowy heights of this room with the carved cornices—this was what Cicia looked at. On a roll-top desk there were snapshots, one of him shaking a finger at a five-year-old Cicia, a pout on her witty little face. Who had taken it? Not Dolly. Dolly took no pictures and let none be taken of her.

Cicia was asleep. Tommy touched her hair, her cheek, forehead, hand. He was not prepared to lose this.

12

Sunday. Sookie was tending a lamb ragout—a *navarin*—
answering letters and listening to a mix of Joni Mitchell and
Chopin on the stereo system which she had installed against
Wursup's insistence that all he needed was the notes—"even
the idea of the notes is enough for a real music lover"
—though when he heard one of his Beethoven sonatas coming through, he said it would change his life: "It's like getting
glasses for the ears. Where have I been?" And more, which,
had he recorded it, might have got him the set and a few dollars more from *Musicraft*, such raving endorsement being
hard to come by.

This was not the day to recommend commercial endorsement to him. He was in Central Park, walking off the agitation
caused by reading his piece on James Doyle in the morning's
magazine section of the *Times*. "A blurb," he'd said over
morning hot chocolate (Quick in water). "A political blurb.
With all I know about him, to gush like this. It's even unfair to
him." She told him he was nuts, he always misread his own

pieces, it was charming, even touching, there wasn't a whiff of paid hack work in it. "You write as a friend—which you are. Nothing wrong with that. It's the only way you could learn anything. Is the only honest job hatchet work?" Her praise never helped, for—wisely—she never said anything harsh about what he'd finished with and printed; the consequence was that the only one of her reactions he took seriously was laughter. ("You don't fake laughs. And you've got a great one. You're a great laugher.")

Starting at eight—with a call from Aunt Rachel, who had either read the piece or thought she had—the phone rang with congratulations, which drove him up the wall. Most of the calls had thorns: "Doyle should get on his knees. Only you could have pulled it off."

The phoning hadn't let up: Sookie, like the old mariner, stopped only one in three: "I'll tell him. I know he'll appreciate it." Finally, she unplugged the phone. Sunday was loll day. Let Wursup discover the glories of an answering service. Talk of extra senses. Never did so self-indulgent a man show more contempt for technical assistance. "Would you walk around without crutches or artificial legs? Would you stop reading rather than wear glasses? You're not selling out when you use an electric razor. You talk like a kid in a commune."

He did think abstinence preserved the deeper values. Last night he made fun of her for wanting to check in again with Dr. Snell. All week, she'd been having bomb dreams. Friday, she dreamed the human race was turning into a great bomb, she was the fuse, the bomb blew up the cosmos, God had a terrible headache. A fragment of which woke her up. Fred envied her dreams. "I wish I dreamt poems. I dream De Gaulle's asking me what to do in Algeria. Or I'm helping Johnson with Thieu."

"It may be fun hearing them, it's not fun having them. Something's going on. I want to be checked out."

"If you're going to see the shrink, don't pretend it's for therapy. You just want him to hold your hand."

"Don't say 'shrink,'" she screamed at him. "You can't control, so you diminish." It was the best way of forcing her peace-at-any-price lover out of an argument.

Now she was making up with a grand dinner. The table was set with Veronese splendor—porcelain and silver, flowers, fruit, shakers, cruets, bottles, goblets—and she was tending pot and phone, saving him from the unconsoling congratulations.

It was a pale, mild day, the windows were open, she was at ease. (Maybe she'd keep Dr. Snell on the back burner.) Music was all around; she'd installed the speakers, like Big Brother's eyes, in every room. Joni Mitchell sang "Sitting in the lobby of the Empire Hotel," and then Guiomar Novaes played heart-melting mazurkas; they went wonderfully together, a grand spring ragout. The place too looked lovely. The sun fell through the blinds, sketched lemon ribs on the rug from Isfahan, which was another gorgeous ragout of foxes, lions, camels, birds, so thick with color you could look at it as an abstraction, and it pleased as much. (Some sort of lesson here.)

After declining a California lecture ("But please ask me back next winter") and an apology to her sister for forgetting everyone's birthday, "as usual," she let herself go on the other correspondence. To a symposium question from the Columbia *Spectator*, "How Deep Can You Go?" she answered.

> Till a hole squeezes shut, which is when the rock pores close at a pressure of ten kilobars (a hundred and fifty thousand pounds a square inch) or thirty kilometers down.

How good to be in a profession which could really answer questions.

Diamonds stabilize a couple of hundred kilometers down. Deep mantle rocks are driven up shafts of diamond.

That for arabesque.

Sookie's script—she never typed—looped, spun, twirled. Wursup said it looked like a domed city. "A calligraphic Istambul . . . a city of infinity signs." (It was filled with lemniscate enclosures.) Writing was a kind of freehand drawing for her.

She fished out a request from the 'sixty-six class secretary at Chapel Hill for "NEWS: marriages, divorce—tears—children, jobs, promotions, prizes—cheers—Anything. *Something.*" She didn't like being addressed as "Dear Sisley" by Dorie FITCHEN Clary, who was—maybe—the thin blubber-lipped girl from Goldsboro who always wore skirts; but it was loll day, and her script wrote itself.

> DEAR DORIE,
>
> For the Class Letter: In her recent stay in G–3 (mental) at Bellevue (should be *Laidvue*) Sisley (Sookie) Gumpert (single) particularly enjoyed the Sock Hop, the Chinese Checker Tournament and reunion with her daughter, Phebe GUMPERT Chase. On her release, Sook was pleased to find that she could pick up the thread of her favorite soaps. Her plans are to extend the crack in her sofa and—perhaps—renew her subscription to *Hustler.* See you at the Big Tenth.

Wursup, meanwhile, walked in Central Park through Sunday crowds. It was fifteen degrees warmer than when he'd walked with Cicia three days ago. Yellow wooden horses kept out cars, but every other moving thing in Manhattan was here—bicyclists, dogs, carriages, the greatest range of human

beings in the world. Clowns picked pennies from kids' ears,
flutists played Bach, bongo drummers agitated burgher bottoms, skaters, ballplayers, lawn bowlers, rowers, chestnut sellers, joggers, walkers; the tiniest charges of life and its most
fragile sticks took the sun. Now and then he passed someone
reading the magazine section of the *Times* or using it to sit
on. At first, he'd tensed; then, what the hell, tonight it'd be in
the trash can. And what did anything like that matter in the
face of all this life? He liked it that this terrific park—and so
many others—had been worked out by another journalist: his
namesake, Frederick Olmsted. His parks outlasted his journalism (though that was first-rate). There was nothing like a
public park for human pleasure. Even in the USSR, people
looked happy in parks. (The Boulevar' in Baku—one of the
best—had saved his sanity after two days of interviewing Azerbaijani GOSPLAN officials: he'd even faced down his height
fear and ridden the Ferris wheel, which gave a grand view of
the ruby-tipped oil derricks in the Caspian.) Being among human crowds, at ease or working—but not in armies, chorus
lines or mobs—was one of life's joys. It didn't have to be in
parks. Years ago, he'd done a piece for the *Atlantic* on what
you saw on Upper Chitteranjee Street in Calcutta during an
hour's wait (getting a shoe repaired in the Jolly Shoemaker,
across the street from Dr. Hyra—Specialist in Sex Weakness).
That human glacier offered more life in an hour than many
people would see in fifty years. The idea of the piece was that
among so many other selves, you lost the most burdensome
part of your own.

He'd left the house so bilious he'd wished quick death for all
he passed, but now he guessed his face must show the same
sort of diffuse animation he saw on other walkers and observ-
ers. There must be some emotional equivalent to Boyle's
Law, a gradual dispersion of emotional particles over any human site, so that in time people got to feel the same as those
around them. In time, one could succumb to love or hatred,

if it came in steadily enough. (Or so the Gandhis and Jesuses believed.)

More thoughtful than benign, Wursup was coming out of a flute-filled underpass near the statue of Rin Tin Tin when he heard someone calling. "Hey there, Mr. Wursup." An autograph chaser? Well, as long as he wasn't mobbed. (This had happened only at two carefully staged autograph parties.) The voice had come out of a shaft of sunlight. Then an old party in a shin-long green topcoat and an orange tam-o'-shanter half slid down the little slope pulled by a low, almost snoutless dog with a gherkin hide.

"It's Terence Bennett, Mr. Wursup," said the stooped, chow-faced old fellow, sticking out his free hand. "From *Chouinard's*. Remember?"

"Sure, Mr. Bennett. Glad to see you. Tojo too." He remembered the mutt now. A few years ago, he'd encountered the two of them downtown, and the mutt had gnawed his shoelace off while they gabbed. (Wursup thought it was named Tojo to vent whatever racial angers Terence couldn't vent against Kevin.)

"Just reread your piece this morning. Shhh, Tojo." The mutt was furious at holding up for human nonsense. He loved to pull his shivery old master around.

"Reread?"

"Read it Tuesday or Wednesday," said Terence. Now that *Chouinard's* had crawled over the ledger into black ink, it began taking in publications again. The magazine section was ready early, and no Chouinardian would conceal the privilege of an early peek at it. "A first-rate follow-up to the little story we ran last month."

Since he couldn't bust old Terence, Wursup gave Tojo a boot in his no-nose.

"*Grrraugh.*"

"Tojo disagrees."

"Stop it, Tojo. Right now. Wish we could have afforded to

print it. Still, we did our little seeding job. Best to let you mastodons do the harvesting."

Tojo had the tip of Wursup's shoe in his teeth. Wursup pushed hard against the teeth, and the animal slipped off for a major yipe. Terence bent over—he was partway there to start with—and stroked the bumpy hide. "He's quite a little tussler, my little nipper. I bring him to Rin Tin Tin to show what can happen to a good doggie."

"I better scoot before I lose a leg to him."

"Our little Abby has made a mark, though, hasn't she? She really wakes them up. Our gang is very nervous about her. But it's the gossip era, and she's a master."

"She's quite a digger," said Wursup. "She's got a Winchell pen, too. Very sharp. Glad she's not on my back. Say hello to all the Chouinard people for me, Mr. Bennett. It's grand to see you."

"I certainly shall, Mr. Wursup," said the old fellow, shaking hands, but keeping Tojo on a tight leash by his own feet. "And congratulations again on a fine piece."

The park darkened, his walk was fouled. Wursup strode past the chains of skipping kids, the sunning matrons, the whistling dads. What was the purpose of all this life? Who needed it? Organic swill. Half of it wishing death to the other half: if only the boss would die; if only Granny would turn it in and leave me a bit of dough; politicians waiting for rivals to blow away. All over the world people were breaking one another's bones, blowing out babies' eyes in Belfast and Biafra, wiring genitals in Rio and Kampala. Half the governments on earth tortured enemies. What were most governments anyway but elected hatreds? Stalin and Hitler were just cleaner examples of official hate. Look in his own head. He and Tojo were made for each other.

"What ugly thoughts I have, Sook."

Showered, perfumed, glittering in a gold pantsuit, Sookie

173

looked up from the ragout. Bubbles of wine tickled the chunks of lamb, Sarah Vaughan sang "Call Me Irresponsible," a bottle of Beaune sweated in the ice bucket, a crescent of Camembert oozed from its crust, a pile of gold and scarlet apples ate the candlelight of four silver sticks. "Ugly thoughts, ugly girl, but a beautiful dinner. *Venez souper à Sans-Souci.*"

They sat over the feast, Sookie delicate and imperial both, half slut-on-call half Mary Queen of Scots, *"belle et plus que belle,"* her hair heaped into coppery grottos, her eyes enormous with pleasure at her production. The hot, winey odors, the spread of crystal, porcelain, mahogany and silver, the perspiration dots on Sookie's cheeks, the kinesthetic confidence of possession here in their snug little slot of New York space, and now, too, the sense that whatever foolishness he'd thought up in his head between Fiumicino and Kennedy was in the heads of several million readers of the New York *Times* melted away the last harshness from his head.

"It's been a lovely day," said Sookie. "I did my chores, I made the dinner, I listened to music. And they'll love me in Chapel Hill. Listen." She read her entry. "That covers it, doesn't it?"

"No paper in the world could refuse it. You go right to the heart of things."

"I am good at personal stuff, aren't I? But I'm ambitious. I want to expand. I'll start small. Local news. 'This morning on Lexington Avenue, Dr. Sidney Fleischsniffer, dressed to the nines and carrying his swagger stick and shit-scooper, walked his Irish setter, Sigmund, who pissed on eleven tires.' How zat?"

"You can be *Time's* Lexington Avenue stringer."

"Wait'll I do my little petroleum report. Texaco'll have to go into the garment business."

"You're a tiger."

"No," said Sookie. "Just your pal. With a touch of Lyell and Aunt Jemima thrown in to sweeten the pot."

"It's a sweet pot," said Wursup. What was he that he should hunt for gloom in all this golden luck?

In his narcissistic ups and downs, Wursup hadn't thought once how Jim Doyle was feeling about the piece.

13

For Doyle, public life had been a way of screening private life. He was not a lyric poet whose private life was the stuff of his published poems. Yet here he was, spread out naked in the million or so most influential homes of America. How had he been trapped like that?

It wasn't true either that today's news wraps tomorrow's fish. People remembered intimate details for years, long after they'd forgotten your missions and policies. What did he remember about certain celebrities but odd facts and scandals? The Dutch queen's consort was a regal business wheeler and—because he'd lost eight ribs—could put his hand through his belly to his back; the crown princess of Japan had been picked for the prince for her heavy thighs—she'd been instructed to play lots of tennis while he was around—and her connection with one of the great trust families; the silvery tough guy John Connolly was the son of a steer-and-chicken slaughterer, and when he lay wounded in the car in Dallas, Kennedy's blood gushing over his eyes, he drifted back to the

terrifying, bloody days near his father's knife. When Doyle
saw such people, facts like these—learned from gossip or
briefing books—dominated his regard, and it took much to
displace them. Yet they made for foolish distortions. It was
like relying on the evaluations of childhood friends and neighbors. Most of the world's most useful people had overcome
what they'd been as children.

But here he was, laid open in the *Times* among the bras-
siere ads: the father-numbed, father-scornful son, trying,
across decades of oblivion, to figure out how to do the right
thing by someone who—to use Fred's grotesque quotation
from Shakespeare—"put stuff to some she-beggar and compounded thee, poor rogue hereditary." As if his mother had
anything to do with beggary. All right, most readers hopped
over anything peculiar. They were looking for a little verbal
warble in the Sunday drone, and would notice nothing more
than that James Doyle wasn't just a smartass clown in nutty
hats who'd worked for Democrats and Republicans, but that
he'd climbed out of garbage and supported brothers and sisters: and that before he'd redistributed public money, he'd
been on the receiving end of it. Still, here in the Arlington
study, with the pink and silver light dangling spring in the apple trees outside the window, Doyle felt uneasy. The Doyle of
Fred's article was a tragic clown with everything but red nose
and silky pantaloons. That was not the Mayor's dish.

Bobby, his serious oldest son, called from Hotchkiss to say
he thought the piece was wonderful. "I learned lots. I'd no
idea you'd had such a rough time. I think it's great."

"It's all in Dickens, Bobby. You'd do better reading *Great
Expectations*." At least he'd purchased his son's ease. The
more remote you were from the ancestral horse thief, the cut-
er he looked to you. But Bobby might have to swallow a few
fish heads before it was over. "It was good of you to call.
You're a better son than I was." *Am.*

Adele said she thought Freddy did a good job; it was nice to

read a piece about a public figure that didn't caramelize his
life and feelings; most were hidden in fogs of bullshit domesticity.

As if public lives were intended for public amusement. The
running American serial. Look at Nixon. Fifteen years ago,
he'd have walked away as a good, gray president. Now he'd
survive as the American Judas. Not that his life hadn't set him
up for it. He'd told a pal of Doyle's how his old man had wanted to shoot Harding after Teapot Dome, and how he'd taken a
ten-year-old's oath to be straighter than straight. He'd stifled
too much natural meanness. When it all hit the fan, he never
knew he'd been the great pilot film for modern exposure, the
first emperor seen not only naked but arse up.

The call from Chicago came from Edward Nowajewski, the
alderman of Doyle's voting ward. Nowajewski was fox-faced,
imperious, and intricate as a Renaissance councillor. Doyle
had seen him hold court in the alderman's office every Thursday night; he sat like the Godfather, dealing groceries, jobs,
permits, out of the city machinery for his constituents, a master of the simple system that went from precinct to White
House. His sharp-nosed red head was a prominent dot in city
portraits, at banquets, airports, parades. Nowajewski's life was
a consummation of attentiveness and rule; his intelligence
was sharp and narrow, without leeway for sympathies that
could not translate into votes. His speech was the *r*-inlaid Chicago rumble of the man who needs no platform polish, needs
only other men leaning in to hear what he says so that their
effort will italicize their memory and their obligation. He had
once submitted his candidacy for the district congressional
seat, but he too had had bad domestic luck: his son was discovered, by a tipped-off reporter, massaging truckers in a parlor. It was not just neighborliness which led to his being cho-
sen for the call to Doyle.

"Jim, our people don't think it's worth your while to fly out
for a presentation." (Doyle was due to go before the Democratic caucus in a week.)

"Is this the Mayor talking, Edward?"

"It's me. But it could be anyone, including the Mayor. Every man and his dog has a copy of that *Times* piece, and we all feel for you, but the bottom line is, *are the people of Illinois going to slate a candidate who says*—and it's there, black on white—*he has no feeling for his own father?* You know the Mayor, Jim. I don't care what kind of a dog your old man was, and Jim, I speak as a man whose pop laced him with corset stays five times a week regular as school, and I have had certain problems the other way as well; I've come close to shooting father and son in the same week. But I know and you know where we are, Jim, and what we build on here in the county. Family. And in Peoria it's no different. If I didn't turn out eighty-two and -three percent of my people, I would not be here talking to you now. I know my people, know the Mayor. And Jim, they do not play it different in Kankakee or Peoria. We can't have any of this psychological horseshit in the voters' heads. I understand from the Colonel the Mayor couldn't even finish the piece, he was so upset. He said if one of his kids said one tenth of what you said about him, he'd take a cat-o'-nine-tails to him no matter how old he was. Everyone can have a few problems, we're no strangers to boozing dads, and yours was a lulu, but *who has to talk about it to the New York Times?* Maybe if a little story had been leaked here to the *Sun-Times* or the *Trib*, you know, how your old man had had bad troubles, how you tried to hold him up, he just couldn't make it, his brains fuddled up, what could you do, but what joy it was to find him again after all the years— Pop, here I come. It's little Jimmy—that would have been grand, it would have taken care of all these dirty rumors. The Mayor don't give a tinker's turd about that kind of story, long as it doesn't show up in everybody's fortune cookie. But you took the dumb route. We had our problems with Adlai, but he knew the score.

"But still, that divorce stuff gave us plenty of trouble in those days. We don't look for that again, Jim. You better try

somewhere else. Maryland, maybe. Except you got a good
Catholic constituency there too. How about Vermont, or
wherever you have that nice place? Take your pick. But in
Cook County, Jim, you're dead."

So there it was, and there was no more point in asking to
hear it from the horse's mouth than there would have been in
asking the burning bush for clarification.

It wasn't the end of life. Still, it changed many plans. He remembered Pierre Billotte talking about De Gaulle's first try
for power, before Algeria finally brought him in in 'fifty-eight:
"He marched us to the Rubicon and said, 'All right, let's
fish.'" But it wasn't likely that an Algeria was waiting for
James Doyle. He'd prepared thirty years, and now he was a
few pages in Fred's collected works. Well, who knows. Maybe
one of these days he'd be able to take the long view himself.
Look at how many princes counted only because they'd spent
a few hours posing for Titian? But what the hell did it matter if
one lasted? It was life that counted, stretching oneself, and
nothing did that for him but high public office. You could
sleep away a presidency, like Ike, but you could also turn it
into international excitement and make millions deeper, hap-
pier, better. In the old days, the Napoleons and Walpoles
looked like giants because so few people were inspected and
written about. Now, with film and cheap printing, there were
thousands of celebrities. Kissinger and Nixon weren't much
bigger than Marlon Brando or the Beatles. Doyle wasn't
much more conspicuous than the subjects of the three other
stories in the *New York Times Magazine*. Who could say what
would count in five, fifty, let alone five hundred years?

Still, as he wrote Knoblauch a few days later:

> I don't think Fred should have done it that way. It
> made me too serious, too mental. Cook County
> couldn't swallow that. And who knows, maybe no-
> body else will. I may not be able to get an Assistant
> Secretaryship.

Even later, feeling somewhat different—the philosophic re-
alist not only reconciled to the given but looking beyond it—
he wrote Wursup:

> I'm not sure the piece did what we hoped it would,
> but who knows if it's not better that way. I feel as if
> I'd been seen by a fine painter. The piece has a kind
> of beauty independent of me, and though I may not
> think I look quite like that, I respect it for design, for
> feeling. I feel as if some of me was used in a work of
> fine art. Jim Doyle, a special kind of blue. Maybe I'll
> even become a type of personality, a fifth-rate Ham-
> let or Don Juan. (Is my mind running a new way?)
> So thank you, Freddy, and congratulations.

14

Tina Rhome called Monday morning as Wursup was switching the phone to NO RING. "Cicia wanted me to let you know she won't be able to make the appointment." There'd been no appointment. "She's on the way to the hospital."

"What is it? How serious?"

"She was just worn out. She and her father—he came yesterday—thought she'd better go back in."

Wursup called Millie Sollinckas.

"She'll be scanned today and tomorrow," said Millie. "I wouldn't advise seeing her for a few days. The tests are tiring. I'll tell her you called, if you like."

Yes, he would like that.

Yet. Perhaps he was the excess in her brew. Which did her in. Broke her routine and her. Too much cream for that small life. He had no "appointment" with her: it was understood they'd be in touch. (There'd been precious little touching.) "Appointment" was her way of getting in touch with him. With the medical flavor that was the flavor of everything in her life now.

Sookie was in mid-production, bottles unstoppered, brushes whirling, makeup mirror lit. (Even a descent for the mail fired up the factory.) And now she was headed across town, to her place, for the weekend mail, before driving across the river to her lab. "What's up?" (They usually didn't see each other once he went into the study.)

"That girl I was talking with is back in the hospital. It's upsetting. To feel helpless."

"That's what hospitals are for." Abstractly, the attention on the small upward strokes of the mascara brush on the lash.

How much of life do you owe any one person? If you're a father, a husband, a son, a lover, a friend, a worker, how divide yourself, your sympathy, time, energy, money? Is the act of division itself treason?

The Jews suffered after they numbered the tribe. Examine a phenomenon and you destroy it. (One of Hitler's mad characterizations of the Jews—an "analytic" people.) When Sookie was *in analysis*, much of their life together went into analytic chambers, and was, naturally, found wanting. In some cases, improvement followed. But now, no analysis. He *felt* for Cicia; he imagined her pale on a table, in the gray hospital smock, slid like dough into a great machine which, centimeter by centimeter, penetrated and cooked her with awful rays. No choice for her now, no deciding whether to go here or there. He summoned the familiar devices of backing off: *There's nothing to do. Don't become a bottomless hole. I'll worry about it later. First things first.*

He heated up the pot of yesterday's Sanka, lit a rough, thin twist of black tobacco, tugged the red-tipped paper slip of his sugarless-gum packet, watered his six plants, did a few knee bends and went into his little factory, the black and white machine waiting for its morning current.

He had a choice: writing up either an interview with Milovan Djilas about the reasons he'd translated *Paradise Lost* into Serbian during one of his terms in jail (Djilas had given him a piece of the toilet-paper manuscript as a souvenir) or the new gerontological research that chose to regard death not as something given but as a biological error. Dreams of immortality, and not Tithonous—"Me alone cruel immortality consumes"—but permanent vigor. But even that sort of immortality might do away with so grand a life as Djilas's: bloody and brilliant, passionate, thoughtful, expressive, jailbird, minister of state, partisan fighter and impartial tongue-raker of those who'd favored him (Stalin, Tito). The threat would not be removed—an eternity in prison being worse than death—but the ultimate hope would be that death would end your troubles.

There were eighty-three thousand items in Professor Nathan Shock's *Bibliography of Gerontological Research*. Wursup had read fewer than fifty of them, but there was plenty there. Some researchers thought the body "tanned" like old film, forming protein bridges which couldn't be dissolved by cell enzymes; others studied how to dissolve it. The body made war on itself: lysome-membrane sacs of enzymes burst and assaulted cells; antisystems developed from minuscule mistakes in the body-cell system and grew within it. The Medawar-Comfort notion was that humans were inadequately programmed for longevity. Some worked on accumulated static, overcharged networks, confused instruction. Some cell tissue could not regenerate—or could it? Should one accept any premise? Ten million species have existed, perhaps ten percent were even noticed, perhaps one percent studied. Metabolic rates, Weisman's "division of labor," heart rate, cell size, poikilothermism (is the creature the temperature of its environment?). Wursup flipped note cards, whirled pages, typed, smoked, chewed, sipped; mazurkas played over and over on the stereo, filled in by the electric wasp-buzz of the typewriter. Yet the few words from Tina about Cicia made their way through all those that he typed, pushing them farther and farther from him. The unsaid mastered the said.

Usually he worked till noon or one. Today he was worn out by ten-thirty.

A vague, puzzled day, pleasant—like so much middling life—by default of unpleasantness. Wursup walked west, then south on Fifth Avenue. Bunches of blue police, patrol cars. "What's up?" he asked a scholarly-looking sergeant.

"Parade."

St. Patrick's had been and gone. "Which?" Wursup felt the international Policeman's Eye. He looked—except for his mildly unbusinesslike turtleneck—unsuspicious, a well-heeled *flâneur* in a red blazer, no one to insult or take lightly.

"It's the Baltics."

New York was a terrific bouillabaisse, with every chunk of fish crying out its presence. "Everyone gets his day," said Wursup politely. He walked past the Plaza, Bergdorf's, Doubleday's, Jensen's, Saks, then over to Will's office twenty-nine floors up in what Will called "my editorial *sharashka*" where the literary *zeks* worked in small, glassy pens.

A new receptionist, small, squirrel mouthed, cute, lit up at Wursup's name. Green-eyed glitter, flushing smile baring bold teeth, a wordless conspiracy of acknowledged fame. "Mr. Eddy says you know your way."

"Only here," said Wursup sweetly. (Deepening the conspiracy, making an anecdote for her chronicle.)

Will, in a handsome blue shirt and a tie by some Kandinsky-loving designer, shuttled between piles of manuscripts. "Thank God you came. I have so much to do, I can't do anything." A thick blue arm lifted a hunk of manuscript. "Want to read a thousand pages on erotic diabolism? The author's a bagger in a Kansas City Safeway. He researched it all at night, took him sixteen years. Flagellants, orgiasts, millenarians. Pre-Jesus to post-Manson. Imagine all the rolls of Charmin and jars of Skippy paying for it."

"You going to publish it?"

"Sure, soon as we sell sixty thousand copies of this." Holding up a handsome smooth red morocco-bound quarto between whose black fillets was tooled in gold: CHALMERS, POLITICAL ANNALS OF THE PRESENT UNITED STATES. "Schroeder thinks it'll do for bicentennial camp. It's actually a hell of a good book. He's an old Tory who blames the climate for the Americans' ingratitude."

With his red cheeks and pointy white beard, Will looked like Silenus, but a tired Silenus. The eyes were blue slits in a capillary sludge, the faun face looked like it had taken a beating—there was crust and sag in it; the bare road between the side clumps of white hair looked damp and bleak. All morning Wursup had written about the hollowing, stiffening, slowing body, but this was Will, and Will's aging stirred up his own, the slowing down of nail and hair growth, the calcium clumps in the knees and knuckles.

"I've spent the morning writing up dreams of immortality, and I feel ninety-three. That girl's back in the hospital. We had a grand walk in the park the other day. I felt like Mickey Rooney with Judy Garland. But I wore Judy out." Will's handsome old-goat's head leaned into the palm support atop his forearms. "Same old garbage. I know," said Wursup.

"Your garbage is easier for me than mine."

"I've *seen* enough, but what's seeing? Has it changed me? I make my living from it. And not a bad one, as you know. I've seen a guy's head lopped off in an Arab souk, a Korean woman hold her daughter's severed head; I saw a trench three feet thick with human guts. Seen! What the hell is seeing? I'm a' duck's back. It's why I became a reporter. It's easier to see than do. Or feel. At least I do feel something for this girl. A little rumble, and I don't think it's got much to do with hunger or an itchy cock. Just good old sloppy feeling, and I'm proud of it. Nice? Her cancer gives me a chance to tell myself what a fine feeling fellow I am."

Will opened his heavy palms. "I pass, Frederick. I'm all walled up in these lives here"—spreading palms over the manuscripts. "All I see is there's no end to it, there's always something new. Escapes, murders, catastrophes, inventions, love, death. Stories, stories, stories." Riffling the piles, on the right, on the left. "We spend our time selling other people's stories."

And Will thought, *what I could tell him.* The grubbiest story of all: wife and best pal. And not just once, twice, a mistake, a lark. But five hundred times. The sneaking, manipulating.

And he felt a terrible impulse, so strong his teeth showed through the white mustache.

"What's up, Will? Pain?" Wursup leaned over.

"Toothache. I've got to see the dentist." But he hovered around the destructive impulse. There was Wursup, the easy bear in his red blazer and golden turtleneck. Ruffled by not being ruffled. In half a second, he could ruffle him. Lives had turned around in half a second, triggers pulled, treason committed. But here? Now? So secure were their lives, so heavy the fortification, Fred would probably do little more than blink, shake his head, say, "Sure, I guessed." Or, "I understand. I don't blame you. I was away all the time." Yet it would never be quite the same. So what was the point? Why give up the comfort of a real friendship, drinks, dinners, talk? And of course there was the money they made for each other. The manuscripts on his desk were mostly histories of the consequences of such impulses, disasters, or, rarely, triumphs. But they were *out there.* Other peoples' stories.

Wursup, seeing Will look not only old—that was familiar now—but shaky, pained, felt he must do something for the poor fellow. Here he was, shut up in his fluorescent tomb day in and out, buried by other people's excitement. He had to exaggerate his troubles, so Will would feel the pleasures of his security, had to show him that he was not simply living off the fat of fame, love and money, but could hardly function. "I wish I had a toothache. A real pain for a change. My trouble is any feeling at all throws me for a loop. I'm not worth a goddamn."

Will knew what Wursup was doing. It was a good thing to

do, and he played his own part in the performance of grief and consolation. "You're much tireder than you know. Last time you took off, you did a piece. You probably don't think it counted, but it did. It took it out of you. And God knows what you've done since. Wrapping yourself up in all these mortician reports. Your feelings for this kid are a cover for your own exhaustion."

"I don't think so. And I don't think a week lying around Palm Beach is my style."

"Why not? You're not a kid any longer. You can't just turn out pages the way you used to. You were like a singing bird then, staking out your territory. Now it's all intensive planting. Not easy. Not just a matter of looking and writing." Will leaned forward on his elbows and palms. Despite his heavy shoulders, he looked dwarfish among the piles of manuscripts and books. They seemed to absorb most of the office light. Will's blue shirt had less brilliance than scoured shine. His beard looked very white.

Poor fellow, thought Wursup. Dear old fellow, under all that assurance. And suddenly, he himself felt cheerier. "Come on. Let's take a walk. Down to the Battery. Out of the cage. I'll take you to Lutèce."

"I wish I were still young enough to be bribed by a fifty-dollar lunch. Or even good company. It's the mines"—palm on the bagger's erotic diabolism—"for me. I'm not much of a Marxist, but you do become your work. Maybe it's more like turning into one's own suit of armor." Will's eyes dilated, the blue almost snowy. Some of the crust had fallen as he talked. Within the white beard, there were still parts of a young fellow. "Anyway, if us drones don't hang in and do our bit, how are you queens going to continue beedom? And liberty?"

IV

15

Wursup was in Bruges when he heard from Sookie about his father and Mona. Late April: fruit trees flowered along the canals, swans cruised in the Minnelac. "Such beautiful question marks," he said.

Gretchen, the girl from Sabena, didn't follow this, or much else; most of their talk the last thirty hours had gone by them. Their minds met mostly when their bodies did, which, Wursup supposed, was the point here.

Four of the white birds toddled on the grass spit beneath the bridge. The cob rocked its little corporation toward a lady whose hair was the color of its plumage. *"Pas encore, cher ami,"* she said to it, and added in English to the romantic couple, "They look for the crusts I bring after I have feed my parrot. *Une belle famille, n'est-ce pas?"*

"They are very clean," said Wursup. "One can only think of such birds in beautiful towns. Though I suppose they themselves are not really beautiful."

The cob's muscular neck drilled its moronic little head deep into its plumage. "Beautiful as *family*," said the lady. She pointed out Poppa, Momma, and the cygnets. With her snowy dentures, flakey powder and white hair, she was like a piece of fine human lace.

Wursup was pleased enough to be thought Gretchen's spouse, though he suspected the lady's criterion was their sexual aura. It said more for the kind lady's antenna than her acuity. Wasn't it clear that he and Gretchen could not be a lasting couple? To spend a week, let alone half a life, with Gretchen would pulverize a swan-sized sensibility.

They'd come to Bruges for the weekend. At the Hotel Memling, their window was rimmed with scarlet vines; the leaves peered in like embarassed neighbors. Below, tourist boats swished in the canal, and polylingual babble rose around them. Gretchen was a wordless—though noisy—lover; the statistics of wool manufacture, tower heights, and the price of great works of art filled in the silence. In the morning, the keeper of the hotel, Mynheer Reckman, served coffee in great Delft pitchers in the grand dining room. The sideboards were carved with hunting scenes; wainscot niches were filled with pewter mugs, brass horns, flintlocks. The fireplace was as big as a beach cabana. Above it was carved EIGEN HEERD IS GOUD WEERD, which Gretchen translated for him as "Nice shepherd is good weapon." Wursup thought it must be "A mighty fortress is our God," but Gretchen did not know the tune he whistled to test the theory.

The only thing Gretchen did seem to know was that she was supposed to be a look-a-like of the Michelangelo Madonna in the Eglise Nôtre Dame. Another Sabena passenger had told her that on a similar weekend to Ghent, and she was anxious to check it out. After she and Wursup finished buying lace, using the bed, and taking a post-breakfast walk, she was determined to see the immortal version of herself.

Wursup had been to Belgium many times, especially after

NATO had shifted to Brussels. For him, there had been nothing of the amusement park about the country. Its perpetual rain fused with the military gloom of NATO. He was melancholy here, where individual life seemed trivial beside the strategy of terrible weapons. He had talked with specialists about "acceptable losses" of forty, sixty or—in admiration of Chinese abundance—four hundred million people. He remembered a lunch with a Belgian colonel, a red-haired Apollo, who'd quoted that god's speech from Euripides' play *Orestes* to dramatize his thesis that motives for belligerence only masked "life's essential motif: self-purgation." The colonel was slender—except for his trucker's hands—clean and learned. His eight-thousand-volume library filled every room of his enormous apartment. He had read aloud (in French): "'Helen's beauty helped the gods launch the Greeks against the Phrygians, heaping the dead to purge the earth of the insolent superfluity of men.'"

On the terrace, a younger Apollo in Belgian military dress had laid their lunch. The colonel said, "NATO is a series of canal locks controlling the sea, but it's the sea that's fundamental. Our sons"—he was not married and an unlikely father—"have been given the dangerous toy—peace—which has freed them for what De Gaulle called shit-in-their-bed frenzy. And our bourgeoisie converts this spectacle into entertainment. Voltaire said, *'Un des plus grands malheurs des honnêtes gens c'est qu'ils sont des lâches.'*" The colonel spat over the terrace. "Marx and Freud had blinders, but at least dealt with the necessary. Probably the Old Testament in these Jews. If Isaac's throat has to be cut, you cut. The ultimate war is between the organic and the inorganic. War is the unique acknowledgment humans make of the principle." The colonel led Wursup to the table. Apollo Junior poured wine and served the soup and veal. "One way or another," said the colonel, "missiles will purge our superfluity."

They talked of poetry. The colonel was a connoisseur of contemporary literature. (For him, Char, Jacottet, Larkin, Hughes, and Berryman were antiques.) "I adore the innocent narcissism of poets. I infinitely prefer brilliant ignorance to knowledgeable cowardice disguised as love of mankind."

The week before, Wursup had had his only presidential interview with Nixon. (*Drain* hadn't appeared; Nixon would not see him after that.) Nixon had been sober, and impressive. They were in his inner office at the EOB; it was full of comfortable sofas and chairs; the large desk was covered with knickknacks, including a model missile. Nixon said he now had only fifteen minutes to decide about an "appropriate response" to a missile attack. Some of his people were reluctant to divert money to "the shield instead of the sword." They were willing to sacrifice forty, even seventy, million people; he could not. The nine hundred million dollars for ABM would save most of those lives. "At least till the mid–nineteen eighties." When Nixon talked of nuclear exchanges, even Vietnam looked insignificant. That human intelligence could disappear in half an hour was a fact before which every other seemed picayune. Wursup felt overwhelmed by it. The world was so fragile. It was this feeling which made *Drain* more melancholy than amusing.

It was only later that Wursup realized its melancholy sprang as much from exhaustion and the breakup of his family as from his encounters with the technocrats of disaster.

Since then, life had picked up. His literary melancholy had enriched and eased him. His troubles now were those of success, and though they were complicated, they were not so gloomy. Even international life seemed manageable to him. Technology dispelled as well as created shadows. There was a kind of international clarity in the world, despite the threat. In any event, he was no longer melancholy, and Belgium, despite its rain, no longer depressed him.

This time, Wursup had come to Belgium to interview Leo Sleecks, a steel executive who'd been kidnapped by an Argentine terrorist group and kept at the bottom of a well for five months. After Sleecks' firm had paid a half-million-dollar ransom and inserted the group's propaganda in ten newspapers, he'd been freed. Wursup was the only journalist he'd agreed to see, and this because he was an admirer of *Down the American Drain.*

This information had come from Mike Schilp, who'd arranged the interview. Wursup's Doyle piece had reminded Schilp of the piece Wursup owed him.

Constance had been serving Sookie, Wursup and Petey what she called her "gold dinner"—corn biscuits, roast chicken, squash, yams and pineapple-coconut cake. On the phone Michael bellowed his come-on, full of *peronismo,* the *descamisados, fidelismo, sans-culottisme.* Passionate odors floated from the table. Constance waved at him furiously. "All right, I'll do it. I owe you a piece anyway."

"You're the only reporter in the world he'd see. He told me *Drain* was a great book. He read it in Dutch and English."

"I can't resist that."

"You better not 'sist this here dinner. Ah didn't spend no four hours in that kitchen so you be letting it freeze."

"Make the arrangements, Michael."

The meeting with Sleecks took place at a café across from the Royal Theater on the Ketelstraat. Sleecks was in the corner table, back to the wall, a lean, bald man in dark glasses, drinking a mug of beer and eating a plate of cheese and anchovies. "Forgive me for beginning," he said in good English. "Since my stomach is getting back to normal size, I've eaten like a piranha. While I'm awake, I eat." He was half a head smaller than Wursup, but erect, firm-looking. He'd exercised hours every day down in the dark. "There wasn't enough room for pushups, but I pushed against the walls."

In five months, no one had said anything to him after the first and before the last day. The only light appeared when the well top slid open to admit the bucket which descended with his food and water and ascended with his leavings and excrement. "The pulley noise was music. Any sound not my own was music." Sleecks' cheekbones were sharp as elbows. A face cut to its bones. And more than the eyes hid behind the dark glasses. "I'm still unaccustomed to light." He peered out of the glasses, though, to see if he were imposing himself too much. So gentle a rabbit, thought Wursup. How did he survive?

"How did you get through the days? The months?"

"Sometimes I think I'm still there." Peering over the glasses to see if this was too fanciful. "I suppose I kept active. Mentally. I played bridge games, chess. Football games. Belgium won the World Cup many times. I remembered poems from school. When I forgot lines, I made up substitutes. You become a bit of a poet in the dark. I thought of meals, how they were made, where I would have them, the lights, the china, the cooking of the dishes. Ahh, and then, forgive me, I imagined every centimeter of my wife and"—making a gentle gaunt pout—"other bodies, film stars, people I knew, girls I'd seen. There's so much in a person's head. I went over my life. So much that was trivial became fascinating, beautiful. I analyzed what I'd done. So many mistakes. Thought is almost physical in the dark. It's like touching."

An hour later, in the Sabena office, the tall Frisian blonde misread the name on Wursup's ticket as "Mustard." Behind her was a beautiful poster of Bruges. "I think I'll go there for a couple of days," said Wursup. "Could you make the arrangements for me?"

The girl would be delighted to help Mr. Mustard. She herself had never been to Bruges, though she'd been told a famous statue there was her double.

"You should go see it."

"Perhaps I will."

Ah, why not, thought Wursup. He wasn't living in a dark well. "Good. Come along. My treat."

In the Eglise Nôtre Dame, Wursup and Gretchen walked down toward the marble sculpture. A *prie-dieu* kept them fifteen feet away. "They have to protect it," said Wursup. "The Vatican Madonna's behind safety glass since that madman took a hammer to it."

"I can hardly see," said Gretchen, squinting. (She hadn't had on her eyeglasses since she deciphered Wursup's ticket.) Her eyes were little chocolate ponds.

"So much fury in the world," said Wursup. "It's a wonder anything survives. Beauty's supposed to tame people, but I don't know. The fellow who hammered off the nose in Rome was a sculptor."

Gretchen shoved the *prie-dieu* aside. "I'm going to see it." And she went up to it. "Do you think it's like me?" Her long face had the length of the Madonna's, but not its sad wisdom. "There is a resemblance," he said. "Of course, she doesn't have your body."

"We'll never know that," said Gretchen modestly. She put her hand over the Madonna's as if to remove it from the marble boy's. "I wish a baby."

"I don't think you could handle a baby like that, Gretchen. Take a look at that little boy." The two-year-old had human history in his downcast face.

"He is a dollie," said Gretchen, and kissed its marble curls. At which there was a scream which drove Wursup's heart against his ribs. Gretchen's arms hammerlocked the Madonna's head. "*Non, non, non, non, non, non,*" yelled the church. Or, at least, a tiny priest running up the aisle, hands rowing the air. Gretchen clung to the Madonna, the clerical hands turned into fists, the screams into Flemish fury.

Gretchen called, "I do not speak this language." Wursup made out words for "police" and "sacrilege," shouted Gretchen from her perch, moved between her and the priest, found three hundred francs in his wallet and waved it in general propitiation. "Please forgive us. We didn't know. She was worshipping." And more, whatever would fill the space between the little priest's rage and Gretchen's terror. The money was taken. French, English and Flemish growls pursued them to the *Uitgang/Sortie*. They walked down mocha streets, past groceries, lace stores, butchers, up Stoofstraat, past the Béguinage, by the Minnelac and the swans and into a grand alley of immense oaks whose branches interlaced to form a green tunnel. They collapsed on a stone bench, leaning against each other. The branches jutted, tangled, lost themselves; there were layers and layers of them, so thick that only here and there could they see the sublime blue sky. Such lofty intricate green thought. What grandeur, abundance, sublimity. Said Gretchen, "My bottom's cold."

They walked back, past the lake, over the stone bridge, down Stoofstraat, into the cobbled courtyard of their hotel. A woman with a squint sat by the door, spinning lace. The bobbins whirled round little spindles; she pinned, shifted, spun. Wursup, fascinated by the creation, had to be dragged off by Gretchen. "My bottom's icy."

At the desk, Mynheer Reckman handed Wursup a message. It was from the AP man in Brussels to whom he had given his address. CALL SOOKIE GUMPERT.

"My God."

"What's bad?"

"I don't know. I have to call America. Wait for me." Was it one of the boys? Please God, no. Cicia? (Sookie would have called him.) Maybe Will? He put in the call. Bless direct-distance dialing. "What's wrong?"

"It's your father," Sookie said. Her voice was clear; how he wished he were with her. "And Mona. They're dead."

198

"My God. What do you mean? What happened?"

"The janitor found them this morning. It looks as if they took sleeping pills last night. They were just lying in bed. Dressed. Dead. There's a note for you. I'm so sorry, sweetheart."

His reservation from Antwerp was for that night. He went upstairs to the little room over the canal. Gretchen was undressed, naked, asleep, noisy. Inhaling, she snorted; exhaling, she whistled; nor was her rump soundless. Is this the food of love? wondered Wursup. It had been a trying day for her. Gretchen reminded him of Mona. Though not as smart, as spirited, not nearly as *there* as Mona is. *Was*. Mona, a dear thing. What would Poppa have done—how quick the tenses of the past are—without her? But what could have happened? His father was vigorous, and as far as he'd known, not sick, not gloomy. If anything, he was a nut of self-confidence, an old life booster. Maybe he or Mona had something, and they decided to go together. Mayerling. Did they both want to die? How else? Sookie said they were lying dressed on the bed. How did they decide? Over a month? A year? Overnight. What was the last night like? Did they talk while the pills took over? Watch Johnny Carson on *The Tonight Show*? Hold hands? Talk? What did they say? Did they change their minds?

A rumble from Gretchen's rear. It was a beautiful, generous rear. The long legs spread at the groin; the protective tufts peered out. Magnetic. Wursup took off his clothes, and held her, front on rear. She woke up, annoyed, but, feeling his interest, found her own.

Under the sheet Gretchen slept. Vines knocked the wooden shutters, leaves chattered, boats moaned in the canal; voices talked of Burgundy, Charles the Bald, Van Eyck, Memling. The little room thickened with absence. Gretchen grew noisier. A human basoon. Under the sheet, skin to skin,

Wursup thought if only one of her sounds could come from his father's body now, it would undo the universe. His father was gone. And great-bottomed Mona, with all her languages. Little Poppa, who gave him cells, his fat nose, and archless feet. Poppa and Mona, two of the four billion, paying nature's debt before it was due. (Perhaps.)

16

There was a storm in miniature in the ant farm: prosperity had come to *Chouinard's;* and it was insupportable. The snug little eco-system whose suppressed, unacknowledged, never-conceded principle was *failure* was now shaken by success. For years, *Chouinard's* had been a baby Dracula of scorn; scorn was the blood of its eccentric life. Now what?

The staff still assembled every morning in Kevin's office, overlooking MOMA's sculpture garden; they still debated the shape of things past and to come, but now the debates were as heavy with "the responsibilities of success" as were the bronze breasts of the Maillols across the street with bronze milk. That is, just as there was no milk, so was there no genuine responsibility; there was only a heavier illusion.

Before, they had also been serious, but the seriousness had had that feathery exemption from consequence which even seriously playing children feel. The Chouinardians were their own world; they set their own standards; they existed to please one another. *Unsere Leute, Our Crowd, The Subscribers,* would go along with them, as feet follow the will to walk.

"Abby's Corner" had drilled a channel into the world, and the world overwhelmed them. *Chouinard's* had twenty-one thousand subscribers. Paper and mailing costs had gone out of sight, but now they had a page of advertisements, which required a business staff, which needed room. Letters came in; they started a Letters Column, which meant another half page, which meant more copy—for the other half—which meant more costs, more help. Stories were fed to them, and invitations to press conferences, showings, events.

They became an event themselves. An article on Abby led to an article on them. Dame Mae was given five minutes a day on the radio station to analyze business and finance; Libba was offered a job at triple her salary by the *Ladies' Home Journal* and was finding it difficult to turn it down. (Unlike Abby, she could not afford to use *Chouinard's* as her laboratory.)

Worst of all, the trouble was not perceived as trouble; and yet it was seldom felt as fulfillment, or even success. The wild joy which infected the office after one of their stories had been used by one of the mastodons—with or without acknowledgment—was gone. They were cited often and raided more; yet their work was no better, and probably worse. They had their teletype machines back, they had a bigger reference library, a secretary converted their five-drawer filing cabinet into a room-size morgue of complex reference—Susannah called it *el cementerio*—which they clumsily used to cite misquotations and substantiate demands for retraction or proper acknowledgment. Even when they were cited correctly, there was little joy; if anything, they felt victimized: "They robbed us again." (Why shouldn't Washington *Post* readers get the story from the horse's mouth?)

No one felt the misery of triumph more than Susannah. Her salary was up, strangers said "Really?" when she told them where she worked, and she no longer had to rely on tertiary sources for her pieces on Honduran land holdings and Chilean truck drivers; but her spirit had been violated. Susannah's premise was "Adjust to what comes." For months, it concealed the violation from her consciousness. Kevin told the old-timers, "Life is learning. One sees light, one runs to it. More light, more speed. We're no longer festering in the oyster, we're enhancing the world." The very imagery he used repelled Susannah. Ornament, decoration, jewelry. Didn't human beings discover their own values and hold to them through thick and thin? *Haz bien y no mires a quien*—"Do good and don't watch to whom." Oh, she granted that the ignorant could learn and sinners see the light. Maybe she was old hat, maybe what had happened was positive evolution. Yet she couldn't shake the sense that Kevin's metaphors rose from basic corruption; crucial energy went into appearance and camouflage. This was the new energy of the new *Chouinard's*. And before she knew it, she too felt it. Once, she'd built her pieces out of other newspapers, checking them occasionally against whatever expertise she stumbled on, or against her own sense of things. Now she felt she could no longer work at such distance from the events she interpreted. She should have time in Mexico City, drinking in the *pulquerías,* checking out the *vecindad.* What could she write about Argentina if she didn't know the *pampas,* Brazil without feeling the winds of the *sertãos,* Bolivia if she couldn't see the valleys from the *altiplano?* A Stanislavskian furor seized her; she wanted to be Latin American in spirit. What good did it do to write about truck drivers' strikes in Chile unless she knew what being a Chilean truck driver felt like?

Now every sentence she wrote was murder; the words were boulders. She couldn't go on.

And there was small comfort after work. For years she was eased by painting, books, cigarettes, coffee, Saturdays at the galleries and museums. These joys were no longer easy and natural. Her own painting exhibited fatigue and self-estrangement. Instead of expressing—and easing—tensions, it created more of them. Years ago, she had swallowed instructions (draw large, draw small, draw the space between the figures, think depth, think contrast, think line, think density), and then had gone on to paint what was there or what she dreamed up. The pleasure was in the paints, the forms, the activity. Now a canvas was a problem to which she had to find a solution. It lay against the easel and said, *Let's go. Don't muck around. Do it right.* She put the easel away in the closet.

Even the boys brought no ease. Billy was gone, and hardly wrote. When he called, he was sweet but full—naturally—of his courses, his friends, his troubles, of the girl he'd be bringing back during the holidays. (There'd be at least an inner debate about sleeping arrangements. She put off thinking about it.) "Take it light, Ma." (Useless advice for her.)

Petey slid toward adolescence; she could feel the ungovernable energy which spurted into fury or wall-pounding music. (She shut herself in, sometimes with cotton in her ears.) On request, he'd lower the volume, but then "couldn't hear." (He wasn't listening to the music but to his inner racket. As was she.)

She smoked more and more. Petey told her she was addicted. "Addiction's a new idea," she said. "It's a passivity derived from television. You sit back and get everything for nothing. You don't need willpower. If I want, I can stop smoking in the middle of a cigarette. For good and all. I don't want to. I'm not aiming at immortality." Even she didn't believe this. She felt herself stranded in the shallowest part of her nature.

As for Kevin, well, they were still friends, but he was preoccupied with the problems of prosperity. And with its vehicle, Abby. When she spoke at the morning conference, Kevin—in fact, everyone but Susannah—listened as if the words came out of clouds. "Abby," said Terence, "knows where it is."

"What's the antecedent of 'it,' Terence?" asked Susannah. Terence thought she was joking.

Whatever *it* was, it brought Abby so many calls she had to

have her own line. There was also an answering service. She said she didn't want to bother other people with her calls. The messages were numerous; she was gone a lot. Only Kevin knew where.

"Where's Abby?" someone would ask.

"Seattle. On a Teamster story," said Kevin. Or, smiling with pride and delight, the nostrils flared on his handsome face, "London. There's something up in the TUC."

"Trade Union Conference," said Dame Mae. (They never ceased enlightening the recruits.)

"And something even juicier, if it works out."

"Let's hear it," said Terence, agitated, his feculent eyes convulsed with excitement. Terence no longer wore coat and tie to conferences; he dressed in striped turtleneck sweaters from which his grooved, turnip-white face rose uncertainly, as if it might sink forever when the sun did. "Give us the word, Kevin."

"She may get an interview with Macmillan."

"The ex–prime minister," said Dame Mae.

"Jesus," said Terence, "what a girl. We'll make history yet. Imagine that little mouse. Oh my. She is some little mouse."

"She's a born journalist," said Libba. "But fragile. And we don't always treat her right."

This was directed, not so gently, at Susannah. Abby had hinted that Susannah must have spilled the beans to Wursup about her Doyle piece. How else could the *Times* have published his piece so soon afterward? The *Magazine* worked weeks ahead of publication. The rug had been pulled out from under her; she'd been made to look foolish.

"A coincidence," said Dame Mae.

"I hope so," said Abby.

Susannah felt the peculiar looks, the odd pitch in Libba's voice. Well, she'd sown the wind, and must *cosechar tempestades*. It wasn't the first time. In the years with Will, Susannah had learned the power of guilt. She'd even looked the word up: it translated the Latin *debitum*. Guilt was debt. And then guilt paid the debt. And she'd paid. Year in and out she feared discovery. Yet wanted to be discovered. Hester Prynne had it easy. And the French collaborators who'd had their heads shaved. There you were exposed. So you learned to live with it. She got away with it; so she paid through the nose and kept paying.

Susannah despised the unrealistic system of sin and absolution; and yet she felt tormented by both guilt and lack of expiation. Two years of backdoor lovemaking, stripping in the kitchen, lying on floors while little Billy wandered around the house—oh, that was a cakewalk. After a while, she stopped hating herself—there were limits—and hated Will instead. Of course, by now, she'd put it all aside. It was all nonsense; she'd been a dope.

In any event, Susannah was quick to take blame, and though there was no point in going around admitting it, she did move away from the other Chouinardians. She did her work, reported on Honduras and Paraguay, read, studied, wrote and tried to keep out of the way.

Kevin cared for her still, as a pal. They went out to supper a few times, and though they talked only generally, and the evenings were short, they both enjoyed them. There was certainly no movement toward bed. That, they'd had for a few months, and then it just stopped. They weren't explainers or seekers of explanations. Not about sexual matters. They just got out of the habit of sleeping together—what was so complicated about that? Susannah could take it or leave it. (She was no orgasm counter; that was for cattle breeders.) She could use a trip to South America more.

Night after night, Susannah sat in the chair, smoking, getting through *La Prensa* and *O Estado de São Paolo*, taking notes for her reports, bearing up. Something would happen. Just go slowly. What were her troubles next to those she read about? She ate well, had fine sons, a good job. Look at the world. There was catastrophe, terrible division in every country she read about, riots, shortages, starvation, kidnapping, assassination, police death squads, incredible, ever-widening gaps between rich and poor. The world was like a mountain under afternoon sun, its crevasses spreading under the deceptive snow. Everyone knew it, and everyone hid from it. "It's always been like that. There are haves and have-nots, doers and idlers, the lucky and unlucky. It's the way of the world." Like people in a Swiss lounge watching tiny climbers inching their way down the lethal mountain, and thinking, How gorgeous, how beautiful, what a sight. "Beauty," like "tragic vision," was something Susannah hated now. It was a device used by the comfortable to handle dangerous situations. To stay comfortable, no, to hype comfort into something like ecstasy so you could ignore uncertainties, dangers, the peril in the mountains, wars, floods, earthquakes. "What a tragedy. Oh my God." Or, "How beautiful, how thrilling."

Wrong. It was wrong. And night after night, behind closed doors, Susannah held the newspapers and felt the world going to hell.

And then, as if Nature wanted to supply a pathetic totem of human disaster, word came from Fred that his father and Mona had killed themselves.

Wursup asked Petey if he wanted to fly to Chicago with him for the funeral. "If you need me, Dad." Then—a true Susannah—Petey felt guilty at the tepid, and refused, offer. "I should have gone. Poor Grandpa. Why do you think they did it, Momma?" He was in pajamas, which made him look younger and smaller than he looked in the daytime outfits, the sweaters and scarves which filled him out. (Sometimes he wore his heavy jacket around the house.) He hated being so slim; Susannah thought him perfect.

"I don't know. Dad doesn't think they were sick. There's just so much in people that they never let out. You know that. I'm sure it's true of you, too."

"Yep. I'm a real sphinx."

She rubbed his back. "I know that. I'm supposed to know you best, and you surprise me plenty. Grandpa may just have been tired of things. A person can run out of steam. And Mona may not have wanted to live without him. Or vice versa."

"He sure seemed energetic."

"Maybe he wanted to go before he lost it. He was a kind of dramatic type. He liked to make an impression. His poetry. All that. A little fellow who liked to show people he was really there. Dad once said his life was a quest for elevator shoes. Maybe going out this way was another pair."

"Momma!"

"I didn't mean it badly. I always liked Poppa. Mona, too. She was a funny kind of person. They don't seem like suicide types."

Petey lay on his side. So unlike Poppa Wursup, so slim, green-eyed, scrupulous, aristocratic, and Poppa such a blusterer, so pugnacious, and blunt-looking.

"Death and birth are so alike in some ways," she said. "You know, you come from nothing—you do, really; don't laugh—and then you go into nothing. Still, there's only one reason people are born. But there are millions of reasons why people die. And millions of ways. I don't have a clue about Grandpa and Mona. Dad'll probably find out."

17

For Wursup, everything in Hyde Park was also what it had been. Houses, trees, roofs topping one another, chips in walls. His memory was that spring in Hyde Park stormed the little lawns and flower beds, tulips standing up on every other lawn, gold, scarlet, pink, violet, like Rockettes dressed in shakos; fattened begonias burst; the cherry, redberry, magnolia and apple trees blossomed; the streets were all flowery. The steeples of the university poked through the emerald tracery into as blue a sky as he'd seen. The streets had a few more high rises, but they were mostly six-flats, burnt brown, gray, ochre, mixed with small houses, the old wooden ones built before the wood-enjoining ordinances of the eighties, and all sorts of brick ones from the wide, small-windowed planes of the Robie House to miniature English manor houses and French mansards. Odd high rises stuck up suddenly on low streets like big dogs lost among mutts. Everywhere, new greens, reds, whites, golds. It was much too beautiful a time to be in a bronze urn.

RICHARD STERN

Wursup had made arrangements with a crematorium from the airport in Brussels. (Mona's family made arrangements for her.) He arrived late in Chicago and stayed not at the house but at the Windermere, the hotel for the local Aunt Rachels. The next morning he walked to the little gray house on Fifty-fourth and Blackstone (bought in the twenties for what Poppa Wursup said was "the only song Grandpa Schneckler ever sang to me") and waited for whoever had seen the notice in the newspapers to show up.

By one o'clock, only three people came, the Chmilewskis, and a natty little fellow with a hearing aid, Mr. Jautakis. For two hours, .Wursup had sat alone in the empty house, stunned by the absentees. How could it be? He'd sent the notice to the papers himself. Didn't people read them anymore? Surely word got around. Because Poppa was his father, there'd probably been a picture. Poppa was a congenial man, and though he could be difficult, he'd always had friends. Perhaps the mourners had gone to Mona's funeral, on the Northwest Side, and hadn't got south yet. But he felt miserable. After all, he himself knew hundreds of people in this neighborhood. More than that came to an autographing party he'd had here downtown at Stuart Brent's. And now they weren't even obliged to buy a book.

Both Chmilewski and Jautakis had worked at People's Gas with Poppa. Chmilewski, a hardy, well-padded fellow who looked like a benign Beria, told twenty stories about his and Poppa's adventures in the cellars of Chicago. All were encounters with rodents, dogs or sex-starved housewives. (No wonder Poppa spent most of his home life stretched on a bed, falling asleep beside the radio.) Mrs. Chmilewski cut him off at the pass at Story Twenty-one. "Station break, Lester." They left with condoling head shakes and shoulder claps.

Jautakis arrived as they were leaving, shook hands and exchanged sad grunts with them, and introduced himself as "the man on whom your dad tried out his poems. I got, de-

spite this"—touching his hearing aid—"a good ear for good
poems. Which your dad had a gift for." He sat straight, severe
and comic, like the actor Franklin Pangborn playing a suspi-
cious bank examiner. (Beyond this, though, he looked familiar to Wursup, and not till Jautakis left did he remember
why.) Mr. Jautakis refused coffee. He had, he said, sent ten
dollars in Poppa's name to the university's poetry magazine.
"For Simon, gas was not a whole life. He was an ency-
clopedia. But who am I telling this? As if you don't know." He
swiveled around and pointed to the Barca Lounger behind
the dark glass of the television set. "There I sat many an hour
listening. If I only had a good memory."

"Mr. Jautakis, when I come across the poems, I'll have copies made for you."

Jautakis nodded kindly, but not, it seemed, in response to
this offer. Either he wasn't interested in marring his nostalgia
with the poems themselves or his hearing aid had gone off.

After five or ten unconnecting minutes, Jautakis rose without warning (as if some invisible spouse had yanked him up)
and took off with the wordless head-shaking which seemed to
be the form of condolence for employees of People's Gas.
Wursup watched him scoot off down Blackstone, and it was
then he realized that he was at least the facial clone of a Central Asian mountain chief, the Wali of Swat, whom he had interviewed nearly twenty years ago. "Who, why, where and
what is this nutty fellow, the Wali of Swat?" He'd driven a jeep
to the little palace under the cream and purple granite peaks
below Afghanistan and China. Another April. Nomads were
pouring into Afghanistan through the Khyber; it was lambing
time; men who looked as though they'd rip trees out of their
way rather than walk around them held bundles of black and
silver in their arms, the karakul and merino lambs. They
strapped them around donkeys decked out with loops of white
jasmine. The Pathans wore roses behind their ears, and ban-
doliers of cartridges x-ed across their chests. (Shepherds

took guns into those fields.) The bazaars were fantastic. Ten
thousand genetic Rembrandts had made those faces. Sakas,
Chinese Kushans, Turanians, Arabs, Mongols, Moguls, Wa-
zirs, Mahsuds, Pathans, Pushtu, Ðurani. An epic gargle. And
the chieftans had great names, the Wong of Bong, the Nono
of Spiti, the Faquir of Ipi—the last a mean little toughie who
lived in rock caves and gave the English trouble in the war. (A
droop-mustached British attaché had shown Wursup the faquir's wartime receipts from the Axis paymaster, Quaroni).
Half the world moved through the markets. *Provindahs*
picked up duck eggs, sheep, shawls, myna birds in twig cages,
crates of Fanta, Pepsodent, razors, sugar cane, turbans, kara-
kuli, kegs of brown honey thick with bee corpses. Sitting on a
doorsill, Wursup listened to a beautiful unveiled woman
honey-seller play on a lute the size of a pear. For days, he'd
driven in and out of the gorgeous valleys. The wheat fields
sweated blood-red poppies. In the middle of them was the
kingdom of Swat, where the old wali—Jautakis's double—
climbed mountains while his son, Jahan Zeb, ran things. Jahan Zeb wore a tweed jacket and not flannels, but a sort of
green diaper. "My worries are the herdsmen of Chitral and
Dir," he said. "They shoot our sheep. I have eleven thousand
good soldiers. They are not sheep." They ate kebab and honey on a terrace under the mountains. Mr. Jautakis's double,
back from his climb, joined them. They discussed the Afghan
plan to set up Pushtunistan. The old wali did not approve.
"Always these rearrangements." Jahan Zeb said, "Moscow is
more remote from us than the stars. And yet, someone plucks
a string there, and a year later, we vibrate here." All over the
world, high-minded polytechnicians and national liberators
arranged one another's murders. Weeks after his lunch in the
gorgeous valley, Wursup's pal McHale went down in Enrico
Mattei's plane over Linati. The altimeter had been doctored
by Laurent, one of De Gaulle's *barbouzes*. The herdsmen of
Chitral and Dir at least wore their cartridges on their chest.

Wursup's copy dealt as much with lambs and poppies as with them. The world needed at least the dream of serenity.

The phone rang, a woman asking for Mona. Wursup said she was not in, and it was then he saw the People's Gas envelope on the phone table. "For Fred" it read in his father's large blocky script, but the salutation was "Dearest Carlo."

My papers are in Mom's old desk. There's money in Hyde Park Federal and checking accounts in Hyde Park National and University. Plus fifty shares of AT and T. Enough to get us buried (burn me!) and put away. I don't care where, that part's for the birds. I wish I'd been more for you. My poems are in the bureau. Good bye, dear Carlo.

YOUR POPPA

After Jautakis left, it had rained, heavily and briefly. Wursup hadn't heard it. When he went out—nobody else would come—everything was hung low, branches, flowers. Clematis dripped against the iron palings of the house, but the air was silvery, chipper. Wursup walked across Fifty-fifth Street and headed south for the Midway on Dorchester. There was almost no one else in these quiet streets. It was like being inside an ear. The kids must be in school or tucked up for naps. He walked past the gray and white row of Federal houses on Dorchester, then an enclave of glassy houses set at odd angles on miniature hills, like a mimicry of suburban *luxe*. Little Hyde Park. Little Poppa. After all those loud years, no more noise. Poppa had been a small Jewish boy in a west-side Polish neighborhood. He said he'd learned the back alleys "like a mafia man has to, or the way Jewish kids in Germany must have learned to take off at the flash of the wrong armband." He'd learned how to fight: "You gotta break something, come up low, grab the back, then get in the knee while they're falling. Or give 'em the hand heel at the eyes." There'd been no thought of college; Grandpa Wurszup (Poppa had dropped the *z*) was a presser, a muttering little man turned blue by the steam, his right arm, the one that pulled the hot boards, outsize and strong as a fighter's. The year his grandpa died, age sixty-nine, twelve-year-old Wursup arm wrestled him, using both arms and all his weight, but couldn't budge the pillar; the gray gnome had watched his effort abstractedly, just one more mystery in the fog of work and food that appeared—who knew?—to be his life.

Wursup crossed to the Midway. The grass perspired gleaming drops. In front of the lab school, yellow busses snoozed; on the tennis courts a girl in shorts was sweeping off puddles. Wursup walked to the statue of the Polish king Stanislas, hooded in stone like a medieval tank, found a dry spot on the steps and sat looking west down the shimmering green horn beyond which Washington Park lay in a thicket of light. There was a baby-skin smell in the air; the evaporating droplets seeded with hot-bread smells from the west-side bakeries. Belts of glassy light, the grunts of cars, the innocent fragrance of the air. It was beautiful here. Every night Poppa came home in his coveralls with PEOPLE'S GAS stitched in red script. At twelve, Wursup had been humiliated by that; he'd asked his mother to get Poppa to change at work, and she had, saying she liked him so much in his civvies. Such foolish shame in tranquil places like Hyde Park, which made—and rightly— sensations of a mugging here and there. Since he'd left, after college, Wursup had realized how pastoral a place it was, at least for the good burghers around the university. He'd seen such terrible things: between Jidda and Mecca, the dried-out meat scraps of pilgrim corpses along the roads. (Dhow captains dodged the port fees and told the Mecca-bound they were only a mile from the shrine.) Near the Custom House, he'd watched an executioner drive a knife into a man's side.

When the man fell toward the stabber, another lopped off his head with a backhand slash. The popeyed ball of meat was put in a sack, flies sheeted the black blood, and the market crowd went back to its sweets and coffee. So far from Hyde Park.

Sunday nights, the Wursups didn't eat at the rickety table in the kitchen alcove, but in the living room, sitting around the little arched radio cathedral where the popes of Sunday entertainment offered masses. Delicatessen: hot pastrami, German potato salad—freckled with bacon bits—and hot coffee cake, the sugary ice melting into yellow cake pulp. Poppa roared himself purple; Momma had to calm him, open his shirt buttons, give him water. Her black eyes—*his* eyes—shone with the pleasures of things then. Not the sleeping windows they were when he saw her last. (He should—but would not—go to her now. It would be like visiting a bush. Worse, the bush was his mother.) On those Sunday nights, they were made a happy family by Edgar Bergen and Charlie Mac-Carthy, Jack Benny and Mary, Rochester, Don, and Phil Harris. He would always know those voices. During the war, Poppa shifted gear, sat up straight; it was time for Winchell's flashes from Casablanca, Moscow and London (mixed in evenly with Hollywood and Broadway, the voice unchanged for bombed London or a bombed starlet). Maybe his dreamy hunger for the magic cities had grown under the rain of those bulletins. All through Hyde Park High and the university, the need to see them ached. He knew he would get to them, there was no question. (Unlike Billy, who had little confidence and said his friends believed you didn't get what you wanted. "You were born at a lucky time, Dad. In the demographical catbird seat.")

Good bye, dear Carlo.

Never had Poppa spoken as affectionately. Though after he'd spanked him—not often, and always with his backless slipper—he'd come in, pat his head and say he hoped he wouldn't have to do that again. Poppa took him to Comiskey Park and the Planetarium and boasted about his compositions. "I think you get the gift of words from me, though I didn't know I had it till you showed me it was in us." The sillier parts of Poppa's character hardened after Momma's brain dissolved. He turned himself into a character with his rant and his doggerel. Maybe it was the way he competed with the high-powered thinkers of the neighborhood. He became a kook, and Mona came along as his audience and subject.

There were glacial rifts in Wursup, times when he was as unfeeling as the chemicals which made him. A year would go by without his writing Poppa a card. And his mother—whom he'd once loved so much he couldn't bear thinking of her when he was away—he couldn't bear to think of now, for other reasons. What a mystery it was. All these currents, hot and cold, running out of a person's arctic and tropic gulfs. "I became a mystery to myself." That was Augustine at nineteen, but by thirty he'd worked things out. It was simple if you were what Malraux called "a demon of the absolute." And Poppa? Had he ever solved himself? Someone said suicide was the most philosophical human act. Had Poppa figured something out at last?

Wursup shook himself, did a few knee bends—these were getting harder for him—and then walked down Fifty-ninth. The Midway was almost treeless now. They'd cut down the sick elms. But the tennis courts were filled. Hyde Parkers waited at the edge of their pleasures and sprang quickly to them.

He walked north on Kenwood, past the glass widow peaks of University High School toward the houses and lawns. Flowers, berries, buds, leaves, were all smiles again; and the lawns shimmered. Even ugly houses looked lovely in back of these elegant little lawns.

In the middle of the block, there was one awful lawn, full of rheumatoid tufts of grass. An old fellow in a beat-up denim shirt and trousers stooped over them, scything furiously with the blade of a kitchen scissors. Sockless, his veiny ankles soil-stained, the laces of his sneakers drooping perilously, he leaped from tuft to tuft. As Wursup walked by, the old fellow looked up. His gray eyes were innocent, baffled.

Professor Macfarlane. Wrinkled, shrunk, gray, not a red hair left, but the same tough muzzle and child's eyes. *Cultivant son jardin.* In his fashion: hacking away.

"Mr. Macfarlane." The scissors blade flashed defensively.

"Mr. Macfarlane, you don't remember me. I'm an old student of yours. From the survey of western philosophy. Fred Wursup."

Something stirred in the grim old face. Pushing on the lawn, Macfarlane got up, came over to Wursup and examined him. "Of course," he said. He held out his hand, dropping the scissors an inch from his foot. They shook hands. "Are you zuh journalist? I read your book. A good book. Strong, right on the mark. What are you doing here? Don't tell me zuh university's started giving honorary degrees to someone beside old scholars?"

"I'm just visiting. For a few hours. I'm off this evening. I grew up here. It's so nice to run into you. I'm glad you liked the book. I didn't think you'd bother with stuff like that."

"Why? A first-rate book. Full of reality and fact. I'd forgotten completely you were a student of mine. I'll have to look it over again, see if I can find zat I did you any harm. Ha ha. I'm glad I read it before I knew. Wait." And he ran like a mountain goat up the steps, his soles just missing the laces. What a preservative philosophic fury was. In a minute, he was back, carrying the familiar, repulsive dust jacket of the first edition (a soiled American flag with the title scrawled across in purple). "Would you inscribe it for me? It'll make an instant heirloom for zuh Macfarlanes." He had a pen ready, an old Parker, which, as Wursup wrote, dribbled ink from its tattered rubber sock. TO MY OLD TEACHER, PROFESSOR DOUGLAS MAC-

FARLANE WHO, 25 YEARS AGO, RIGHTLY FOUND ME UNFIT FOR
HIGHER THINGS. FREDERICK WURSUP.
"Zhank you, Frederick. I'm sure I found you fit for any-
zing." He closed the book on the still-wet inscription. "It's a
treasure for me. Very few of my students have amounted to
much. Next time, come have coffee wiz me."
What a costume ball time was. The flamethrower of the forties was now a powdery old goat, the fury rent only on his terrible lawn. "Good-bye," Macfarlane called after him. Wursup
looked back. The old fellow was waving the scissors at him.

There were pieces of paper tacked, taped and wedged into
the front door, and on the steps were five or six plants and two
dishes wrapped in silver foil. "The Seidmans were here," read
one piece of paper; another, "The paper said you'd be receiving at three. Guess there was a mix-up. We came to say our
sorrows to you. Our hearts are with Si and Mona." It was
signed "The Beckers, Norm and Alice Fryberg, The Hams,
Esther Keller."
Wursup took in the papers, the plants, the dishes. There
were thirty-five or forty names. He copied them into a notebook—people he knew, people he didn't.
Upstairs, he started going through drawers. In Poppa's bureau, under his socks and handkerchiefs, was a cardboard box
with tie clips, collar fasteners, cuff links, a gold ring, pictures
of his parents, of Momma, of Wursup as a boy. In the corner
was a fifty-year-old marriage manual.
Three days ago, Poppa and Mona had been walking around
this room. He was probably inhaling some of the molecules
they'd breathed.
He telephoned the lawyer, asked him please to get someone
in here to pack up all the personal things and send them to
New York. Except for one chair he'd mark—the seat had
been embroidered by Momma—the furniture could be dis-
posed of with the house.

* * *

He called a taxi. "O'Hare." They took off along the green powdery lake, along the IC tracks, past the Douglas pillar, the museums, Soldier's Field, then west on the Eisenhower and under the post office to the Kennedy turnoff and the truck-heavy northbound traffic. The low, foolish hindparts of the city spread west and north of them; east, the heavy coppery muscles of the Loop. Then they were out of it, into the backside of jumbled brick, where Poppa had grown. Red-brown, thick white, the knobby towers of the Polish churches rose from the throbbing tundra, warehouses, factories, Chevy dealers, merchandise depots, printing plants, the files and files of brick houses.

"Bear right," said Wursup. "Take the Edens."

"You said O'Hare, right?"

"Right, but I changed my mind. Get off at Winnetka."

Momma sat in the garden with her Volunteer, a girl from Mundelein College. The matron brought him out. "We haven't seen you for a very long time." Momma sat on a bench, holding a glass of milk, watching, or seeming to watch, two ladies whacking vaguely at croquet balls. "Momma, darling," said Wursup. His mother looked up. Oh Lord. Grandma. All iron gray, her hair clipped but touched up, wavy—there was good care here. The little black eyes, the features thicker, closer to the portrait of Grandma on the floor of his closet than to his sense of Momma. She looked at him, not recognizing, no, but seeing him. "Momma, dear." He bent and kissed her cheek. Dry, grainy, a bit of Momma's smell.

"It's an honor meeting you, Mr. Wursup," said the girl, who was small, sweet-faced, eyeglassed. Her hair was beautiful, deep red and waterfalled down her back. "I've been with Mrs. Wursup for three months now. Every afternoon but Wednesday and Sunday."

"How good of you," said Wursup. "How lucky she is. How do you find her?"

"Oh, just fine. She's really wonderful. No trouble at all. Very sweet. She drinks her milk; she buttons her smock. She just doesn't talk. But I think she knows her way out here. I think she prefers this bench. And knows when to go back inside."

Wursup knelt beside his mother and looked into her face, which looked at his. It sensed something; he was sure of it. It was not unhappy, not scared. "Momma, darling," he said. "It's Carlo." He took the milk carefully from her and handed it to the Volunteer, then held her dry light hands. "Momma, dear. Poppa died. My poppa. Simon. Si died, Momma." The black eyes were on him. Was there curiosity, attention, puzzlement? The mouth was neutral, easy, but the head seemed to move a bit from side to side. Or did it? Had the words passed through her ears? Had they moved slowly into her brain, fallen somewhere in the dark pool of old events? "Momma, darling," said Wursup. "Momma, dear. Poppa died." Then, worn out, absolutely worn out, he let his head drop into his mother's green lap. Only for seconds, though. There was just no point in it.

18

The De Witts and Tommy Buell were giving a hail-and-farewell party, the hail for Cicia, who was back after three weeks of radiation therapy, the farewell for Gopal, who was flying to Calcutta. Tommy needed the party for himself. It had been a somber time in New York. He'd stayed at the hospital till Cicia said it was better to stay away. He'd tried everything in New York to divert himself from what was happening to Cicia, and that included a try at plunging in deeper, sitting in on a doctors' conference in which Cicia's case was debated. The radiologist wanted to pour in "more rads", the immunologist—a flamboyant Serbian lady with ghost-colored hair—said they must "smash it with everything we've got," which, as far as Tommy followed, seemed to be ten or fifteen other diseases competing for her corpuscular defenses. Pictures of his daughter's innards filled the wall of the little conference room: dense settlements bordered by bleak spaces and epigastric mews.

Tommy was dazzled and nauseated at these frightful versions of his baby, but he'd asked for it, and the bald, green-eyed surgeon, Dr. Giessen, said, "I suppose it's a breach, but what the hell." Tommy tried to follow the interpretation of the sick terrain, the debate about fibrous adhesions, white-cell counts, bone scans, but gave up, thanked everyone, said he left it to them, they were wonderful caretakers for his daughter. He walked down the hospital's L past the beeping monitors of dysfunction to Cicia's room. No, he couldn't go in; there was a frightful weight in him. He'd tried to make his daughter into what would slake his curiosity, a subject. (Would he write about her in his pamphlets, describe the doctors, the conference?) He went to the window at the end of the corridor (wood sashed, single glazed); it was dark outside; his face shone in it—so old with its ugly dewlaps, his chin docked in ports of fat. What had happened to him? Had he been deflected, like Solomon, toward alien gods, and been punished with burnt seed? (His wonderful daughter seared by terrible machines.)

He opened Cicia's door. It was dark, but he could make her out, asleep, shorn, shrunken, battered. He couldn't look, but bent over her blanketed foot and kissed it.

A week later, Cicia was recovered enough to go home. Tommy had given Tina carte blanche to get Cicia what was needed to make herself "fit to be seen," and he stayed away till she said she was ready to see him. He, Tina and James DeWitt planned a party, and—partly to lighten their own spirits—began thinking of vacations she might like to take: Paris, Rome, Greek islands, the sea, the mountains. "The idea's to spread life out for her again," said Tommy. "Things aren't over for her. The doctors haven't given up." He'd never liked spenders of other people's money, let alone other people's lives, but the doctors he saw weren't generals or belligerent senators sending the young off to die. They competed to save her; he could feel that Dr. Giessen cared deeply for her. "It's not Cicia's beauty but her life that counts," he told Tommy, his little green eyes full of feeling. Giessen loved Cicia and hated her cancer; Tommy would swear by him. "Whatever will is," he said, "Cicia has it." Tommy knew about renewal. He'd been in the reclamation business. And he had seen people farming on the battlefields of two wars. He believed in life's regenerative power. At the Hiroshima Museum, he'd seen pictures of the city after the atom bomb. It was an ocean of smoking rubble; the only *things* preserved were toilet bowls, thousands of them, glittering in the sun. But outside the museum was the newest, loudest, liveliest city in Japan.

Cicia too would have a museum of damage within her; but it could be a strength, a reminder to renew.

"We'll just have to remind her what life can be," he said to Tina and James. " '*Despontar o dia*,' they say in Brazil for the first drink. 'To take the edge off the day.' "

Wursup hadn't seen Henry Knoblauch's son more than twice since he'd known him as the boy genius of the American School in Rome. Little Benny had been a charming, wide-eyed boy with a large mouth, "the mouth of the Knoblauchs," said his father, "and I have the dental bills to prove it." Splinter-legged little Benny said, "Poppa, the size of the mouth diminishes the size of the bills. More room for the teeth to spread and the dentist to work." Benny skipped half a dozen grades. Only the saintly naiveté of brilliance had kept him immune from the resentments of classmates and age-mates. Here he was, a skinny, redheaded little frog dealing with the drug problem at the school: Doris had found him, age ten, puffing away experimentally at marijuana; she'd thought it was a cigarette—horror enough—but Benny told her it wasn't tobacco: he was trying out "the least powerful of the cannabinols." Sister Jennifer supplied the translation. Doris hit—not Benny, how could a mother hit such a child?—the ceiling. "Your father will deal with this." Wursup, in Rome to do a piece on the Vatican Congress, had come home with Knoblauch, who summoned his huge-eyed little *Wunderkind* to the terrace, where he and Wursup drank Orvieto amidst blooming frangipani.

"Do you understand the meaning of drug-taking?" Knoblauch asked the little boy. "What it does to your system?"

Said Benny, "Not entirely, Baba. I'm not into glycolate esters, though the notion of euphorohallucinogens is exciting. I know what happens with substitutions around the ring. And you can bet I'm scared of any suppression of left hemispheric powers. Still, I have so little artistic power, it might be a good thing for me to rev up my right hemisphere."

"What can be done?" crowed grinning Knoblauch.

In Benny's room were tomes—hauled in from the American library or bookstores—that weighed large fractions of his eighty pounds: treatises on economics, the mathematics of traffic, chemistry, thermodynamics. Benny also read five or six novels a week, though what he made of Heathcliff, Prince Myshkin or Emma Bovary, Wursup could not imagine. Benny shied clear of nothing—comic books, his parents' friends, music, painting, Italian football games. The world was one pleasure dome of excitement; everything that existed enchanted the blue-eyed little frog who was so clearly a human prince.

Wursup saw Benny again when the boy first came to the States to attend Grinnell College, in Iowa—he'd wanted to "become American" and thought the best way was to go to a good small school in the middle of the country, where he could do the requirements with one hand, or an index finger, and chart his own course with the other. The Wursups had put him up for the night and then Susannah put him on the plane. Wursup hadn't seen him again until Benny had delivered a package of Via Cassia Vecchia figs from his father when he was doing his one-year doctorate in theoretical physics at Columbia. Benny had come by Wursup's apartment with the cellophane sack, and Wursup didn't recognize him.

The little boy—he'd been that till his last year at Grinnell—was lost in a great benign bulk, and the red hair was so clearly sparse that one could feel it as a kind of irrelevant brightness of sky minutes before storms break over a city.

Now, at twenty-five, Benny was still large, though thinner; his head was stippled with red; the froggy jaw had not been much altered by the dental work. The mental works still went full blast. He'd come down to Wursup's in a bus with an "interesting number," and spilled off the operations which made these apparently casual digits a key to—if Wursup remembered—some sort of "non-Abelian marvel" about "self-generating fields." (Benny himself—Abelian keeper of numerical sheep—was a kind of perpetual generator of himself. What essential relation did he bear to Henry Knoblauch or bitter Doris?)

So when Benny called with news neither of his father nor of the universe but of a party in honor of Cicia Buell, his miraculousness took on yet another coat. "I was also surprised we had friends in common," said Benny. "The odds are hard to calculate. It'll be nice to see you again, though the auspices aren't the happiest."

"You mean, Cicia hasn't much time?"

"I know next to nothing. At least she's out of the hospital and feeling better. The party is also for my friend Gopal. That is a definite farewell."

Benny said he'd pick him up. "But you're on the West Side, Benny."

"It gives me a chance to walk, and to see a part of town I seldom see. And to talk with you."

Three good reasons. Benny had become more worldly, but not to the degree of the simple delivery of wishes (which, unlike reasons, were undebatable).

So, on Saturday, there was Benny, in his party outfit, his great persimmon head coming from a steak-colored turtleneck and dice-squared jacket, (quick pickups from an

Army-Navy store on Upper Broadway, priced for disposal before merciful disintegration). Benny had been chewing a salami; there were meat flecks on his large lips, and he exhaled spicy aromas. "The high-tide doomsters will have to postpone disaster day" was his substitute for "How are you?"

"Hi, Benny. I don't follow."

"It's a beautiful day. These climatologists are rewriting history on tidal charts. High-tide eras bring cold weather, cold weather brings saviors."

It was refreshing to get down to cases. It was like a Dostoevski novel: no hellos, just enter the drawing room and make for the other man's throat. Or, in Benny's case, for his theory. (Perhaps it all began as a fortress the little boy built to keep out the silent animosities at home. Why fool with civilities if they were just sugared poisons?)

"Shall we walk? At fourteen m.p.h., I should lose a fifth of a pound. Which gives me a little cake margin."

"Maybe we should get down there early," said Wursup. "Cicia might tire." On a walk, Benny would formulate questions about every third inch of New York; theories would smother the avenues; he'd arrive at Cicia's so logy with cerebration there'd be no room for his feelings. Whatever they were.

"Right-o," said Benny. "Does the Lexington train get you to the shuttle?"

"I'm loaded," said Wursup. "We'll take a cab."

It had been many weeks since he'd seen Cicia, and the intensity of the first meetings had evaporated. He was even somewhat surprised to find himself included in a return-home party. Had there been that much established? He'd forgotten. He'd been to Belgium and Chicago; much had happened. And Cicia? Well, she'd also gone a long way and come back.

Such motion didn't allow for rootage. Nor did their sort of absence make hearts fonder. Loving wasn't that easy. *Opening up, letting go, giving in*: all these seam-busting partici-

226

ples, as if one were a sack with a fixed number of emotional goods, the only problem being distribution. The other notion was as bad: emotions like muscles had to be exercised. Keep in emotional trim, feel deep, feel big, fall in love and treasure hatred. Otherwise it's emotional obesity, the heart's death. Yet anyone who went out hunting emotional truffles was a pig. There should be no strategy for feeling. If you turned yourself into the cold eye at the edge of other people's frenzy, you became what every good actor became—a cynic who believes that everyone is, like himself, a performer of significant gestures. Newspapermen had an added vice. Knowing they could not only spot the telltale gestures but put saleable words to the most complex negotiations, the most beautiful humans and the most stupendous disasters, they felt wiser than the negotiators, more beautiful than the beauties, more wicked than the disaster bringers, more human than its sufferers. Understanding everything, committed to nothing.

Benny bent toward the cabbie, who was telling him that a Mets pitcher better stick to pitching. "Seaver's posing so much for the menswear he can't throw his fucking curve." The sun was wedged in the Macy's-Gimbels gulch. Benny said he'd never followed baseball. The driver, Louis Schneider, number 86739, said he wasn't missing a thing but aggravation. "What do you do for a living, kid?" He failed to beat a light at Fourteenth. A plump girl in a blue Avanti squeezed in on his left. Schneider called out, "What else did Dad give you for Christmas, Gloria?"

"I'm a physicist," said Benny, making it easy.

"Good boy," said Schneider. "Keep it up."

"You've got a very strong number there," said Benny, looking at the shield. "Eight-six-seven-three-nine." And he told Louis where the number fit in the great scheme of integral permutations.

"I'm glad you like it," said Louis. "To tell you the straight truth, it never occurred to me." At the Washington Square arch, a blond girl dressed like a Chicopee squaw was playing a recorder among the sandal sellers. "You like that?" asked Louis.

"Like what?" asked Benny.

"That blond Indian playing the flute there. Is that something?"

Benny looked back and said Marie Antoinette and her attendants dressed up as milkmaids. "It's a form of apology to have-nots. And perhaps propaganda."

"I could listen to you for days, kid," said Louis. They turned into Charles Street, wound past the pens of decabbed trucks and pulled up in front of DeWitt's house. "Watch yourself around here, kid," said Louie.

Benny said he usually watched other people, but thanked him for his advice and the pleasant drive.

Tina opened the door. She carried a half-filled highball glass and was—or sounded—unsteady. She wore a yellow dress, and her voice was cheery, if not her eyes. She gave Benny a one-armed hug and pecked Wursup's cheek. "It's a grand shindig," she said. "Get ready to whirl. Take off your clothes, eat, drink, dance. Let wine put peonies in your face. That's a poem." Wursup hoped she was only the doorkeeper, not the keynoter.

It turned out she was whooping it up for a somewhat bedraggled lot. There were eight or ten youngish people standing around, drinking and talking, but not much more gaily or fluently than the DeWitt family portraits. Tommy and Cicia were sitting on a sofa in the darkest part of the room. Tommy had a highball; Cicia's mouth touched a silver-rimmed cup frequently, but without getting anything out of it. Gopal, in necktie and black suit, stood with a small red-haired girl and drank vodka. James moved around, stirring whatever conversational coals might ignite. Wursup and Benny were what he

228

needed. They made their way to Cicia, then were taken in hand by James and put at the center of other groups. Soon there were two conversational bonfires. Benny made his own fire; Wursup excited one. Questions and compliments came his way like forms to fill out. He managed for a while, and then the weight of Cicia, sitting quietly on the sofa, made this unbearable. He went over and sat with her.

She did not seem to be looking beyond the rim of her cup. Very still. And Wursup felt there was somehow less of her than there had been, more than just weight loss. There was even something askew in her, he couldn't tell what—the pallor, an odd stiffness in her hair, an aura of fragility. When he'd first shaken hands with her, she looked at him only a second and then said drinks were across the room. Now Tommy moved over on the couch and Wursup sat beside her and asked when they'd have another walk.

"Even wanting to take one will be nice," she said.

So it's down there, thought Wursup, down in that dendrite soup where all the connections boiled into the will. The soup had cooled in Cicia, as it must have in Poppa. It was the deepest trouble of all. He'd seen a Montagnard village days after a murderous raid. Everyone there, whatever age, was old. Babies flopped at breasts; childrens' eyes looked nowhere. In concentration camps, the term for the will-less was "the Moslems." Cicia wasn't that far gone. Even if the primary mechanisms had been tinkered with, there were others. Find another pilot light, and the soup could boil again. Wursup had gone back to the Montagnard village eight months later, and life had started up.

Cicia was dressed in a green velvet pant suit. She wore lipstick and rouge, and she responded. Perhaps she was even testing despair, like an artist, to see if she could manage there. Not to use it, but as a form of vaccination. Will Eddy made mental lists of terrible alternatives on the principle that nature always surprised you. Perhaps Cicia was vaccinating herself with a small death to keep off the large one. "You look fine enough to want anything."

"Tina and Daddy went shopping. I've got lots of nice new things. A bit like a costume exhibition. And not just the clothes."

"Cicia," said Tommy. "Your energy level is low. Naturally. But you're beautiful, and you're structurally sound. What would get her back on a faster track, Mr. Wursup?" Tommy's own flesh glowed; he looked superb in soft flannels and a polo coat that no assembly line produced, but his voice was shot with a puzzlement that made the gorgeous colors a Pagliacci front.

"Would you like to go somewhere quiet and talk for a while?" asked Wursup. "We could go to your room."

Across the way, Gopal was seized and asked to make a farewell address. He looked fragile in his black suit, a teak figure wrapped for shipment. Alcohol had fed his melancholy with a certain boisterousness, and he rippled with excitement in his thin black suit.

Sinking Cicia, ballooning Gopal, baffled Tommy, reeling unhappy Tina, and Benny, sprinkling intelligence over students, lawyers, musicians, accountants: these added up to a party. What a strange affair society was. All over New York, there were gatherings more or less like this, display cases, proving grounds, ceremonies of foreplay and farewell.

Gopal went behind the lacy table full of cheese and nuts and fat white shrimp. Tina stood dreamily, a champagne glass in hand. He took her other hand, lifted it a bit, and she said, "It's time to speak up, Gopal." Gopal's black eyes seemed half his fine little face. Ruefully, they surveyed the beautiful room, the scarlet carpet, the plumes and ruffles of ancestral De Witts, the rainbow of petits fours, the silver scoops, the faces of his American friends, the square, softly skeptic face of Tina, her little eyes like punctures under her heavy brow.

He shook his head, made the *namaste* gesture, palms together, swung to and from the chest. "I'm staying," he said. "I won't go."

There were cheers, yes-yesses, laughs. Tina said, "You'll go, but you'll be back soon. Now a little speech."

"Let's listen to Gopal," said Cicia, and she called, "We'll miss you, Gopal."

And Gopal, noticing Cicia directly for the first time, said, "I will miss you, Cicia. All of you. Can anyone imagine how much?"

"Help us," said Tina. "Tell us."

"An occasion has its own brain," said Gopal. "If it means me to speak, I speak."

"Speak, occasion, speak," said the red-haired girl (one of Gopal's sexual safety valves).

"The grotesque idea has spun out of my destiny: I must go home. I am Hindu and Marxist. How can I be propelled by an occasion? I can. Marx said commodities fell in love with money and wooed it with their glances. So departure has fallen in love with me. It's seducing me. Or trying to. Maybe I will fall in love with it. So I will depart now, and then, who knows, be departing from where I arrive. Then the love affair will be over, and I will be back with those I love because I was made to love them. At least, in this phase of my soul's progress. Man is born American but is everywhere in Delhi, Malaysia, the Congo. All we must do is unite, throw off our foreignness and melt in the American pot together. May it not be so long."

Tina put down her glass, took Gopal's little head between her hands and kissed him on the lips. There were hear-hears and other cheery bustlings. James opened more champagne.

"Want some?" Wursup asked Cicia. She shook her head. "Want to talk, then?"

She got up, a kind of velvety meadow. Wursup trailed her into the high, girlish room with the posters and—now—his postcards tacked and taped to dressers, walls, bed rests. "If I take off here," she said, "it'll be among masterpieces."

"You're psyching yourself up for something," he said.

"Nope. I'm too tired. I get little flashes, and I don't have the energy to blink. What the hell. They poured half a star into me."

"You'll throw lots of that off," he said, drawing on old draughts of Lew Ayres and Lionel Barrymore in white uniforms, frowning deeply over the troubled innards of Hollywood emergencies. "But you looked mighty forlorn down there. You worry a pal."

"I could worry a pal plenty more. But we better lighten up here a little." She reached for, but couldn't reach, a lamp; he did, then lit up four or five. Their shadows ran up the twelve-foot walls; the daylight scarcely appeared on the slats of the French doors. "Cicia's cave," said Cicia. "I should make you something magic, turn you into a pig, but there's nothing but tea. And you'll have to do it yourself. In the cabinet, the one behind Mishima."

There was a picture of the almost nude Japanese writer lying on a rock by the water. He looked like a city of muscles. "So Cicia has her dreamboats, too. Very revering. I knew him."

"You're so lucky. How could he have sliced up such a body?"

Wursup boiled water. "I only saw him a few times. In the fifties. He was a charmer. Very Western. He told me a story I wrote up. About the general—I forget his name—who'd performed the last ritual suicide. Mishima was absolutely lit up about him. I thought he was putting on a show." He took two packets out of the little orange trunk of Twining's Ceylon and dropped them in mugs, poured in the water and brought them over to the couch. Cicia just managed to hold on. "Cheers," he said, touching his turquoise mug to her green one. Some of the fumes mingled. "It was the day the Japanese cabinet voted to surrender. The general opposed it, but the emperor cast the decisive note. General Anami—that's the name—helped write the emperor's speech. It was the first time the people had ever heard the emperor. The idea that God *had* a voice was mind-splitting. The speech itself was full of the antique idioms reserved for imperial usage. 'The war has developed not necessarily to Japan's advantage.' Anami didn't hear it. He wrote a farewell haiku, something like, 'Basking in the Imperial Sunlight in life, I have not a syllable to bequeath.' A friend came in while he made the other preparations, some colonel who told Mishima the story. The general put on a white shirt the emperor had given him, folded his coat around the picture of a son who'd been killed in the war, read the colonel his poem, went out on the verandah and pulled the sword across his belly. Then he drew it out and tried to cut his neck artery. Mishima said no *gaijin* could appreciate that refinement."

The tea, or the story, or maybe the thought of Mishima's astonishing body had put better color in Cicia. She leaned into her pillows, not as if exhausted but with ease. Her long, green-velveted legs were crossed at the ankles. "You look beautiful, Cicia. You are beautiful, but now you look it." A little squirt of something like fright went across her face. "It's so. A special sort of beauty. I can't remember seeing it anywhere."

"Two days ago, I dreamed I was a shark—the one in *Jaws*, I guess—and I was swimming around the world trying to bite off limbs to make me human. It was terrible. Then I was sixteen criminals sitting around talking criminal. Each one missed some part—an arm, a nose, a breast."

"It's awful stuff, Cicia."

"It's awful what's happened."

"It doesn't show. It hasn't come to the surface. Maybe you're fighting it off in those dreams."

"Sure."

She drank awhile; they said nothing; then she handed him the cup and started—he thought—scratching at her head, working at it. When he was about to ask what was wrong, she lifted the blond hair all the way off, and looked at him, as he, breathing hard, felt his insides smacking themselves.

Her skull was egg bare, egg white. And her eyes, under the astonishing yawn of skin, were great blue arcs. He tried to say something, but just touched her leg. She said, "I read that when Mary of Scots was beheaded, her red wig fell off, and the executioner held up her old gray head. At least I won't get gray."

"Oh, Cicia," said Wursup. "How hard for you. But at least no one can tell but you. And hair's the thing everyone does something with now. You can have a transplant, like Proxmire or Sinatra, if you want."

"Maybe."

"You're beautiful," he said.

"Some beauty," she said, and moved her palm slowly up her skull; it seemed to take minutes. "This is your little friend. Nobody had a magic herb for her. They threw their stuff into me, and here I am. Baldy Buell. 'Miss me, miss me, then you have to kiss me.'"

It must be something like seeing your parachute not opening, thought Wursup, the shock and terror. Instead of the lips and noses and eyes framed by the gold, there was a totally different perspective. Unfair. He was already adjusting a little to it, but no, it was unfair of her to do it; it was unfair that it *was*. It didn't matter. Nothing matters. Fame doesn't change you. Losing your money doesn't change you. Of course it changes you, deeply. Maybe essentially. You aren't what you were. Now you're poor, or old, or lame, or famous. Everything has to change around that. Sure, money can buy you legs, a face-lift, a wig, but it takes time to catch up to that. It's almost easier for a transsexual to have the transforming operation: at least he is now what he always felt himself to be. All this went

234

into a few seconds, and at the end, he was already a little easier.

He leaned over to kiss her. She turned away and put the wig on. "That's over for me." There was a kind of laughing cough, and then, *boom*, a sob, an awful sob. Her legs pulled up, her face hid behind her knees, and the wig, not fixed, moved on the fleshy egg. The skull flesh was studded with purple marks. "Cicia, Cicia," he said. "It's okay, kid. It's okay. Let it go." And he put his arms around her velvety arms, and tried to get his own face against hers, managing only at the bared ear. Instead of stroking her hair, he stroked her back.

When Wursup came downstairs—he'd tucked a blanket around Cicia, put out the lights, and, with a relief at which he felt ashamed, gone softly out—the party had broken up into little groups. Gopal and the chubby redhead were melting tragically and amorously toward each other; Tina and a girl in old pilot's glasses were reading each other's palms. On the couch, Benny had taken Cicia's place beside her father. At Tommy's request, he had explained some of his work until even Tommy's considerable capacity for appearing to absorb what he couldn't understand was exhausted. But they had struck up a strange bargain. "Benny and I are going to do a joint autobiography," he told Wursup.

Upstairs, his scalped daughter was weeping herself to sleep, but a man can't throw himself into a grave, can't shave his own skull. Tommy, his own white fleece convulsive with light and excitement, had seen a new way to discover and display the form and meaning of his own life. Years ago he'd failed with Walbank. That timid infant couldn't face up to himself and had thrown in the towel. Now here was this fabulous dynamo of invention, this Magellan of universal geometry, and in almost every way Tommy's opposite number. It was a perfect match. This Ariel of numbers had been raised in Rome by a German-Jewish-American businessman; he, Tommy,

235

was an Americanized Italian who'd spent his life cruising the coasts and surfaces of the world, a businessman whose very business was the protective, invisible shield, the clear glass—there and not there at the same time, its aim its own invisibility. Oh, it was beautiful. He had been raised on the brim of thugs, two-bit thieves and *pezzenovante*—"big shots"—his family an operatic parody, full of phony tears and phony fury. All by himself, he'd made a certain distinction, through muck and luck and buying and selling, through picking to inside straights and bamboozling rubes. He'd even got to educate their almost-uneducable children, prying them away from weekend car washings and ballgames, touching their clotted heads with luminous ambassadors from a mental world that was closer to them than they'd been taught to think possible (by the world's Walbanks, hired to conceal, mystify, shore up in snobbery the manna of great thinkers). He, Tommy, had come out of muck to cross the chasm between these laboring lizards and the Benny Knoblauchs. "So what do you think? He'll do a boyhood chapter—you know, what he saw and did in Rome, what his parents were like—"

"Are," said Wursup. "I've known them thirty years."

"*Are* like . . . what it meant growing up as an American stuck between Italians, how arithmetic and all that took over, what it meant, whatever, wherever. And then I'll do my story, the racket of the mills, growing up in that smell, so thick you thought you were dying; the army, poker, buying and selling junk, old mattress springs, busted hardware, going into hock for a little furnace, hiring men as they walked out of jails, dodging the unions, and making it, inch by inch, and all of a sudden, there you were, a million, two million, and you didn't even know it, and waking up and saying, more, more, there's plenty more, all of that's junk, and now I'll make sense of it, do something. Seeing the world, books, music, and still more, pulling up the others, organizing minds the way I organized the plant. Not bad, huh, Fred? Not a bad story. Not a bad pair of stories. You know publishing. This is a big book, isn't it? Something that would go, that would take in a lot of life, a lot of America? Right?"

"Sounds terrific, Tommy."

"Maybe you could even put in some of the superstructure. A preface, maybe, showing how the two parts fit together, what they mean?"

The handsome little fellow was bursting. All the leaden melancholy had been bombarded with ideas. The pigeon's-blood flannels, the hundred-dollar shoes from Milan, the Pacific tan, the white hair, the blue cotton shirt out of the Burlington Arcade, the five and a half decades of push and shove and agitated mentality—it all came back and obliterated sullenness, gloom, his poor, sunken, bald daughter. And he had agitated compliance from a cosmos-drunk Benny. "Sure, who knows, why not, Tommy. You and Benny'll be the Barnum and Bailey of the biography business."

That was the old human principle, thought Wursup. A slot opened on earth; it meant there was room for a new plant. You buried the father; you buried the daughter; either one enriched the ground. This was better than Hindu wheels of fire, progressive etherialization toward perfect nothingness. Benny looked like a big, heaving tuna on the end of Tommy's line. He'd learn to function out of his ocean, long enough anyway for Tommy to get his chapters out of him.

Tommy was no brute; he'd let himself sink far as he could with his daughter. He'd tried—doctors, wigs, parties, whatever was possible he'd still try, but he knew you couldn't go down to hell with Eurydice. Or at least only one Orpheus in a trillion could, and then what good did it do?

Wursup himself had surrendered Cicia upstairs. She was almost as far away as Poppa and Mona. He'd toss off that article for Mike Schilp now. It was just another verbal turn. A hunk of subject he could chip into a lively piece. Another "How To" piece. *How to Cook Spaghetti alla Vonghele, How to*

Make an Outhouse, How to Raise Begonias, How to Marry, Divorce, Tell Your Children about Santa, Bury Your Father, Face Up to the Death of the Beautiful and Young. Quotes from Epictetus, *Hamlet*, Einstein, a few squiffs of one's own, and Schilp would have another dozen pages of his July issue tucked away, and there'd be another assignment waiting for Wursup, and another, until he felt his own insides curling up one morning and someone saw a little shadow on his tomogram, and the great parade suddenly came down to one little marcher watched by himself, beating his own bass drum, commemorating nothing but his own departure.

20

Wursup drove up to Swan's Island a couple of weeks after—
and partly as a consequence of—Susannah's wedding.

The wedding itself was a consequence of tenancy arrangements. Both Susannah and Kevin's leases were up at the end
of May, and Abby was vacating her place to move to Chicago.
Ideal. Everything worked out. They'd have wedding and wedding party the day before the movers came; the furniture
would be padded, the carpets rolled up, and they'd dance in
the new life. Abby's apartment would do just fine. Firstly, it
was only three blocks from the office. As for room, well, Billy
was home only a few days a year—he could sleep on a
couch—and Petey wouldn't mind a small room. In four years,
he'd be in college. And high school—which he'd start in the
fall—would take up most of his life; after a few days, he
wouldn't notice the smaller quarters. Abby's place was expensive, but the cost wasn't much more than their combined
rents. And they'd save on bus and cab fare.

A new life in a new place. Perfect. Kevin hesitated about

moving into Abby's but didn't have the nerve to say why. As for Susannah, she wasn't one to be troubled by love's old shadows. What had happened had happened. Watch for ghosts, you'll see them. Keep your mouth shut and the flies out. (*En boca cerrado no entran moscas.*)

Wursup had been invited to the wedding party—the ceremony itself was rapid, civil and unattended, even by the boys and Susannah's mother—but only by way of Petey. Not that anyone received cards of invitation or announcement. Might as well write it up on subway toilets. Susannah's mother had only learned about it because she'd called to say she was en route to Cape Cod for a month with her sister. (Which settled another problem for Susannah: her mother could take the boys for a few weeks so she and Kevin "could settle in with each other.")

"She's so efficiently careless," Wursup said to Will. "So elaborately unceremonious."

He found himself peculiarly absorbed in the event. It was not just the removal ten blocks south. (He wouldn't admit even to himself that he'd miss watching them from the roof.) They were all certainly big enough to live ten minutes' walk from one another (though he knew the extra eight and a half minutes would often be what would prevent their seeing one another, for wasn't convenience the essence of 'home'?). No, it was Susannah herself. "I'm going to miss her," he told Will.

"Miss her?"

"I mean, not that I see her in the street or anything, but it was my house, too. I'll miss knowing where she and Petey eat breakfast, where the toaster is, how you go from room to room. I'll even miss the sense of her around the street. Susannah may not be Madame Curie, but there's sure less crap in her than in most people. She's of a piece. Maybe not a big piece, but the same wherever you tap."

Will, who had tapped there, said he supposed so. It was his least-favorite subject. He had been shriven in church, but he would have given plenty to have confessed and been shriven by Wursup. His daughters laughed at such old sexual shadows. At their parties—he understood—it might be that everyone had slept with everyone else. (Of both sexes, if this noun still functioned outside of the laboratory.) He could not imagine such intricate intimacy. Was it just like eating together? It must be wonderful. Yet why did his daughters cry so much? Maybe there was a given quantum of human unhappiness rigid as Planck's constant? Each human system distributed it differently. (This idea would undo the world.) If he was mangled by old operatic guilts—the term now was "hang-ups"— his daughters had just as bad times with their straight prose.

"It's not Susannah you're going to miss: it's those twenty-five years."

"I don't think so. I'm a happy tenant of the present. And the best thing about it is remembering. All the cozy sentiment free of factual grit. I sure don't want to be twenty again."

"So you're sweetening memory with regrets. One way or another, you cash in."

"Sure, a lot of it's just a middle-aged guy's fear of losing unimportant habits. But be simple. I like Susannah, and I don't think I'll see her anymore."

The evening of the wedding reception, Wursup was up on the roof, concealed—for it was still light—by a chimney from which his field glasses spookily poked. The wedding party yakked, danced, champagned. The *Chouinard* geezers hotfooted with the rest, bending, bumping. There was Dame Mae, a shepherd's crook of white hair dressed in black, but by no means mourning. Her ancient, corsetted keester rocked against Petey's innocent apples. Billy, surely looped, used his six feet as if each of them was independently at the music's disposition. What a dancer. He snuggled up and down with Libba, who appeared to take him as no joke, then with a tiny, gorgeous black girl—one of the recruits? his date?—who was herself no slouch. They were each other's extensions—what a

241

performance. Then Susannah slipped in, stiff and giggly, not so much dancing as advertising the idea of it.

Well, she hadn't spared the champagne. Caterers walked with trays of it: Mumm's and Piper Heidsieck—he read the labels. What a surprise. Someone else must have ordered it; Susannah's grapes would have come from no farther away than Syracuse. (Yet they had had grand parties in their time; but then Susannah hadn't been morally to the right of Cato the Elder. If they made her mayor of New York, there'd be no dangling by the financial short hairs.) Now, though, if she didn't exactly swing herself, she wasn't freezing swingers out. There were tamer scenes in Nero's Rome (at least in Seneca's neighborhood). You couldn't find a stodgier pack of mice than the Chouinardians, yet from the rooftop, it looked like a Fellini party, the antiques rattling the juveniles (though, thank God, more motion than sex).

Susannah was all lit up. And, though he couldn't *feel* it, beautiful, still boy-slender—a boy with balloons. And, wonder of wonders, she wasn't in apron or business skirt and blouse. A gold-green dress with a glittery gold sash. "All in gold, my love." The furnace must be hot. She sashayed around, maybe no poem of fire but at least a tinkle of glints. The face—he held the glasses on it—wasn't grooved with thought, or suffering either. And it wasn't just makeup. Without trying, Susannah was in that All-American land between sixteen and sixty, unassignable by grooves, rings or teeth. It was honorable to be smooth-faced in America. The eyes, lime-dense, flashed "go," though—he told Will later—"everything else in her gives you speeding tickets."

Will remembered otherwise (though didn't want to). "I guess it's celibacy that's kept her young."

"That's only for plants, I thought. She is really more vegetal than anyone I know. 'My vegetable love.'"

"Better a live cabbage than a dead dog."

The cabbage was being swung and kissed by the recruits' companions. Goddess of Misrule tonight. Good for her. This old sun of his family life. He'd known her before he'd voted, had loved, plowed, married, sown, and cropped there. And never was she much more than a familiar stranger. Until the end, when she simplified into an enemy. And that was brief. Now again she was intimately distant, more distant than intimate, but not all that different. As if a rock had a mental and sensible life. Yet a pal, like these pet rocks they sold. Loyal, straight, never a flick of doubt about her, and when it came down to domestic brass tacks, who could touch her? They'd lived all around the world, and Susannah adapted better than American Express. There must be a Cartesian exoskeleton on certain people which makes them instantly and internationally recognizable as trusties. Susannah could do things every travel manual warned you against—showing her heels in Java, patting heads in Saigon, flipping through the Koran in mosques. It didn't matter; the worst she got was a cautionary finger-wagging. She had no more language skill than a parrot, but in *chowk, souk, épicerie* or *Käserei,* Susannah got service, smiles, help. Unconvertible, she appeared to every proselytizer the ideal convert—Hindu, Shinto, cannibal or Christian *naturaliter.*

Nothing but eyes and memories, Wursup watched her till it grew dark and cold. So long, Sue-sue. . . . Toodleoo, kid.

He came down through the bathroom at ten, stiff, red-eyed, sinuses dripping phlegm out of spit range. No pill taker, he forced down five glasses of water and a glass of rum, and then, sweating, got under the blankets. In the morning, he felt better. Moving day. He went up on the roof, and there they were—two red and white trucks sandwiching a brown van that could have held an Olympic pool. On the sidewalk, the green leather chair, the prayer wheel from Bhagamat, the mosaic table, the sandstone Garuda bird from Bali, chairs and tables that were like chips off his heart. "So long," he sent across to the leather chair (flipped like an empty box to a huge mover's head and then lost forever in the van).

Wursup descended to his cold. Yes, his head was full, his

lungs filling. He went back to bed with a pot of tea. Not enough. The cold swelled. He called his doctor. "Leo, I need a shot." Leo Vietch had retired but kept a handful of old patients whose medical delicacy didn't travel well. Tiny, great-domed, sensitive, Leo was a doctor-prince, thermometer and thermostat of his patient's psyches, knowledgeable, comforting, modest and secure.

"Frederick. You haven't even been veighed in five years." The accent was deeply Hungarian, though Leo had lived in New York for forty years. "You must really be low. Can you meet me at Lenox Hill, or shall I come to you?" He still consulted at Lenox Hill and had staff privileges there.

He met Wursup in two hours, looked, tapped, poked, palped, wrote out a prescription, and, "as long as you're here," took his blood and sent him up for X rays. "You should be completely vell in three or four days. If not, call me. Call me anyway." Unsmiling, though everything in Leo was a smile. "You look a vee bit peaked to me. Maybe you should go out in the country. It's beautiful now. Take some valks. Relax. I know you. You come together like this"—Leo made a little fist—"and everything vich has lived quietly in you starts shouting, 'You're sick.' "

"I have to drive the boys to their grandmother, on the Cape. Maybe I'll go on up to Will Eddy's island. He's been inviting me there for twenty-odd years, and I was there only once for a few hours to see his father. I've got good feelings about it. And I'd have it to myself."

"That's the ticket. If anything acts up, you can reach me in minutes."

"I wish you could take charge of every part of me, Leo. I feel a hundred percent better already."

"The Braginsky Effect," said Leo. "You know it?"

"Tell me."

"The act of measuring a body—in physics—disturbs it. In this case, it's the opposite: being seen by the doctor is the cure."

"Not *the* doctor. It's a Vietch Effect."

The cold was still there, but he felt fine. A wonderful day, seventy-five or so, and a sweet breeze. Sails up. Maybe he'd even take out a sailboat, though he'd never been much of a sailor. Windy journalist. Wasn't the journalism episode of *Ulysses* set in the Cave of the Winds? Unfair. Joyce had done good journalism himself. Plenty of other good writers, too. Dostoevski, Marx, Orwell—millions of them. Mandelstam, the poet, had done a wonderful piece on Ho Chi Minh back in the twenties. He'd used it in *Drain*. There were more hot-air poets and novelists than reporters. At least reporters didn't use their own breath. He'd drive north with the boys, have a few days by himself, and then maybe Sookie would come up. Or even Cicia. It might be just the ticket. Good sea air, lobster. They could read Professor Eddy's books—it was one of the best libraries in Maine. Better than looking for rabid squirrels in the park.

"You are enthusiastic, Frederick. I can see it in your eyes."

"I'm an easy read, Leo. Always have been. Lay out your dime, you get all I have, plus news and features."

"You're blessed, Frederick. The human Kabbalahs are on the couches. If there's anything to report—which I'm sure there won't be—I'll get your number from your friend."

"You've had my number from day one, Leo. Thank God."

21

The usual phone sound on the island was a loony whine. "Get use't't," said Mr. Stinton, the Eddys' caretaker. "Wait't out." When the whine stopped, you could phone. That wasn't the end of the trouble. The phone had it in for the English clause, at least for the five- and six-word clauses of Wursup's callers. Every fifth or sixth word—or, more likely, word part—was dropped. It was as if conversation were hauled to the mainland by small-mouthed fish which discarded what they couldn't carry. (When Sookie telephoned Wursup about Cicia, he heard only the "eech" sound and thought Sookie was telling him Leo Vietch had found something on his X rays.) "Fesser put 't'n. Durin't wawr," said Stinton of the phone. "Call'm middle't night." (The fish probably carried Stinton's speech intact.) Stinton's mouth was a long seam between his fallen cheek flesh. When he spoke, the stitches gave reluctantly till the inner, cautionary thread pulled back against the menace of aperture. (Is it fear of giving anything away, wondered Wursup, or just northern caution about taking too much cold air into the throat? Mainland Maineacs weren't celebrated for loquacity, but by island standards, they were chatterboxes.)

In any event, he didn't get much of Stinton's conversation. Nor of any other islander's. The Eddy house was isolated, half a mile from Stinton's, which was up on the main—the paved—road. And when Wursup took his afternoon swim in the limestone quarry, there was little more than amiable nods and "Good afternoons" from other swimmers. In the little grocery store, there'd be another "Good afternoon" or two, and that was the conversational quota till he ordered his lobster and crab rolls at the closet-size diner at seven o'clock.

"Come soon, Sook. I'm going batty."

" . . . any day . . . convection . . . data . . . write it up and then . . . "

"I wasn't expecting Paris, but there isn't even enough for a good Vermont village here. The houses sit out on the road as if they're waiting for the moving van to haul them off to a real place." (How much of this the fish delivered, he didn't know. Sookie was more intent on her reasons for not coming to him.)

"Why don't you . . . the island belles . . . amusing."

Belles. Bells, more like it. Interbreeding had evolved an island shape. It did not clutch the heart. A short, browless head on a tiny neck turret, narrow shoulders swelling into a largish torso and then the grand finale, an enormous rear end. Wursup felt the very knell of desire in these flesh bells. He observed them diving off the rocks, great bottoms up. What clappers could stiffen to sound them? Not his.

The house was fine. (That he remembered.) It was elephant colored, elephant high, a shingled box weathered with foamy blotches. It stood three yards back from a private cliff which slid into a bay of coppery rocks. Ducks massed and gulls skimmed for fish in its red arms. Now and then, a bulge of water shifted, dipped, bulged. "Porp's," said Stinton, pointing one out the day he showed Wursup the house. Occasionally, sailboats, bloated with blue, rose and orange spinnakers, flew toward the green shoulders of Placentia Island, ten or twelve miles across the snowy ocean.

There was less life in the house. The presiding deity was a stuffed blue heron, its foolish, wicked bill indicting the walls of books, the tables of instruments. "A house of unremitting instruction," Will called it. Wursup had remembered the handsome timber walls with their skin of books; but after days surrounded by omniscient authority, he began to share the heron's rage at the wordless—no, silent!—oppression. The range of the books was staggering. (Professor Eddy must have been a one-man university.) There was also an unparsable assortment of magazines piled into corners and under tables. Old *Lifes* and *Looks* sandwiched *Yachting,* the *Mercure de France,* the *American Physical Review, Perspectives in Biology* and *Medicine, Neue Deutsche Rundschau; Maine Facts* lay under *Yale Reviews* and *Diogenes; Dedalus, Scientific American, Partisan Review, Better Homes and Gardens, Saga Schriften* (with some of Professor Eddy's translation of Snorri Sturleson) mingled in periodical orgies. (Perhaps everyone who came to the house had to bring ten different magazines.) Nailed to the timbers were maps, charts and guides of every sort, manuals of reptiles, birds, ferns, tides, weather. ("High visibility over salt water means rain," Wursup read above his bed. "The salt haze is dispersed by unstable air currents.")

Yes, he would learn much; but little that was current. There was no newspaper; no current magazines came in; there was no television set; and until Milton Buffman told him about the radio, he had no access to daily event but the compromised calls to Sookie. It was fine for the first days. He did lots of work on the sheikhs and oil moguls; and the massif of his white note cards sank while a new white mountain of pages formed.

He typed from eight till two, ate a sandwich and went off to the quarry for ten laps and his critical inspection of island flesh. He came back via the grocery store, then doused his head with Bug-Off and went for his walk through the woods. In the dazzling gold layers of late afternoon, the trails were invisibly animate: grass tunnels closed behind unseen tails; pebbles scuttered in lower wakes; all around was the viewless racket of the woods—crickets chipping away at themselves, bullfrogs juridically honking, wasps and bees making small-saw noise. Wursup was haloed by bugs probing the odorous perimeter of his flesh. (They wanted his blood, but at least showed themselves.) The woods were spectacular. Wursup knew few tree names but he identified fir, white birch and the stunted juniper heavy with blue berries. Wild raspberries peered from leaves, ferns collected gauzy nets. Now and then the ocean popped up around a corner; the trail bent toward it, the racket of the waves covered that of the woods, and then the trail wound back along the ins and outs of the island's body. "It is beautiful here," he told Sookie (after waiting out the whine for two hours). "Especially if you're a bug or a frog. What's new in the world?"

"Nothing but . . . lympics. You're not missing a . . . "

"I miss. I miss."

One day in the grocery store, a round-backed little fellow with beard enough for a Marx and a half and a forehead like Shakespeare's dropped a box of Bran Flakes in front of Wursup's cart and apologized. "Milton Buffman," he said, sticking out his hand.

Milton was an off-islander, but had built here twenty years ago. He knew the Eddys, knew everyone on the island. He was a carpenter and taught biology in a Portland high school. Mostly, though, he regarded himself as chronicler and philosopher of the island. Wursup went back to his house, a beautiful one-story cedar affair hugging a hill which overlooked the Lobster Co-op dock. They sat in chairs Milton and his son had built, handsome, back-breaking walnut versions of Mies and Breuer chairs. "Only the best models," said Milton. He was a teetotaler; they drank Diet-Pepsi and watched the white putt-putts coming in one by one to the dock, the high-booted lobstermen hauling the slatted crates of the miserable red creatures to the scales. "Used to cost two cents apiece," said Milton. "Now two-fifty a pound, and the old lobstermen say you're paying mostly for water." He was a champion of the old islanders, the old ways. "Things started slipping here when the ferry began."

"What did they use before?"

"A bimonthly boat from Rockland. Now it's all ferry. Not sun and moon, but boat schedules." Milton was sincere, but also amused at his sincerity. (You knew because a gold front tooth showed in the chaos of hair around his lips when he smiled.) "The idea of islands is self-sufficiency. Making do. Bucky Fuller comes right out of Maine island lore: Spaceship *Earth*, ship technology, garbage as treasure, recycled waste, the humus toilet, self-supporting domes. That's what it's all about. More Pepsi?" The great forehead flushed. "I'm not entirely self-sufficient. I don't stint on the groceries." He invited Wursup to stay and see, and they fried hamburgers, heated baked beans and finished off with vanilla ice cream and Brach's chocolate mints. "Nothing but the best." (No gold tooth.)

Wursup commented on the island shape and the dangers of interbreeding. "Where are all the hanging jaws? The bug-eyed stares?"

The gold tooth fired up. "Right-o. The danger in all these places is endemic cretinism. The islanders figured it out long ago. Or nature did it for them. They take in any stray who comes along—sailors, lumbermen. Dad goes off for the lobsters and Mom or Daughter—sometimes both; *I know instances*—refreshes the genetic pool. You'll see very unisland-looking types here. Probably take them for visitors. Right down there in the co-op store there's a girl who's the spitting image of Dorothy Lamour in those Polynesian pictures."

Milton had a good radio. Mahler thunder filled the house during supper; Stockhausen plinks riffled the genetics lecture. "Maine Public Radio's terrific. Music, news, BBC-type features. In the morning, it's five hours of Baroque. The farmers wrote in to say the cows give more milk to it."

"I'll have to go off-island and get one," said Wursup. "I can't go long without music and a little news."

The gold tooth went wild. "You haven't found it yet? Ha ha ha. No wonder. Look at your toilet paper. The holder." Wursup had noticed the odd, perforated box. "The prof was learning every minute. I nearly fell through the hole when I heard Handel coming out of the thing. It's not exactly high fidelity, but it does the job."

That it did. Every morning now, Wursup came downstairs and moved his bowels to Vivaldi and the world's news. What a joy to hear the day's remote calamities: floods washing campers out of Colorado canyons, earthquakes killing thousands and thousands of Chinese (as the dying Mao shivered with premonition). There were bashed heads in Spain, acid-blindings in Detroit, tornados, mysterious plagues. Martian soil gushed pent-up oxygen, sailing ships assembled for the bicentennial voyage up the Hudson, there was gymnastic perfection in Montreal; a Toronto professor tracked the monarch butterflies of the hemisphere to their winter congregation on a Mexican mountain where they piled so thickly branches collapsed under them.

So now Wursup's days flew by to Bach and the world's doings. He typed, drank coffee, ate tuna from a can, worked out the politics of Africa and Asia from his cards, took his swim, his walk, and waited for his new pal, Milton, to come for supper. He'd buy six lobster rolls and open up the New York State Chablis he'd brought in from the mainland. (Maybe Milton's temperance was only economic.)

When he got back from his walk, the phone was ringing.

Milton. His generator had broken down; he was going to catch the last ferry and drive to Bangor for parts. "And I might as well drive down to see Jerry"—his son—"as long as I'm off-island. Sorry about supper. Be back in a few days."

Wursup felt amputated from the universe. Solitude rose from the water, the walls. The heron snorted it at him.

Usually he called Sookie at eight, but he called now. Or tried to. The loony whine. The ocean visibility was terrific, perhaps the microwaves were tangled up with the coming rain. Yet there were no clouds anywhere. He tried again; the whine. Every five minutes he tried again; it was a bad hour. At eight, he got through, and there was no answer either at her place or his. Rage. Irrational, helpless. If he were on that Mexican mountain, he'd have wiped out the Monarchs of the Western World.

The genocidal thought eased him a bit. "Regicide. Lepidopteran regicide. Ha Ha. 'The rage of dreaming sheep.'" (A sentence of Baron Stein's, about the Prussians under Napoleon, which he'd used for his Algerian chapter.)

He picked up the regional phone book and went through it. Who knew who might be up here? In two minutes he found half a dozen familiar names—people he'd met, even interviewed (David Rockefeller—separate listings for pool and stables; a former secretary of defense; a critic who'd written a decent piece about him). He worked out a spiel. "This is Fred Wursup. The same. I'm up on Swan's Island. Staying in a friend's house. Oh, great, I was just going to invite you over here. I can't get over till tomorrow. The last ferry's gone, and I don't have a boat. No, no, I wouldn't think of it. I'm beat tonight. Terrific. See you tomorrow." The imaginary dialogue almost substituted for the real thing.

But not quite; and he couldn't bring himself to call; he didn't know them well, and besides, loneliness showed in your voice and scared people.

Then he saw ELIZABETH FARR. MRCR'S BAY.

252

Joy. He could call Elizabeth. They were colleagues, pals, lovers. Relief wiped out all her defects, her sexual scorecards, her nervous, avian head, her claim that every shiekh, shah and minister she interviewed made for her tits and sheets. He thought only of her beautiful skin, the way she pulled off her dress under the bat-winged fan in the Strand Hotel, her stillness under the great golden turnip, Shewe Dagon, while the bells tinkled and the monks in saffron whisked brooms over the pavement.

Elizabeth answered the phone. "What a surprise." Her voice was goosey with delight. (And the phone transmitted flawlessly; the fish must respect locals.) It would be grand to see him; yes, she knew the island, though hadn't been out since she was a girl. She'd come after the weekend; her mother was giving a July Fourth party. Why didn't he come to it? Though it was mostly antiques, plus poor droopy-balls Angus Hunnicomb, who'd been trailing her since she'd tripped over them in Rome. Monday, then. She couldn't wait; she'd take the first afternoon ferry.

Two and a half days, but he could wait now; the sense of having someone was what counted.

Rain, a cozy, small thumping noise. He switched on the toilet-paper holder. The end of *La Bohème.* Just the ticket. He'd once seen it broken up in Palermo: an old Sicilian had thrown his shoe into the tenor's face in the middle of "O Soave Fanciulla." Sicilian higher criticism. Wursup heard himself roaring. Why not? Live it up.

He thumbed a section of books: Trollope's novels; *Rats, Lice and History*; Plutarch; Macauley; *Crabbe's Poetical Works.* He thumbed through the latter and read five hundred couplets of "The Newspaper." It was good stuff. The old boy had newspapers down pat before Washington took the oath of office. These old boys could write. What confidence. That had gone from prose. Anne Frank's *Diary of a Young Girl.* When it came out, he'd tried it out of piety, but he was too old. Three years ago, Sookie had dragged him to Anne's hideaway house on the Prinzengracht, and in the mean yellow room with the pictures of the blond movie stars and the little English princesses, Sookie had broken down, sobbing. He skimmed the pages: so scrupulous, such receptivity, good cheer, such sweetness and funny alertness. A voyeur—*voyeuse*—also, spying on the neighbors across the courtyard: a girl after his own heart.

The phone rang. Sookie. "I've been . . . for an hour."

"I called *you*. There must have been interference." Blushing. "These damn fish. I was just thinking about you."

"Listen, hon, there's something . . . eech . . . bad way . . . better come . . . so sorry, baby."

A pincer closed on Wursup's innards. His X rays. Dr. Vietch had found something. Serious. He would not have summoned him lightly. This was it. His fatigue, his irresolution, his loneliness, the long infatuation with the death material—it had all been part of it, an inner, premonitory buckling. His eyes were lead balls; his stomach felt the murderous tumors. "Why did he bother you? Why the hell didn't he call me directly?"

"Who? Her father? . . . know where you were . . . called you at home."

"I gave Leo the number up here."

"Leo? . . . you mean? . . . Cicia's father . . . Buell."

His eyes melted; his insides unwrinkled; he breathed deeply, wiped his forehead on his sweater sleeve. Safe.

But Cicia. Cicia was not going to leave the hospital again.

" . . . zero prognosis. The stuff . . . over her. Liver, heart . . . huge tumor in the left . . . icle."

Mr. Buell thought he would want to come down before it was over. They were at St. Vincent's, going into the Coronary Care Unit.

"I'll come now. Tomorrow. The first ferry. The last one's left. The poor girl."

"I know how . . . so sorry, baby."

Wursup called Elizabeth, told her there'd been an emergency: he'd been called to New York; no, it was a friend. If he came back, he'd call her, though it looked as if they were meant to meet only out of the States; so, until Bogotá or Brazzaville, or, who knows, Rangoon or Rome, take care.

He unplugged and closed up the typewriter, packed his note cards and manuscript. The toilet-paper holder announced a Beethoven quartet—F major, Opus 135—and the announcer read from the record jacket. (Wursup, a scholar of jackets, knew the style.) Finished in October, 1826—the announcer threw in "a hundred and fifty years ago"—five months before the composer's death, written in the country where he was staying with his hated brother and adored nephew, the sick old man terrified the servants, strode around the hills singing at the top of his voice; twice, the deaf man had stampeded oxen. "Must it be?" he'd written on the score, and "*It must be*"—a joke about the landlady's call for the rent.

Some joke.

The little wall box rasped but did its stuff. Wursup unlatched the window and went outside to listen.

The grass was wet, but the sky was clear and almost solid with stars. They filled every branch space and studded the long arch down to the horizon. Notes the dropsical, bilious deaf man had inked a century and a half ago on score paper were stroked on catgut by four men, agitated the air, made electric pulsings, scratches on oiled platters. And how many other losings and findings till the contents of that ear-blocked, in-turned head in Austria became the inside of another one on this land dribble of the American coast? Instead of mess, there was something lit and lucid. Connection. A handshake of the species across years, languages, space.

Five hundred miles south, another head was checking out, cell by cell. Off to a country of no music, no correspondence, no connection.

Cell by cell, as would every other cell, every drop of sea, every star, one by one.

*　*　*

There were only four other cars on the six-o'clock ferry. Wursup stood at the bow, beside a merry-looking woman his own age. "Beautiful day," she said.

"Yes, indeed."

She was driving home for the Fourth, to be with her daughter's family. Was he living on the island? She hadn't seen him. She was an oldtime off-islander. Too bad she hadn't known he was there; he could have come over. Though she was afraid she wouldn't have been much company: she'd been writing up her research. She was a physiologist, a student of sleep.

She had a fine, small-chinned face half covered with the enormous glasses of the day, and beautiful dark hair parted in the middle. He asked her about her work. (Heavy with Cicia, he was still receptive, eager.)

Was he really interested? It really was too bad they hadn't met earlier. Her husband was a lawyer who forbade all mention of her work. She said no one really knew what sleep was; the old notions were all wrong, including Freud's "hydraulics"; dreaming did not seem necessary to the psychic drainage system; many people hardly dreamed, and there were healthy specimens who slept but minutes a day. She herself was tracking sleep through different species to see what evolutionary development it accommodated; she'd reached the lizards—good sleepers—so sleep was not a thermofacient adjustment.

Fascinating stuff, spieled out charmingly as they plowed the turquoise water past islands and into the dock at Bass Harbor. "Have a good Fourth," she wished him.

He took Route Two to Bangor and drove south on Ninety-five through Maine, the eastern corner of New Hampshire, around Boston and Providence. He drove straight through, stopping only for gas and coffee. By six, he was in Manhattan. The traffic was heavy for Saturday evening, people going into New York for the flotilla tomorrow. He drove down the East

256

River Drive, and was tempted to go on across the Brooklyn Bridge and have a drink with Will. What a view he'd have for the ships. "Cicia," he said, "Cicia." (Forcing himself to feel the girl behind the name.) He drove up Twelfth Street—no space, no garage—and pulled into a Hospital Emergency Zone, locked the car and ran up to the CCU. No one asked him for a pass.

It was a large room—he remembered it, except now it was decorated with patriotic bunting and posters of cocked hats, flags, the Yankee Doodle trio. Behind this was the machinery of human crisis: wall-size monitors full of dials, a bank of television screens where two nurses and a doctor checked out the dying hearts.

There were five cubicles. Wursup glimpsed people tubed, swaddled, linked to instruments. He said Cicia's name. A nurse pointed him to a curtained cubicle on the left. Dizzy now, throat closing, he held off a second, took a breath and went in.

She was breathing. Tina stood at her head, holding her hand. Tommy, shaggy, eyes red, sat by her feet. On the other side of the bed was an older woman, gray, severe-looking. Cicia's eyes were closed; a transparent plastic mask covered her nose and mouth. Her breath was heavy; she was pale, gaunt, but looked tranquil and beautiful. Tommy and Tina held his hands, and Tommy introduced him: "This is Mrs. Buell, Cicia's mother. Fred Wursup."

The woman nodded sharply. Her face was open and clear as Cicia's, but there was something extra in it, a kind of inside knowledge held in the corners of her eyes and mouth. Her eyes asked what he was doing here.

Indeed, he asked himself that. He had known Cicia quickly, maybe deeply, but for less time than this woman had had her in her body. Had Cicia called for him?

The air was full of the bleeps and hums of Cicia's machine. The screen of the Hewlett-Packard Monitron showed four lines, two of which were flat. Purple balls made waves on the other two. In a slot, light-beaded numbers ticked every half-second: 67, 66, 67, 67.

"We've been here since Wednesday," said Tommy. "Tina and I. Mrs. Buell came yesterday."

Cicia's mother would not acknowledge she was being talked about. Her world was enclosed. (Though it apparently included the daughter she hadn't seen in years and never wrote.)

Across the room, in another cubicle, a loud voice insisted, "You remember me." Wursup looked out and saw an old black woman leaning over a tubed mummy. "I was with you Christmas 'fore last. At George's. You remember."

Cicia's breathing raised and lowered the sheet above her breasts. The bought blond hair looked natural. He went past Mrs. Buell and touched Cicia's arm above the white band her wristwatch left. It was warm. Tina, across the bed, said softly that the trouble had started ten days ago with a bad cold. Cicia had felt awful, bloated; she could hardly breathe, wouldn't eat. "I called Tommy."

"I'd gone back home for a week."

"It was pneumonia, and we came here. Of course, they scanned her. The stuff was all over. Everything was breaking up inside. You could tell. She smelled sour. Even then, they told us they'd pull it off. They'd knock out the pneumonia, then throw everything they had into her. That was Tuesday. She was conscious all the time. Yesterday the nurse asked if she were in pain, and she said, 'No, there was just a little trouble getting her breath.' Wednesday she told me she wished she could have finished her work with you—she called it 'work.' She felt she could tell you so much now. Last night, *she*"—Tina looked at Mrs. Buell with an entomologist's distance—"said Cicia should compose her thoughts, she was dying. Cicia said, 'You're scaring me.' That's the last thing she said."

Wursup went back to the foot of the bed. He watched the

purple balls and the numbers. After a while, he squatted and shut his eyes. Tommy came over and squatted beside him.

Wursup fell in and out of dozes. Then Tommy was shaking his arm, pointing to the Monitron. "It's going down." The beaded lights flashed: 54, 53, 51, 47, 45, 45, 41, 32.

Across the room, a man groaned, "What time is it?"

A woman said, "It's nine-thirty."

"Eight-thirty?"

"Nine-thirty."

Tina's eyes were enormous. She took off Cicia's mask. The Monitron read 10; the lines were flat; there were no more bleeps, just hum. Tina kissed Cicia's lips. Tommy leaned against Wursup's shoulder, then went and took Cicia's head in his arms and kissed it. He and Tina embraced. Wursup came and touched Cicia's arm. It was already cool.

Mrs. Buell sat in a powerful stillness, her lips turned into each other. Then she went to the bed and pulled the sheet over her daughter's face.

Death, the Sniper.

Back in the fifties, Wursup had interviewed an assistant of Von Thadden, the German descendant of David Hume who headed a right-wing neo-Nazi movement. The assistant, Schabacker, was a dark, thuggish-looking fellow who looked a little like Wursup himself. He told Wursup that he'd fought at Stalingrad, that his platoon had been pinned down in the snow for a week by a sniper they could not find. "There was no place to hide. No trees, no bushes, no tanks. Only corpses, men and horses." Every day one or two men were shot. One night, they located the rifle flash. Two of them crawled toward it and found the sniper in the body of a dead horse. He'd been shooting through the empty eye sockets, living off the horse flesh. We shot his brains into it." There was a plaque on Schabacker's desk. It was a quotation from Plato which he translated for Wursup: "Though human affairs aren't worthy

259

of great seriousness, it is still necessary to be serious. Man is God's toy. And that is the best part of him."

Wursup's car was ticketed. He drove home, had the doorman call his garage and went upstairs with his bags and typewriter.

The place was dark; Sookie must be at her place. He wasn't hungry, thirsty, tired or lonely.

There was something else: some need.

He went to the back bathroom, stood on the lidded toilet, shifted the bolt in the ceiling and pulled himself through the hole to the roof.

The dark was shafted, scarfed, wedged, with city light. Fountains of it burst from the avenues, and, cell by cell, the skyscrapers held small starcups of it. The stars themselves were blotted out.

To his right, the Carlyle looked like a great ship upended in the sea, going down with all lights on. Wursup looked across Lexington, at his old apartment. It was dark. The new tenants were out. Or perhaps it hadn't been rented yet.